LEOPOLDO GOUT

genius

THE GAME

FEIWEL AND FRIENDS
NEW YORK

A FEIWEL AND FRIENDS BOOK
An Imprint of Macmillan

Our books may be purchased in bulk for promotional, educational, or business use. Please contact your local bookseller or the Macmillan Corporate and Premium Sales Department at (800) 221-7945 ext. 5442 or by e-mail at MacmillanSpecialMarkets@macmillan.com.

Library of Congress Cataloging-in-Publication Data
Names: Gout, Leopoldo.
Title: Genius : the game / Leopoldo Gout.
Description: First edition. | New York : Feiwel & Friends, 2016. |
Summary:
   "Three underprivileged young prodigies from across the world with
   incredible skills in technology and engineering team up to become the
   heroes the world never knew they could be"—Provided by publisher.
Identifiers: LCCN 2015026921| ISBN 9781250045812 (hardback) |
   ISBN 9781250086884 (ebook)
Subjects: | CYAC: Adventure and adventurers—Fiction. | Genius—
Fiction. |
   BISAC: JUVENILE FICTION / Action & Adventure / General.
Classification: LCC PZ7.1.G69 Ge 2016 | DDC [Fic]—dc23
LC record available at http://lccn.loc.gov/2015026921

Endpaper credits: Eye photographs © JR-ART.net; illustrations © James Manning; brick wall © Shutterstock/Dan Kosmayer

Illustration p. 225 © Jonathan Sager
Photo p. 295 © Chia Messing, design James Manning

Book design by Liz Dresner and Rich Deas

Feiwel and Friends logo designed by Filomena Tuosto

Rex's Complex Code, RSA cipher, and Malbodge code examples provided by bMuse.

First edition—2016

10 9 8 7 6 5 4 3 2 1

fiercereads.com

To Ines Celestia, Leopoldo Valerio & Caitlin:
Los amores de mi vida.

Albert Einstein once said, "The true sign of intelligence is not knowledge but imagination."

He's right. The people I know, they always led with their creativity. And they didn't let age stop them, either. Kim Ung-yong studied astrophysics at NASA when he was eight. Taylor Wilson built a nuclear fusion reactor when he was fourteen. How insane is that?

As for yours truly, I created a computer program that can find missing people with the click of a button. Oh, and I'm still under the two-decade mark.

They call us "special," but we're still like you. We go to the movies, we get in fights with our parents, we have crushes, we wish we could skateboard better. We also just happen to have brains that the white coats have dubbed "organic computers." Wasn't like we chose to be this way.

And here's the kicker: We're the ones everyone else threw away. Twenty years ago my friends and I would be forgotten. Me because my family's poor, my friends because they come from places nobody cares about or everyone hates. What's different is now we have the tech and the tech sets us free.

Give me a computer and I can build you any program you've ever dreamed of. Give my friend Tunde some spare watch parts and he'll build you a working cell phone. And my friend Painted

Wolf, you give her a problem, any problem, and she'll solve it.

The world our parents grew up in is history. All the old rules, we've thrown them out. We're the ones making the future. We're the founding fathers. Hand us unlimited bandwidth and honey garlic chicken wings and we'll fix the world.

We'll get to all that good stuff a little later, though. Just wanted to send this while I had a second. See, there's a reason my status online is: *Running for my life.*

Thing is, when you bake a cake you have to break a few eggs. And there're some people who really hate it when you break eggs. A few of those people have Taser shotguns and are chasing my friends and me across the world at this very moment. And, frankly, that's the least of our problems.

The revolution's already here. Welcome aboard. And, uh, get ready to run.

See ya,
Rex Huerta

*Any sufficiently advanced technology is
indistinguishable from magic.*

—ARTHUR C. CLARKE, *PROFILES OF THE FUTURE*, 1961

PROLOGUE
THE VANISHING

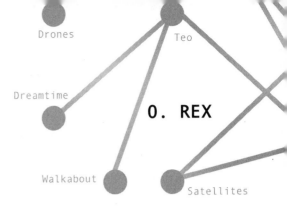

Drones

Teo

Dreamtime

0. REX

Walkabout

Satellites

The night Teo disappeared started off just like any other.

I was at my desk, trying to finish a few projects before I got too tired, when the front door opened. The hinges were rusty and the screech they made was like nails on a plate. Ma had begged me to put some oil on them but that would've defeated the purpose. Those hinges were our alarm system.

Just hearing the door creak open wouldn't normally have given me pause.

A lot of people came over to our house. Sometimes they'd even show up before breakfast. But this was near midnight. The town was asleep.

It was silent.

It took a second for the fear to creep in.

I switched off my desk lamp and glanced down the hall at my parents' bedroom. Ma and Papa were asleep, curled up together, him snoring.

Teo's door was closed, and he only closed it when he slept.

So who just opened the front door?

I leaned back in my chair to peek around the corner toward the front of the house. It was hard to make anything out in the half-light.

I scanned the room, my eyes making out rough shapes as they adjusted to the dark. The couch. The TV on its stand. Nothing out of the ordinary . . .

"That you, Uncle Bobby?" I asked, trying not to be too loud.

No answer.

Uncle Bobby (who's not really my uncle) would sometimes show up at our place drunk. And when he was drunk he sang Mexican folks songs, *corridos*, as loud as he could with his big, thick gringo accent. I think, deep down, he was a Meximorphic and he really believed he had an inner Mexican begging to escape. He and Papa connected because they understood the land. It was fun to watch them differentiate hundreds of trees and plants by their possible "medicinal" qualities (aka booze content).

Papa would say things like, "Did you know that in Europe they throw away all their corn if fungus grows on it? I'm serious! In Mexico, *huitlacoche* is like caviar!" And Uncle Bobby would just nod in agreement.

Thing is, Uncle Bobby never came by this late.

That's when my chest tightened.

Okay. Okay. You can handle this. Just need to wake Papa.

My hands scrambled over my desk for something, anything to use as a potential weapon. I found a screwdriver. It was dinky, but I had nothing else.

One . . . two . . . here goes nothing.

I got up and crept into the front room, ready to scream at the top of my lungs, left hand balled into a fist and—

It was Teo.

I instantly relaxed, then got really mad.

"You scared the crap out of—"

Teo put a finger to his lips and shushed me. Glancing out the window as though he was reading the darkness, he said, "I want you to go to your room until morning. Don't come out."

"What do you mean? Why?"

"I'm leaving, Rex. I don't want Ma and Papa to know."

"Where?"

"On a walkabout."

I was confused. "Walkabout? What do you mean? How long?"

"Forever."

I should have asked, "What's wrong?" But I didn't.

I was too stunned to say anything.

Teo led me back to my bedroom, sat on the edge of my bed, and frowned. "I don't want Ma and Papa to get too worried. I'm fine. I'll be fine."

"I don't get it. Why aren't you coming back?"

Teo just stared off into the shadows. "Something big is coming and I need to be out there to be a part of it." Then, looking me straight in the eye, he said, "World's going to change, little brother. We're all going to have to shift out of our default settings and I just hope I can wake everyone up soon enough to realize it. Good-bye, Rex."

"What about Ma and Papa?"

"You take good care of them for me." Teo stood up.

"Wait! I don't understand. Why are you doing this?"

"I have to."

Then he left.

I heard the door to the house screech one last time, then it was silent. I looked out my window, searching for Teo in the darkness, but I couldn't see anything.

I was tired. Confused. And scared.

Too scared to move.

After that, I guess I just passed out.

0.1

The next morning I wasn't surprised that he was really gone.

That word, *forever*.

Man, nothing's worse to hear than that.

Teo's vanishing act hurt. Deep like a knife wound. And the days just after were filled with fear, worry, and panic. Panic because calling the cops would mean exposing my parents' immigration status to the world, and not calling the cops meant we were somehow giving up on finding my brother.

We debated it endlessly, watching the hours tick by, and finally decided we had to call. The police did what they could, but without any evidence of a crime, Teo was written off as a runaway. And that was it. Even with California's lenient immigration laws, we knew we couldn't call again.

Amazing how you can get used to something, though. Even torture like that.

Eventually, the pain turned to numbness and then, finally, tears. Every meal Ma would have to stop halfway through and go to her and Papa's room, biting her bottom lip to try to hold the tears in. Everything she cooked was bland, like her tears had washed the flavor from her cooking. And Ma loved to cook. She worked at a Thai restaurant a few blocks from our house and used to love spending the weekends piling our kitchen table high with a crazy smorgasbord, where stuff like *jim jum, chiles en nogada, panang gai,* and *papatzules* sat side by side. But that was before.

Got so bad that Papa and I couldn't eat, either. We'd just sit there and listen to Ma cry until Papa pushed his chair back from the table and knocked on the door to their bedroom real soft.

I wouldn't see them for the rest of the night.

I'd put myself to bed, or more often fall asleep at my desk with my head on my keyboard and a half-eaten Oreo in one hand.

There were the usual stages of grief.

First it was denial.

We sat around the phone just knowing it would ring at any second. That Teo would be on the line and laugh and tell us how

10

sorry he was for worrying us. He'd say he was coming home, that it was one big, crazy adventure and he couldn't wait to tell us all about it.

That quickly turned to anger.

I found myself endlessly replaying my last interactions with Teo. They weren't good. The months leading up to his disappearance were filled with antagonism and disappointment. He'd just gone through a series of knock-down, drag-out battles at college over politically motivated hacking, and dropped out. Bitter, he kind of gave up on biology, too, and instead spent almost all his free time online in hacktivist and anarchist forums. He got really into this group of radical hackers called Terminal. Terminal was shady. It ran defacement and denial-of-service attacks on multinational corporations and totalitarian governments. But Teo defended them, said they were bringing power to the powerless and actually accomplishing things.

"Yeah, bad things," I'd tell him when he said it.

"They just look bad," he'd reply.

Unlike Teo's anger, however, ours dissipated. We couldn't hate him for long. It took months, but for Ma and Papa, that sadness eventually transformed into a numb sort of acceptance.

Papa, he got real into work, breaking his back in the winery as the harvest cellar operator. His nose got him that job. I sometimes joked Papa could sniff an aroma from a grape when the plant was still a seedling. Regardless, he worked harder than anyone else in that place once he got the promotion.

Ma, she built a shrine to Teo in his room. It was nothing fancy, more like one of those things you see on the side of the highway where someone crashed into a pole or flipped their car after a drunken night out.

That shrine, it said more about Teo than he'd ever admit about himself.

11

It had his least favorite picture of him. He looked too thin, his hair was kind of goofy (and Teo spent a lot of time on his hair), and his smile was all lopsided. One of those "in the moment" photos, and even though it didn't capture how cool Teo could be, it captured who he was. Underneath all the fussed-over detail, he was one of us, someone who wanted to be liked, someone who wanted to belong.

About eight months after Teo had gone, his name started to drift. Soon it wasn't Teo this or that, it was "your brother" or "our son." The shrine started to gather dust.

In their own private ways, Ma and Papa had grown used to the idea that Teo was gone for good, that he wouldn't ever come back to us, that our family was shattered.

But not me.

Sure, I went on the same emotional roller coaster.

I found myself lying awake at night, bargaining. Making ridiculous offers for a swap—me for Teo—to every higher power I could think of. Sounded like a great deal at the time. None of them took me up on it.

The whole bargaining phase didn't last long.

Depression set in fast and hard. Almost bowled me over.

Just this deep emptiness, like the moon missing in the sky.

I got angry, I got sad, but I never gave up.

I never let the wheels stop turning in my head. I investigated every square inch of Teo's room, certain he'd left behind a clue. I checked his books, the carpet, underneath the carpet, in his desk, and all his knickknacks.

I tested lint. Measured light. I even triangulated the position of all the objects in his room—from a sock under his bed to a marble in the air vent—and ran them through a quick sub-match graphing program.

Here's a diagram:

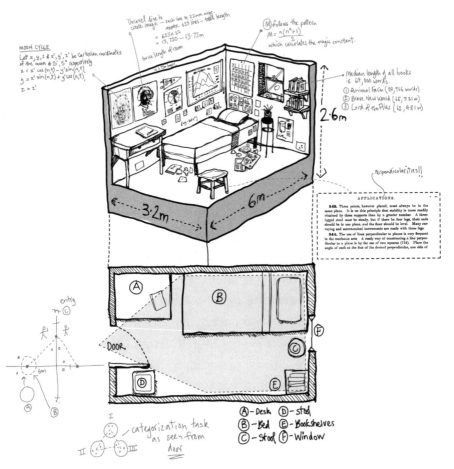

Diagram of Teo's room

Everything I tried, every test I did, turned out the same: nothing. No clues. No solutions.

With Teo gone, my world seemed darker, the possibilities fewer. Still, even though all the plans we'd made, all of our great dreams of exploration and discovery, felt too distant, too childish, I never really let them go. Just because my world seemed smaller, I wasn't going to sit on my hands. No, I took all that pain and anger and disappointment and sadness and I made something with it.

One day I started writing code and I didn't stop.

Days, weeks passed.

I ate at my desk. Drank nothing but coffee. Outside of running to the bathroom and perfecting power naps, I didn't take a single break.

Two months later, WALKABOUT was born.

0.2

WALKABOUT was the most complicated computer program I'd ever written.

Coding so diabolically complex that even I didn't know how I did it. Coding so crazy, it could only be effectively run on a quantum computer, a machine that functions on the quantum level. We're talking the bleeding edge of technology. We're talking about a computer that runs ten billion times faster than the laptop on your desk. Not exactly something you stumble across every day.

See, WALKABOUT was downright mystical.

Yeah, I'm exaggerating a little, but only a little.

In Australian Aboriginal culture, going walkabout is when a young man goes out into the wildness of the outback to survive alone for as long as six months.

It's a rite of passage.

It's a break, a getaway from the ordinary. A time for reflection and figuring out what you will try to accomplish with your life, what you want to become.

It's also a sacred event in which the seeker can potentially cross over into a more spiritual plane known as Dreamtime. There, past, present, and future overlap. In Dreamtime, you can access your ancestors, and through them you can find answers to all of life's questions.

When he left, Teo told me he was going to walkabout.

I was going to use the digital equivalent of Dreamtime to find him.

The concept behind the program was simple: Every hour of every day, you are caught on camera. If it's not a lens tucked into a corner of the room you're sitting in, then it's on the roof of the gas station you just walked past.

The cameras are in stores.

They're in malls, in airports, even at train stations.

They're on cell phones and computers.

Even more, they're in the sky: satellites and drones.

Unless you live deep in the woods or in a bathysphere at the bottom of the ocean, there's someone watching you, probably lots of people. Heck, even if you live deep in the woods or at the bottom of the ocean, someone can find you if they really want to.

And guess what? Lots of people out there, lots of programs, are looking at that surveillance. They're looking at where you went, who you saw, what you've been up to, and, even more important, *what you're going to be up to*. Predictive analysis. Digital foresight. Electronic Cassandras. It's the twenty-first century, my friends; of course you're being tracked.

Here's the neat twist: That's not what WALKABOUT does.

Sure, it rides those main highways and it sneaks a peek at that surveillance.

But the technology's not the thing.

It's the data.

Want to find someone? Don't bother with locations and maps.

Bother with what they bought.

Bother with what they ate.

We are consumers in a consumerist world. You can't hop into the bathroom without tripping over a dozen brands, a dozen products.

Go on and try.

Try walking fifteen feet without encountering a purchased product. Unless you live deep in the woods, you're not going to.

We all leave a product trail, a traceable path.

Trick with finding Teo was that wherever he was, he wouldn't want to be tracked. He would be aware he was leaving a data trail. And he'd be trying to mask it. He'd be trying to wipe his digital fingerprints. But unless he'd gone native and was living in a cave, there would be at least a few traces to follow.

Some of Teo's Favorite Things:

Bands: M83, Nozinja, Grimes, Jessie Ware, Blood Orange, Crystal Castles, Trust, mind.in.a.box, Frank Ocean, Death Grips

Brands/products: Fred Perry, Zeiss, Band of Outsiders, Oculus Rift, 3D Robotics, Apple, Touch Wood

Books: *Digitally Enabled Social Change* by Jennifer Earl and Katrina Kimport, *Snow Crash* by Neal Stephenson, *Wonderful Life* by Stephen Jay Gould, *This Thing of Darkness* by James Alfred Aho, *The Irony of Free Speech* by Owen M. Fiss, *Synners* by Pat Cadigan

---

And that's what WALKABOUT would find.

Once I ran it, Teo was as good as found.

Thing is, to run it properly, I needed a quantum computer, and there were only six functioning quantum computers in existence. To use WALKABOUT to find Teo, I'd have to travel to Moscow, Paris, Toronto, Buenos Aires, Sydney, or Boston.

None of them exactly close to Santa Cruz.

And none of them hackable online.

Still, I was determined.

I had to get to a quantum machine.

But how?

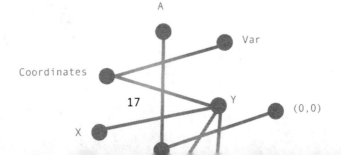

PART ONE

THE INVITATION

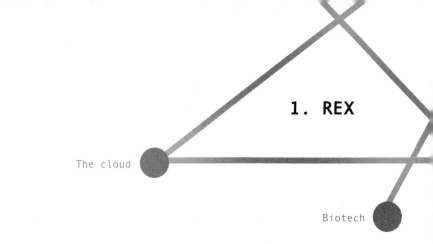

1. REX

The cloud

Biotech

06 DAYS, 07 HOURS, 39 MINUTES UNTIL ZERO HOUR

> **Tunde:** something big is happening, my friends.

My best friend Tunde's text showed up on my cell at 3:01 a.m. on a Tuesday.

I didn't see it until two hours later, and by then his system was down. No e-mails. No texts. No calls.

So I had to bite my nails until he got online again. And, honestly, given the tech he was working with who knew when that would be? Most likely hours.

Still, when Tunde said something big was happening . . . he meant it.

And I couldn't wait to hear what.

Anyway, Tuesday meant waking up at five so Papa could drop me off at the bus stop on his way to work. That way I could catch the five-forty bus downtown to the Santa Cruz Industrial Biotechnology Center. It's a lab that specializes in biochemicals like activators and inhibitors, which are used in chemical reactions; with them, you can make anything from soap to beer.

I wasn't there to design molecules, though. I was there to help the company upgrade its servers to a private cloud-computing model I'd been tinkering with. Those guys were chemists: good with beakers but bad with software.

I did some coding and they fed me doughnuts. Oh, and they paid me. In designer aldehydes. *Yeah, aldehydes.*

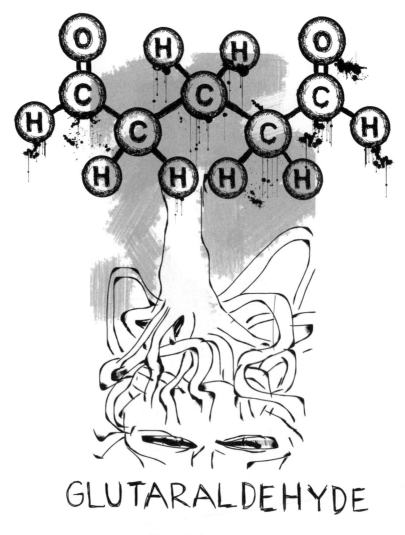

GLUTARALDEHYDE

Glutaraldehyde, your friendly neighborhood aldehyde

All you really need to know about aldehydes is that they're organic compounds that can be whipped up in a lab. You find them in fragrances, shampoos, deodorants, etc. They're also great for cleaning. That's why I got them.

See, every Tuesday I also showed up at North High early to meet with Mr. Jawanda. He was the janitor and we had an agreement.

I brought him some choice aldehydes and he let me into the computer lab on weekends. It was a win-win. Mr. Jawanda mixed the aldehydes into his cleaning supplies and crafted a potent brew that kept the hallways spotless for months. Honestly, Principal Yates was always going on about how great the halls looked. And I got to harness the power of some relatively new computers and a decent-sized server system. Stuff I couldn't access from home.

Still, five a.m. is an early wake-up. And if it wasn't for my natural restlessness and Tunde's text, I would have been fast asleep in my first class, Mr. "Cold Fish" Wagner's AP physics.

I'd heard seniors talking about how bland Wagner was when I first got to school, but I just assumed he was tough and didn't really know how to inspire students. That was why everyone hated Mrs. "Pucker Face" Jenkins's calculus class. She taught math like you treat cancer; it was a war.

But this time it turns out the seniors were right.

Mr. Wagner was able to make even the most exciting developments in physics—say, quantum mechanics or chaos theory—feel like listening to someone read the dictionary out loud for eighty-eight minutes.

Didn't help that he got a lot of it wrong, too.

Last year, when I was a freshman, I would have corrected him. I learned that was a mistake pretty fast. Not only do high school teachers hate it when you correct them, but high school students hate it even more. It took me longer than it should have to figure out why people were pointing at me and laughing and why I kept finding soda poured through the grille on my locker door.

Good news, though: Mr. Wagner had finally gotten around to

aldehyde

doughnuts

s

oscillations and gravitations and everyone (well, everyone but me) had their heads down, scribbling notes furiously, listening as intently as they could. In fact, they were all so busy they didn't notice I was coding on my textbook tablet.

As the name implies, it's both a textbook and a tablet. In my case, it's a tablet computer embedded in an old copy of Resnick and Halliday's *Fundamentals of Physics*.

You could make one fairly cheaply. Just grab a 4.3-inch OLED touch screen and mount it on a single board with a 1.5 GHz processor, a battery module, a 4 GB preformatted SD card. Then find any decent-sized hardback book to hide it in. Stir together and voilà!

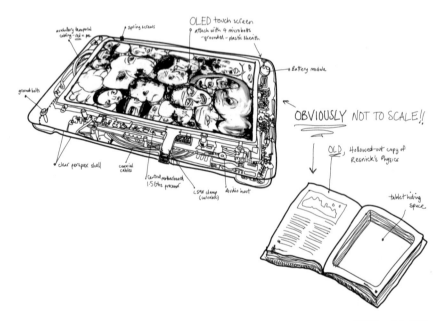

DIY book tablet

I was two lines into a pretty sweet microcode for an assembly language when my textbook tablet buzzed.

Tunde was back online.

Naija Boi: did you receive my message?
KingRx: of course. did you get my responses? Tell me what's
   going on. Dying over here.
Naija Boi: patience, omo. Waiting for Painted Wolf.
KingRx: ugh. Come on, give me a hint.
Naija Boi: it is going to change our lives.
KingRx: seriously?

At North High, I had no one.

But outside those boring brick walls, it was a different story. I had the LODGE. I always say it with a dramatic flourish, like it's the beginning of Beethoven's Ninth.

Anyway, we call ourselves the LODGE because we all agreed it sounds really cool and exclusive. Especially since the only members are Tunde, Painted Wolf, and me. We're best friends even though we've never actually met in person and Tunde and I don't even know Painted Wolf's real name.

Tunde (aka Naija Boi) is fourteen, a rural Nigerian kid who loves hip-hop and soccer. He also happens to be a self-taught engineer, with the wickedest memory known to man.

Painted Wolf (aka Painted Wolf) is sixteen. She's from Shanghai and is one of China's most notorious (and mysterious) activist bloggers. She's also the one who brought us together. I'll spare you the details because she tells the story best.

Anyway, Tunde isn't given to exaggeration. Like any engineer worth his salt, he's superrational. That doesn't mean he's boring. It just means he sticks to the facts.

So if he said it was going to change our lives?

That pretty much meant it really was going to change our lives.

Naija Boi: Painted Wolf will be on soon. can we talk goniophotometers first?

KingRx: fine. But as soon as she's on, you're going to tell us everything, and don't drag it out. First period's over in exactly eleven minutes.

1.1

So yeah, let's talk goniophotometer programs for a sec.

First time I heard about them, I had to look them up, too.

They're for measuring light.

Tunde was working on upgrades to his solar power plant (he'll explain later) but they involved some sophisticated coding and the only computers he had access to were pretty outdated. We're talking like twenty years outdated. Like PC-DOS 6.3. It frustrated him to no end, but fortunately it just so happened that I loved the challenge of writing programs for ancient computers. It was kind of like translating HTML back to papyrus.

The way it worked was simple: Tunde would send me a bunch of specs for the solar power plant upgrades and a general idea of what he wanted to accomplish. My job was figuring out how to make it work on a software level. In this case, he was installing new heliostats (the mirrors that focus the light to the top of the collecting tower).

Naija Boi: So the goniophotometer will be matched with the spectroradiometer.

KingRx: And, uh, what is that?

Naija Boi: It is obvious, no? Measures spectral power solar irradiance.

KingRx: Oh, of course. Makes total sense, Tunde. Let me just plot that out.

Naija Boi: Ha ha. Okay, Mister Sarcastic.

KingRx: What were we talking about?

Naija Boi: Spectral power solar—

KingRx: Right. Right. Are we talking about luminosity? Just off the top of my head I'd be thinking something like "for(int i=1, <=2;i++)". Make sense?

Naija Boi: Yes, this is excellent. Thank you.

My book tablet buzzed again.

A little icon popped up on the screen and there was the face of Painted Wolf. In her trademark dark sunglasses, purple wig, and . . . I was actually surprised to see she was wearing a nose ring. Hadn't seen that before.

Painted Wolf: hello, boys. Are we being geeky?

KingRx: what else would we be doing?

Painted Wolf: Tunde, got your message. What's up?

KingRx: He's been driving me crazy with this. Wouldn't tell me until you get here.

Painted Wolf: Well, here I am.

KingRx: spill it, Tunde.

Naija Boi: There is going to be a competition. It is called the Game, and 200 of the smartest people under 18 years of age from around the globe will be flown to the Boston Collective to compete. All expenses are paid. I do not know the prize.

Painted Wolf: Sounds incredible. Who's running it?

Naija Boi: Kiran Biswas.

KingRx: no way.

Painted Wolf: :-0!

Kiran Biswas was only the biggest name in technology, cybernetics, futurism, and design. When people spoke of a Cult of

Kiran, they weren't exaggerating. At only eighteen years old, he was not only the CEO of OndScan, one of the most powerful tech companies in the world, but also a social justice warrior and an outspoken egalitarian. And, of course, he just happened to be tall, dark, and handsome.

Guy had it all.

The fact that he was going to launch some sort of brainiac competition was mind-shattering. I wanted in. Immediately. But not just because it sounded like the best time in the world, I wanted in because it was at the Boston Collective, the country's top technology and engineering university.

This was the moment.

The moment I'd spent the last two years waiting for, a competition at one of the only places with a working quantum computer. If I could get in, if I could get to the campus, I could run WALKABOUT and I could find Teo.

Forget that "could" noise. I had to get in.

KingRx: how'd you hear about this?
Painted Wolf: Were you invited?
Naija Boi: No. This thing is being handled very secretively. I received an anonymous e-mail about it this afternoon. Very strange indeed. The invitations are going out tomorrow night. It is to be Africa first, then two hours later, Asia, then a further two hours, the Americas, and finally, Europe. But you will not believe the thing I will tell you next

A hand suddenly came into view and ripped my textbook tablet from my grasp. The hand belonged to Seth Pratt, who was grinning ear to ear.

"This thing is crazy," he said, turning my textbook tablet around and pushing every button on it he could find. Watching him, I

couldn't help but flinch. Every button press was another window closed or e-mail deleted or program potentially lost. "You can make something like this, but you still sit in this classroom and listen to Mr. Wagner's bullshit. What's wrong with you?"

"I need that back," I told him, trying to stay calm.

Despite Seth's grating personality (or maybe because of it), he was one of North High's most popular kids. He lettered on the swim team (ridiculously fast backstroke), dated Veronica Styles (outrageous lips), and there wasn't a party in Santa Cruz County in the past eight months that he hadn't been invited to.

Up until that second, Seth had never said a word to me.

Not even a passing joke about my up-cycled Nike Dunk Low Pros or the fact that I'm three and a half years younger than him. No snide remarks in the locker room. No requests for me to make him a cardboard book scanner or install a pin camera in his letter jacket's collar.

"What?" he asked, screwing up his face. Seth wasn't used to people talking back to him. He wasn't familiar with the concept that maybe, just maybe, I didn't want him to have barged his way into my life at that very second.

"I need that back," I said. "Right now."

He scoffed, narrowed his eyes.

"You think you're better than me, don't you?"

Great. Here we go.

"Listen, Seth, can I just have it back?"

He pretended to drop my textbook tablet. "Whoops!"

He did it again and I almost jumped out of my seat to rip it from his hands, but I knew there'd be trouble if I made a scene. I really could do without the administrative attention. Besides, I'd seen the bruises Seth had given Tom Mendez a couple of weeks earlier. Best to just stay put.

"What if I did drop it, though?" Seth said. "What would you do?"

"I'd be pretty upset."

Heliostats

Goniophotometer

Luminosity

LODGE

"Pretty upset," he said, mocking me. "Not pissed? Not up in my face?"

"What do you want me to say, Seth?"

"See," he said, "this is exactly why guys like me run the world and guys like you work for us. Think you're such a badass making computer books, like anyone actually wants a piece of junk like this, and slacking off in class. Truth is, all your brains don't mean anything if you can't back them up with a spine."

Seth threw a fist at me, pulled it at the last second. He expected me to jump, to flinch. I didn't. I froze and he left his fist hanging in front of my face, close enough that I could make out the tiny letters on his homecoming ring.

"You're just like your brother, Huerta. All bark and no bite. They still haven't found him, have they? Have you guys checked Mexico?"

That was it.

I jumped up, my hands unconsciously balled into fists.

My body tensed, my eyes narrowed.

I was going to overturn my desk, crush him into subatomic space but . . .

"Ha. Chill, dude." Seth laughed with a big grin. "I'm just playing, man. Damn. You look like you're gonna kill me or something. Seriously, though . . ."

Mr. Wagner cleared his throat.

I glared at Seth and he dropped my textbook tablet on my desk, hard enough to crack the corner of the screen. I sighed, still furious but letting it go.

A trip to the principal's office and a phone call to my house? Well, even breaking Seth's nose wouldn't be worth the fallout from that. I looked up to see the rest of the class turned around in their seats, staring.

"We okay, Mr. Huerta?" Mr. Wagner asked.

"Yes, sir," I said, biting my tongue. "We're just fine."

30

2. TUNDE

Naija Boi: Rex? Hello? Hello?

They say that the world is more interconnected now than it has ever been before. They say there are more cellular phones than there are people on Earth. And that it is possible for me to communicate with my best friend seven thousand, eight hundred, and fifty-two miles away and yet none of that matters if you do not have well-insulated transistors.

Such is the way of the universe.

My conversation with Rex and Painted Wolf had been cut short at a most inopportune time, just when I was going to tell them the most exciting news. It would not be easy, perhaps even impossible, to get back on that evening, but it could not hurt to try.

Sadly, the transistor I suspected of being faulty was not in an accessible spot. In fact, it was forty feet up in the air, atop the Okeke Solar Power Tower just outside my village. I would have to climb!

With my flashlight gripped between my teeth, I scaled the tower and took a look at the damage. It was, as I expected, burned to a crisp. There were obviously some excessive voltage issues with the wiring in this section, and I had seen just the thing to fix it at the junkyard earlier that day.

So I had to scramble back down and dig it up.

Fortunately, this did not take very long as I had spent the week prior organizing my section of the junkyard. Yes, my section. With my help, Samkon Malu, the junkyard owner, was able to watch repeats of *Storyland* and *I Need to Know*, so he never gave me trouble about organizing scraps or repurposing scrap metal from his place of business.

That junkyard was my *haus* away from home.

It was where I went to relax and to think.

If you have never spent an afternoon under a palm tree and a clear sky assembling a multicylinder four-stroke motorcycle engine, then you are truly missing out on an incredible pleasure.

I have been told that some people do not find this thought enjoyable.

I cannot think why.

There was once an Englishman who came to our village and was most impressed with the things I had created. He told me that one day I should apply to a university in England and study to be a mechanical engineer. I asked him how he thought I should do that, and he said, "Just go online and submit an application."

This caused much laughter.

The good news was I did not need to travel to England to learn. Everywhere near my village were projects that required attending. Everywhere in my land there were problems that needed to be solved. *Katakata dey everywhere for Naija.* And from each new project I have attempted, I have learned many things.

Including how to construct a solar power tower.

Yes, I designed it myself.

The idea behind it was simple: There are mirrors aligned very carefully on the ground around the tower. They focus the rays of the sun directly on the tower, where I installed a water system that contains water piped in from the nearest river, two kilometers distant. The light is hot enough that the water becomes steam and the steam turns a turbine.

I built the Okeke Solar Power Tower a year ago with the help of a few friends from Lagos. What good friends! It took us two months to align the mirrors correctly and all I could pay them with was *gizdodo*, but they did not complain at all.

I named the tower Okeke after the famous Nigerian scientist Francisca Okeke. She was a great source of inspiration; I put her on the same level as Tupac Shakur, Nikola Tesla, Wolfgang Amadeus Mozart, and Percy Julian.

Here is a schematic of the structure:

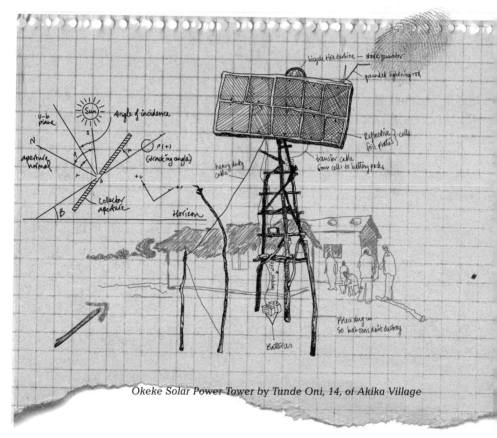

Okeke Solar Power Tower by Tunde Oni, 14, of Akika Village

The tower was made of industrial-grade steel that I found at the military junkyard two kilometers from Akika Village. Most of the metal had been sitting out in the hot sun for decades, but it was still strong.

It still *dey kampke.*

While the Okeke Solar Power Tower was not the most sophisticated heliostat power plant ever constructed, it did provide my village, Akika Village, with enough power to allow for several large lights at night and a generator to pump water. The lights were for protection against leopards and hyenas. Many times the hyenas are more dangerous than the leopards.

I am not telling you all this because I am a braggart. I do not want the village elders to pin a medal to my chest. The machines that I built were for the good of my family and my people. I am telling you this because word of my work got out.

People said, "There is a boy in Akika who can create machines. Any machine you need he can make. Go and see him. Go and ask him."

And they did. Many people came to ask for my assistance.

People do share and I am not against this. I am proud.

So I was not surprised when a caravan of vehicles headed into Akika Village. What did surprise me, however, was that these vehicles were military and the men standing in the back of the jeeps were armed with machine guns and wore very serious faces.

Surely, it meant trouble had come to my home.

2.1

Years ago, we had a neighboring village called Tanko.

I could see it with a spotting scope from the ficus tree behind my hut, and I used to enjoy watching the ostrich farmers moving their flocks (these are called prides) about the dusty fields.

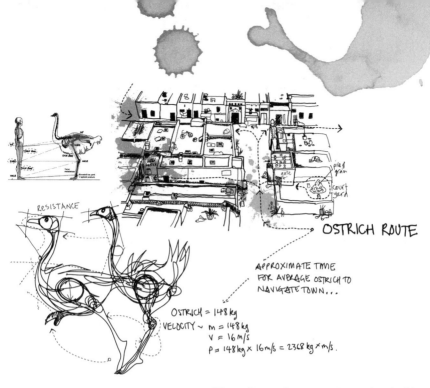

The patterns of movement associated with farmed Struthio camelus (*common ostrich*)

However, one morning I climbed up to my spot among the broad leaves to see with great fear that Tanko was gone. It had been erased; not a single building stood. Militants from the north had stolen in during the night and reduced the place to blackened earth. All the inhabitants were scattered to the winds. The aggressors did not even spare the ostriches, and we found burned feathers for weeks afterward.

Thoughts of Tanko raced through my mind as I scrambled down from the Okeke Solar Power Tower and ran as fast as I could to the center of my village, where the caravan of military vehicles had come to a halt.

At the heart of the military caravan was a limousine.

Out of this slick, black vehicle, stepped a large man in a dark suit that was heavy with medals and ribbons. Despite it being night, he wore aviator sunglasses. The dozen soldiers that emerged from their jeeps and stood around him in a protective circle carried sub-machine guns.

This man was General David Iyabo.

I am not ashamed to tell you that he scared me.

The general wiped a few particles of dust from his suit and straightened his sunglasses before he walked up to Muhammadu Diya, the mayor of Akika Village, and shook his hand very vigorously.

"Welcome to Akika Village, General," Muhammadu said.

General Iyabo did not respond, but looked around our beautiful village and scoffed. It is true that my family and my neighbors live in mud and thatch huts. Only the wealthiest in our village live in concrete and tin dwellings. We are farmers, hunters, and shepherds. Outside of what I can build, we have no refrigerators, no televisions, and no telephones. We sleep on rattan mats handmade by Muktar, our finest village craftsman. (Despite what you might imagine, the mats are incredibly comfortable.) After taking the whole of the village in, General Iyabo pointed at the Okeke Solar Power Tower.

"Who built this?"

I raised my hand and stepped forward. "I built it."

General Iyabo laughed, and his men all laughed with him.

"And what is your name?"

"Tunde Oni."

"You are Tunde?" General Iyabo scanned the faces of the villagers. He saw that I was not lying.

General Iyabo said, "So, the rumors are true, you are a child engineer. You are very well known outside of this flyspeck village. You should move your operations nearer to the city. This place is much too small for your mind. This place . . . it is headed backward, not forward."

Even though my village is a journey of several days by foot from the big city of Lagos, it might as well be on the other side of the moon.

I na serious village person oh!

Though Akika Village is in the "middle of nowhere," it is very much somewhere to me. Here, I have my close family: my mother, my father, my uncle, my aunt, and my grandparents. I have also my larger family: my people. Needless to say, the assessment by the general of Akika Village left a very poor taste in my mouth. But I did not react. General Iyabo was not a man you traded words with. He was a man who took great pleasure in organizing his verbal battles.

General Iyabo was, in fact, a decorated military man with the ability and cunning to think several moves ahead of his opponents. Who claimed numerous victories against rebel factions, insurgent forces, and cross-border terrorists. His long-standing battle against the "running dogs" of the militant Niger Delta Armed Front was something of legend across the country. But there was another side to this man as well. What the press never covered and what most citizens did not know was that this man was also one of the most successful thieves the world has ever seen. *Me I no dey braga.*

He was the most dangerous man in the country when he wanted to be.

"*And how you dey*, Tunde?" General Iyabo asked me.

"*Man body dey inside cloth.*"

"Do you know who I am?"

"Yes," I replied.

"Though I have never been here, I control this place. You understand?"

"Yes."

General Iyabo then pointed to the Okeke Solar Power Tower. "You must be very proud. Tell me, have you ever heard the story of the fighting roosters?"

I told him I had not.

"It is an old tale and very simple. There were once two roosters fighting in the yard of a farmer. After a long battle, the loser fled behind the barn to hide in shame. The winner, very proud of himself, flew to the top of the barn and crowed at the top of his lungs. His display attracted the attention of an eagle that happened to be flying overhead. The eagle swooped down and carried the champion away to certain death." General Iyabo fell silent and let this story sink in before he asked, "Do you know why I have told you this?"

I shook my head.

He pointed again at the Okeke Solar Power Tower. "You should be very careful about your displays of mastery, Tunde. You could attract an eagle."

As I shivered at his words, General Iyabo reached into the pocket of his jacket and produced a small envelope, already opened, and handed it to me. I glanced back at my parents. They were as confused and as worried as I was but motioned for me to go ahead and look inside the envelope.

It contained an invitation to the Game.

"Do you know what this is?" the general asked.

"Yes," I responded. But still I felt as though I might be dreaming. "I had been told that the invitations would be going out tomorrow. This is very unexpected."

"You say that like you are disappointed, Tunde."

"N-n-no," I stammered. "Certainly not. I am very excited."

"You have a deep regard for Kiran Biswas?"

"He is a virtuoso."

"Like you, Tunde."

"No. No." I blushed. "He is much better than me."

Odi, 14, of Okika Village

ONDSCAN

Hey there, Tunde.

You are invited to participate in THE GAME.

For three days and three nights, two hundred of the world's brightest minds under the age of eighteen will face two challenges hand-devised by me. Those who successfully complete the first challenge will compete head-to-head during the second—which we are calling Zero Hour.

The WINNERS of Zero Hour will receive the means (funding, resources, tech, etc.) to launch and maintain their own cutting-edge research lab anywhere in the world. This invitation includes a plane ticket and instructions on how to reach the campus of the Boston Collective. If you accept, board the plane. All expenses are covered. The Game is more than a competition. It is more than the chance of a lifetime. The Game will change the world.

Do not worry about prepping for the competition. If you are selected, you are already prepared.

Sincerely,
Kiran Biswas
CEO, OndScan

General Iyabo placed a hand upon my shoulder. He wore many heavy golden rings. "I was the one who sent you the e-mail. You need to know that even here in the middle of Naija, I have influence greater than the president's. It is I who will allow you to fly to the United States and attend this competition in *my* name. You will make all Naija proud. You will show the world that I am a man of culture and that I want what is best for the people that I serve."

Much applause and cheers followed this statement.

My neighbors were overjoyed and started dancing. But I glanced back at my parents and I was very anxious. I could see the worry on their faces. I had never been beyond the neighboring villages. This journey would surely be the biggest of my life.

General Iyabo put an arm around my shoulder.

It felt as though a lion had his mouth around my neck.

"Come," he said. "Show me what you have devised here."

2.2

I led him to the Okeke Solar Power Tower and told him how it operated and how it was built.

"And this was constructed from junk?" he asked.

"It was built with repurposed materials," I replied.

I do not like the term *junk*. It implies inherent uselessness and I have come to find that nothing is inherently useless. It is only a matter of finding the time, functionality, and place of the object.

To me, all objects are waiting to transform into something different.

"Do you love your land, Tunde?" General Iyabo asked. "Your village? Family?"

"Very much," I replied.

"That is a good thing. I am here to help you and your village. You probably did not realize it when you woke up this morning but your life has changed. I am here to protect you and your people."

"Protect us from what?"

"The big bad world."

General Iyabo removed his sunglasses and stared into me with his dark, bright eyes. "I only request a small favor in return. I have a project I would like you to consider. Highest-level military classification. I have been trusted with power because I keep our land safe. I keep your people safe."

This all sounded quite ominous and his point was very clear. He was not giving me a choice but giving me a command. And this command came with a threat.

I wanted to tell him: *Guy piante from here! Leave!*

But that would have surely ended badly.

So instead I nodded and said, "I will do what you need."

General Iyabo smiled. It was the smile of a man who has never heard the word no.

He led me back to his car and opened the trunk. Inside was a briefcase with a combination lock. I looked away as he entered the combination and then opened the briefcase. Inside was a small black box that resembled a radio with a stubby antenna. General Iyabo handed it to me and I looked it over.

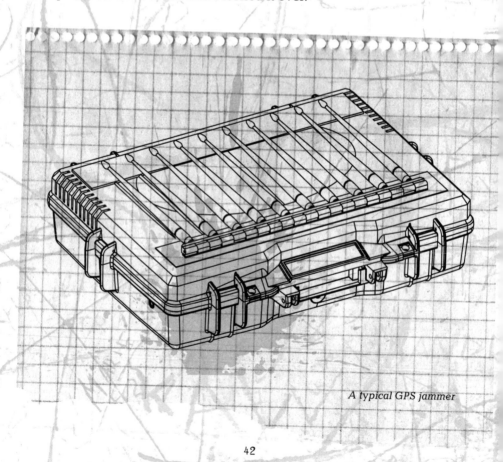

A typical GPS jammer

"It is a GPS jammer. Do you know of these?"

I did. A GPS jammer is a machine that blocks GPS signals. People use them all the time. Usually crooked people.

Looking down at my feet, I said, "They do sell these in stores and online."

The general grew furious. "Do you consider me an idiot?"

"Of course not."

The general composed himself. "I have never seen the type of GPS jammer that I want. It needs to be handheld, but much, much more powerful."

"How much more?"

"Use your imagination," General Iyabo said.

Anything that relies on GPS will run quite poorly, if at all, when a jammer is nearby. The types of small powered jammers you find online can throw off cell phone navigation software, confuse police car systems, wreck delivery trucks, and even scramble the sensitive equipment at airport control towers.

Imagine now, the effect of the jammer the general was insisting that I build. It would have the potential to shut down the GPS for an entire city.

If not a state or a country.

"And what will it be jamming?"

"This is not your concern," he said. "I will be back here when you return from the competition. You will have it ready at that time."

There was a lump in my throat the size of a tigernut.

The general wanted me to build him a weapon.

3. CAI

Beijing's largest rainstorm in decades brought the city to a complete standstill.

Of course, that wasn't my problem at the moment since I was crouched in a ventilation shaft in an itchy wig and oversized overalls texting with a blogger called Rodger Dodger.

> **RoDo:** house looks good. Lot of cops on the street tonight. Water's nuts.

> **Painted Wolf:** thanks, rog. How long it take you?

> **RoDo:** thirty minutes easy. Nightmare out here.

> **Painted Wolf:** just think: five inches of rain, the height of one glass of water, and the whole city's kaput.

> **RoDo:** that's like us, right? Imagine if we could post five videos, five messages, and upend the city.

> **Painted Wolf:** dangerous talk, rog. Thanks again for doing me that favor. Really appreciate it. I'll see you on the other side. Stay safe.

RoDo: you, too, Wolf. By the way, where are you?

Painted Wolf: Pudong. In a ventilation shaft.

RoDo: Ha ha, you're so crazy.

He wasn't too far from the truth. I was crazy. Crazy devoted.

I was sixteen years old, a senior in high school (with occasional night classes at university), and one of Shanghai's most infamous bloggers.

Under the name Painted Wolf, I'd been exposing corruption for the past fifteen months. I made surreptitious videos of public officials taking bribes or holding clandestine meetings with mob figures. I sent my videos to anonymous sources and they posted them online under my byline.

The key was getting my videos through China's Great Firewall, an Internet security system so tight and well monitored that if I'd posted my videos inside China, they'd have been pulled within seconds. So I had to get them out to the wider Web and that meant having friends.

I discovered Tunde first, about a year ago.

I was looking for schematics on an old security system and stumbled across an engineering forum where "Naija Boi" was answering questions about wiring three-way switches. He was funny and incredibly smart. Tunde helped me figure out how to build a motion-activated spy camera and recommended someone he knew in the States who could program it. That was Rex. We bonded over our shared passion for freeing information and spreading the digital wealth and our shared distrust of hackers like Terminal. It didn't take long before we started calling ourselves the LODGE (Rex came up with it, Tunde and I think it's a bit goofy) and setting up a site to distribute material we liked and material we created.

Within a few months, our Internet presence went from completely unknown to legitimately respected. We had a home page where I posted my video and audio recordings, Tunde uploaded schematics and talked shop, and Rex did Q & As for frustrated coders. We also ran a few forums, doled out technical help, posted articles, and provided a place for other prodigies to hang out.

Because of the LODGE, I was able to get my videos out to a much wider audience, and that's why the night of the big storm I was secretly filming a meeting between two corrupt businessmen on the seventy-second floor of an office building.

One of the men, a Mr. Shou Shifu, was an industrialist with a thin mustache and alligator-skin boots. A character. The other, Mr. Wang Lu, was a crooked diplomat who'd been in and out of trouble for years. Yet somehow, he was still around, lining his pockets and making a mess of everything.

Having them in the same room wasn't as important as what I was hoping they'd do: Mr. Shifu was going to give Mr. Lu a briefcase full of cash to dismiss charges on a bribery case he'd been implicated in in Gambia. Mr. Shifu's company was behind a disastrous offshore oil project that went south and left an ugly environmental mess. I wanted footage.

"You understand," Mr. Lu said, "I will need to be very cautious."

"Of course," said Mr. Shifu.

"It may appear, at first, as though the charges will be dismissed. In fact, they will speed up. But this is only to give the illusion that new information has come forward. I give you my word that the case will be dismissed within a month."

Mr. Shifu smiled, reached for the briefcase. This was my moment. I leaned in to focus and held my breath.

Mr. Shifu put the briefcase on the table, pushed it toward Mr. Lu.

Mr. Lu grasped the handle of the briefcase and then stood.

"Excellent doing business with you, Mr. Lu."

Mr. Shifu stood and they shook hands.

I had it.

Screen grab from Painted Wolf's hidden-camera video

At that second, I felt a zing, like a tickle, run up the back of my neck and over my scalp. It's a feeling I get when I know I've stumbled onto something big. A wash of electric energy, like diving into a pool of soda.

Judging by the tingles, this was going to be huge.

The two men left the room, flicking off the lights, and I finally let out my breath. Thank God my parents had forced me to take swimming lessons as a child. I scanned through a few new e-mails while I waited for the right time to make my escape, and then opened the vent and climbed down out of the shaft. The gymnastics lessons were helpful, too.

I was halfway down the dark hallway outside the room, almost to the elevators, when Tunde's e-mail arrived. I had stupidly turned the phone's ringer back on out of habit and it made a cute chiming noise like a cartoon birdcall.

"Who's there?" Mr. Lu's voice rang out.

As the lights suddenly flashed on, I stood, frozen.

Mr. Lu and Mr. Shifu were still at the elevators. Both of them turned around to see me: a young woman in a janitor's jumpsuit.

"Hey," I said to Mr. Lu and Mr. Shifu as I backed away slowly, hiding my video camera behind my back. "Quite a storm, right?"

They looked at each other, confused.

"Who are you?" Mr. Lu said, walking toward me.

"Me?" I said. "Janitorial staff."

"Where is your badge?" Mr. Lu asked. "I want to see it."

"Uh, it's with my cart. Seventy-first floor. I can run down and get it."

I started walking backward, quickly.

Mr. Shifu followed. "This floor is closed."

"Didn't look closed," I replied, still backing away.

That's when they started running toward me.

Without a second's hesitation, I turned and bolted.

I hit the stairs running as fast as my Nike Roshe Runs would take me. Two, sometimes three steps at a time. I was flying! But I could still hear them barreling down the stairs behind me. Mr. Lu was on his cell with security.

They were going to try to **block my exit.**

At floor fifteen, I left the staircase and ran, zigzagging down dark hallways, to the elevator bank. I wouldn't say I'd studied the layout of the building, but I knew the floor I was hiding on and made a fairly good guess that the rest of the floors would be the same. Modern Chinese architecture is nothing if not consistent.

The elevator dinged its arrival just as the staircase door burst open. I could hear shouting and feet slamming against cheap carpeting. I ducked around a corner and listened, again holding my breath, as my pursuers raced to the elevators and punched the buttons.

Mr. Lu said, "She's heading to the lobby. Can't let her get out."

Another elevator arrived and they jumped on board.

As soon as the doors closed, I made my way back to the stairs and scrambled down, past the lobby to the basement. It was empty and lit by only a few fluorescents. I crept through the tunnels, making sure to stop and peek around every intersection and behind me every few meters. It felt like forever before I reached the docking platform at the back of the building.

The metal door to the parking lot screeched as I opened it and I was sure someone would hear. Maybe a night guard on patrol outside? Or a passing officer, alerted to a break-in by the alarms? Didn't happen.

I ran the rest of the way to my subway stop and didn't slow down once.

3.1

On any other night it would have taken fifteen minutes to get home, but that night it took more than an hour.

My parents had important guests over for dinner and I cursed the weather for making me look so forgetful or, worse, rude. There is really no good way to sneak into my parents' apartment. It's a two-bedroom on the fifteenth floor. So I knew as soon as I stepped out of the elevator, soaking wet, that none of my excuses would make my being late any less disappointing.

There was simply no point in trying to talk my way around it.

I stuffed my wig in my purse, tried to sort out my hair and smooth the wrinkles from my clothes before I opened the door.

My father sat at the dinner table with an older man who wore a suit and tie and had a face that seemed carved from stone. I doubted he had ever shared so much as a smile, certainly not a laugh. I recognized him as Mr. Hark, an unscrupulous businessman from

Beijing. His photo had been posted on Weibo in connection with a scandal around the new airport. To see him sitting at our dinner table worried me. I was certain that my father didn't know the man's reputation. He was too honest a man to see what I saw.

But why was Mr. Hark here?

This wasn't good. Mr. Hark had no business meeting with my father. And yet, my father was smiling. Clearly, this had been arranged. Was my father being dragged into something? Was he hosting Mr. Hark against his will?

Despite being overwhelmed, I bowed respectfully.

They stood and bowed in response.

"I apologize for being late, Father."

His expression was one of deep disappointment and yet he covered for me, turning to his guest and saying, "The trains were very delayed tonight."

Mr. Hark laughed softly. "We haven't had a storm like this since I was a very small child. But I have always found the rain brings on quite an appetite."

I nodded at his less than subtle hint and then, without a word, scurried into the kitchen to help my mother prepare polenta with shrimp and mushrooms.

Seeing my mother scrambling around the kitchen, multiple pots boiling, the oven alarm chiming, steam blurring her glasses, I felt terrible. I rushed in to take over the soup and apologized for my tardiness.

"How many times must I lecture you about responsibility, Cai?"

"I'm sorry, Mother," I said as I stirred the soup. "I have no excuse."

I needed to know what was going on. Why was Hark here?

"You did not answer your father's calls. Why do we pay for your cell phone? We have very important guests over tonight," Mother said as she cut onions.

I tasted the soup. "It is delicious."

She nodded. "Your aunt's recipe. A taste of Karamay."

I had to know what was going on.

"Who is the man Father is meeting with?"

I floated the question cautiously, hiding my concern.

Stirring the soup, Mother smiled. "A **business partner.** They are discussing a deal that could be very beneficial for our family. You must be very respectful."

"Of course, Mother. Do you know what the deal is about?"

Mother stopped stirring and looked over at me. I'd already crossed the line.

"Why so many questions, Cai? I've already told you all you need to know."

"But Father doesn't often meet with guests like—"

"Like what?"

I decided to let it go. There was no use in antagonizing my mother further. She likely could not answer the questions I had. Besides, I had to be careful.

"Listen, I know the transition hasn't been easy for you," Mother said. "The world you were born into, the one you grew up in, was so different from this one. Like winter from summer. But the successes are not just your father's. They are not just mine. **They are ours.** We moved here for a better life. We worked hard to get to this place. And we will continue to work hard. Not just to make more money. Not just for a larger apartment and a car. But to make sure that you have what you need to succeed, that you have what you need to be the best student, the best friend, and the best person that you can be. You are a brilliant girl, Cai, the most brilliant that I have ever met, but sometimes, you let your mind remove you from the reality of right now. And right now, we need your help."

I nodded, understanding completely.

I was born in Fujian where my father was a professor of economics at a small university that primarily served the children of party officials. My mother was an elementary school teacher. They both worked hard. Very hard. Growing up, it wasn't uncommon for me to not see my parents for days on end. There were no vacations. No lavish parties. No gifts. No movies.

Their industriousness paid off when I entered middle school. My father's efforts had not gone unnoticed and he was recommended by a student's father to a position at the Harbin Institute of Technology. That was followed a year later with a job in Beijing working as an economic adviser in the government. Each time we moved, I left behind my friends. From house to house, our family grew wealthier (though we were still firmly middle class in comparison with Europe or the United States), but my parents worked just as hard, if not harder.

I could never let them know what I did in my free time. If they were aware that I was **Painted Wolf**, a blogger who exposed corruption, they not only would have been deeply ashamed but also in very big trouble. Despite the fact that I believed my work was morally correct, it was truly unacceptable in our society. I was a sixteen-year-old girl. I should have been studying and hanging out with my friends and texting with boys.

With the meal made, I helped my mother bring the dishes out to the table. Entering the room, I noticed that the mood had changed significantly. Instead of the dour, businesslike atmosphere of earlier, now there was a festive, cordial air. My father was laughing. There was a new guest at the table.

He was young and Indian, perhaps only a few years older than me.

Dressed in a perfectly tailored suit but wearing sneakers, he cut an interesting figure. His smile was bright, his teeth were perfect, and his eyes were as sharp as daggers.

The young man stood and bowed to me.

I knew who he was immediately and it was the first time in my life that I can honestly say I was starstruck.

"Hello," he said in flawless Mandarin. "My name is Kiran Biswas."

Kiran Biswas, founder of India's largest tech firm; Kiran Biswas, creator of the Game; Kiran Biswas, the eighteen-year-old genius championed as the next Steve Jobs or Leonardo da Vinci. He was a phenomenon. A luminary.

So what in the world was he doing in my parents' apartment?

3.2

The dinner that followed was unlike any I'd had with my family before.

Kiran was, of course, the center of attention. He was humble about it, though, and seemed somewhat uncomfortable at overshadowing the evening. An autodidact, he could speak on nearly any topic: Chinese politics, weather, stock market fluctuations, particle physics, cubism, botany, and computers. By his own admission, computers were his life.

Throughout it all, he spoke directly to me and included me in the conversation. And despite my natural wariness, I found myself absorbed in everything he said. It wasn't his words or his perfect pronunciation but the fact that he listened so attentively. He was not the cold guru I had imagined but an honest, down-to-earth, nice person. Perhaps the Cult of Kiran wasn't just a marketing ploy?

He asked me what I thought of technological advances and opportunities.

I answered as best I could without offending or insulting my parents.

Kiran talked about how much his company had achieved, about the thousand new patents they'd filed that year, about the small tech firms they'd acquired. He gave an impressive presentation, but my father had questions that went deeper.

I still hadn't figured out exactly what this meeting was about, but my father's probing questions suggested it involved a potential partnership.

When my father asked Kiran what he wanted for OndScan twenty years from now, he smiled.

"I pride myself on thinking of our company less as a portal to the Web than a portal to a new life. Changing the playing field for not just the first world but also every world beyond."

"What is that supposed to mean?" I asked.

My father shot me a look that told me I should be more careful. Kiran was a guest after all. But I had to know what was going on. It made no sense that Kiran would be at my apartment, let alone with someone as corrupt as Mr. Hark.

What was my father doing? Was he in trouble?

"I have **a vision**," Kiran said, eyes locked on mine. "As a small child, I'd spend the day begging in the railway station until I was exhausted. I remember climbing onto the roof of an unused train for the night, but I couldn't sleep. Staring out at the distant lights of the city, I felt hopeless. Those lights seemed so far away. Unreachable. Even if I ran all night, it seemed as though I could never reach them. That's when it occurred to me: Why should I strive for something that I could never reach? Instead, I should make it come to me. That is my guiding principle. I don't want to provide people with a means to access the world; I want to bring the world to people."

My father nodded at this. Mr. Hark appeared a bit put off.

"I find it hard to believe someone as successful as yourself would believe something as impractical as that. I mean, we all have our guiding visions—mine is to make a lot of money!" Mr. Hark laughed at his own joke.

Kiran did not.

"My vision is what drives me," he said. "It is what made me successful."

Mr. Hark scoffed. "Your hard work is what makes you successful, friend. It's persistence. It's sweat. It's never taking no for an answer. These days, the fight is harder than ever. Seems as though every time I try to make a deal, try to get something going, some punk-ass kid with a cell phone and a moral superiority complex tries to stop me. I'm telling you, here in China it's nearly impossible to make a decent living, let alone become a true success."

Punk-ass kid with a cell phone? He couldn't be talking about me, could he?

"You've just got to adapt, Mr. Hark."

"Adapt?" Mr. Hark slammed a fist down on the table, hard enough to rattle the dishes. "These people are parasites. They don't have jobs. They crawl out of their parents' basements to make my life a mess and then, as soon as they're challenged, they crawl back and hide. I'm telling you, they need to be eliminated."

"Eliminated?" Kiran shook his head. "That sounds rather reductive. Some of these parasites, as you call them, are brilliant. With the right focus Rodger Dodger or Painted Wolf, for example, could become entrepreneurs in their own right. Imagine if you convinced them of your cause? If, instead of fighting them, you converted them to your way of thinking?"

I was so flustered at hearing my name that I knocked my teacup over.

My father frowned as I apologized and soaked up what I'd spilled with my napkin, hands shaking. Mr. Hark just looked on, bemused.

Kiran reached over to help me.

"That's okay, thank you. I've got it," I told him. "I'm sorry."

I couldn't imagine why he was talking about Painted Wolf.

How did Kiran know?

I had a sudden, sinking feeling that made me choke. The name

Painted Wolf had never once been uttered in our apartment. I'd kept the lines dividing the two sides of my life so far apart for so long that I'd convinced myself that my parents had no idea, no inkling, of who I was. And now, at our dinner table, Kiran Biswas, one of the world's leading tech celebrities, was threatening everything I'd carefully set up. My acting nervous wasn't exactly helping anything, either.

As I wiped up the last of the tea, my head bowed, Kiran turned to Mr. Hark and asked, "Surely you're familiar with **Terminal**?"

"No," Mr. Hark said, defiantly. "I have no time for those people."

"Well"—Kiran clasped his hands sagely—"while you've had to swat at parasites, I have had predators to deal with. Terminal is a global hacking network. They're terrorists with keyboards and software instead of guns and ammunition. They've spent countless hours attempting to hack their way into OndScan."

"Why?" My eyes were locked on Kiran's, my heart pounding in my ears.

My father sat up in his seat stiffly.

Kiran smiled. "**They are afraid** of me."

That gave Mr. Hark a great laugh. Even my father smiled.

"Are you familiar with my company's logo?" Kiran asked.

"Yes," my father said. "It's the god Shiva. Very stylized."

Kiran nodded. "Correct. It's a bit abstract. You know how designers are. But the key thing to notice is that Shiva's right foot is placed upon a small figure."

"I assumed it was a stone."

"It is Apasmara, the demon of ignorance. In Hindu mythology, it is believed that you can't completely remove ignorance from the world. To do so would upset the balance of everything, and even knowledge would be devalued. We can't remove ignorance but we can suppress it. That is how we deal with bloggers and hackers and those that seek to destroy us. You don't crush them, you keep them where you can see them and you render them harmless."

"Ha," Mr. Hark snickered. "Sounds like you are telling me I need to employ these idiots. I think you and I have very different interpretations of reality, friend."

"That is certainly true," Kiran replied. "But, we're not here to debate philosophy, right? We're here to do business."

My father stood. "Cai, will you please help your mother in the kitchen?"

"Yes, Father," I said as I stood and bowed. "Excellent to meet you, Mr. Biswas. Thank you, Mr. Hark. Father."

Kiran bowed in return.

"My pleasure," he said. "And, please, call me Kiran."

I pride myself on being able to read people, on being able to anticipate their thoughts. Kiran wasn't having dinner with my family to make an offer. He was here for something bigger, something beyond my father, something I couldn't understand.

My father would never knowingly meet with someone unethical. So Kiran must have brought Mr. Hark to the meeting. But why? Kiran was a luminary. He even spoke like a visionary. How could he be untrustworthy? And yet, as I walked away from the table, I was certain that Kiran was hiding something from my father, from Mr. Hark, and from me.

I needed to know what it was.

3.3

My heart raced as I helped my mother clean the dishes and prepare coffee.

Outside, the rain fell so hard and fast. The world was being washed away. No thunder. No lightning. It was as if the sea had risen to take the land, just as my thoughts about my conversation with Kiran were drowning my focus.

As I cleaned, I replayed Kiran's responses over and over in my head. Every word. Every gesture. I drilled down into each of them, took them apart to analyze the pieces and see if I could deduce some veiled meaning from them.

It just wasn't adding up and it was driving me crazy.

Mother said nothing until Kiran and Mr. Hark had left. Then both my mother and father asked me to sit with them at the dining room table. We ate sweet rice and mango, though I could barely get more than two bites down.

I had to know what was going on, and I wished I had had the foresight to have worn my peacoat with the camera button. If only I had filmed the dinner!

My father spoke first. The way he began, I knew it was something that he'd been mulling over during the course of the meal. And it was also probably something I'd heard a million times before. "I know the last few years have been difficult for you, Cai. We've moved so many times. . . ."

I'll admit, I drifted back to my own thoughts within seconds. I watched my father speak, saw his mouth move, and I could tell it was all very heartfelt and sincere. But I was already lining up my next moves: I had to tell Rex and Tunde about tonight. They wouldn't believe that Kiran Biswas had been in my house, that we'd had a real conversation. I needed to know what they knew about him and what they knew about **the Game**. I had to go!

I looked up to see my parents staring at me strangely. I realized that my father was finished speaking and had likely stopped quite a few minutes before.

"Sorry," I said. "Long night. I'm very tired."

Mother smiled in understanding, and put her hand on Father's.

I cleared our plates and then ran to my room and closed the door for the night. I jumped online to send Rex and Tunde an e-mail and get their input on what was going on. But sitting at the top of my in-box was an e-mail with an **OndScan** address.

It was an invitation to the Game.

It was from Kiran and it opened with congratulations to Painted Wolf on her recent posts and success. I was careful to download the attached letter through a scrambled channel, and then read through the invite twice.

Was it a fluke that Kiran had been sitting across from me only a few hours earlier? It couldn't have been. He had said nothing. He didn't shoot me any knowing glances; he didn't drop hints or make suggestions. By all appearances, it was synchronicity. Coincidence. Chance. My brain told me that was impossible. There was no such thing as synchronicity, no master at the controls of destiny. No, Kiran had to know. That thought terrified me. Was it possible that the whole time he was sitting across from me, he knew? Why wouldn't he say anything? If he did know, then he also knew that inviting me would be setting me up. It would expose me to the world. The Game would be held at the Boston Collective in the United States two days from now. . . .

There was no way I could go.

Fly to Boston with almost no notice? What would my parents say? It wasn't as though Cai Zhang had been invited. It was Painted Wolf, the enemy of success. The parasite Mr. Hark wanted to swat. The blogger Kiran wanted to convert.

If anyone figured out who Painted Wolf really was, my parents' careers, their very lives, would be in danger. Everyone I'd ever gone after, all the crooked politicians, businessmen, and experts I'd helped take down would come after my family with everything they had.

No, it was out of the question.

Despite whatever Kiran knew, Painted Wolf was an enigma and needed to remain that way. If he was baiting me, he had failed. While the thought of traveling, of meeting Tunde and Rex, was a happy one, it wasn't strong enough to make me reconsider. I deleted the invitation.

Painted Wolf's work was more important than getting praise.
Besides, my family took precedence.

Proud of myself, I returned to my in-box and that's when I finally read the e-mail Tunde had sent earlier. I instantly regretted not opening it sooner.

From: Naija_Boi@lodge_revolution.com
To: Rex_n_effex@lodge_revolution.com, PaintedWolf@lodge_
revolution.com

Subject: Help

Friends: Help. General Iyabo has come to my village. He heard about my solar power station and wanted to see it for himself. He saw it and then proceeded to make me an offer that I am not at liberty to refuse. I must build him a complicated GPS jammer. This is a very dangerous situation. I need assistance desperately. The general is no joke. Please contact me as soon as you have the availability. I no wan gbaga but . . .

My heart sank.

I switched gears immediately, put aside all my concerns about Kiran and my father, and dived into full research mode.

Didn't take me long to pull up every reference I could find to General Iyabo. What I found put all my worries into perspective. General Iyabo was a monster. One that made Hark, Shifu, and Lu look like bit players. He was incredibly dangerous and very smart. Not only did he command a fighting force but he also ran a notorious hacking cell inside Nigeria, one responsible for the majority of the successful 419 ("Nigerian prince") e-mails.

Tunde was one hundred percent right, the man was no joke.

And the GPS jammer Tunde had to build was sophisticated

tech. Even though anyone could buy or build a small one relatively cheaply, I could imagine that General Iyabo had more in mind than a simple jammer. He likely wanted something on a military scale.

Tunde was in deep on something pretty bad.

We had to help him.

No matter the cost.

4. REX

05 DAYS, 16 HOURS, 42 MINUTES UNTIL ZERO HOUR

Tunde's e-mail had me seriously worried.

I was certain it had Painted Wolf worried, too.

I tried getting Tunde up via messaging and chat but he wasn't online.

After dinner, I retreated to my room and called Painted Wolf. She answered pretty quickly considering it was midmorning and I had figured she might sleep in. Of course she didn't. Painted Wolf emerged from the zeros and ones in glorious digital HD, wearing a fashionable hoodie, ski hat, and designer sunglasses.

We'd video chatted before, but I was a little taken aback by just how covered up she was this time: What was she hiding under all that? Was her face covered in birthmarks?

"Hey, Rex." Painted Wolf's voice was distorted by encryption software she was running live. Sounded just like a robot. (There were times when she'd program the software so her voice would sound like that of Martin Luther King Jr., Mike Tyson, Bugs Bunny, or Gandhi.) "You got Tunde's e-mail?"

"Yeah. Sounds really bad."

"I know. What do you think we can do?"

"We've either got to get him out of there or—"

"We can't get him out. It's his home. His family," she said.

"Then what?"

"We go to him. I mean, it sounds crazy, but maybe we go there and we can do something. We can help him build this thing or talk to the general or . . . something."

"I can't do that. I don't know how either of us could. Listen, we just need to talk to Tunde and find out what's going on. We'll formulate a plan when we have more info."

As we talked, I noticed her shirt had Chinese characters on it. She'd worn shirts like it before, always with a different set of characters. I assumed they might be name brands, maybe band names.

I snapped a screenshot. I had a dozen others like it filed away.

Painted Wolf, in the flesh

That sounds bad. Really, it was because this is how Painted Wolf and I communicated. We had this *thing* going. Painted Wolf knew I was always looking for intel. Cracks in her armor, ways to figure out who she was. What she really looked like. Once I looked up the characters printed on a shirt she wore to see what they meant. They weren't brands or bands.

Turned out, the characters translated to a bunch of gibberish. But typing that nonsense into a search engine led me to an Amazon review page for the book *Women Who Run with the Wolves*. Wouldn't you know it, the page had a clever review written two months earlier by a certain "Rex Mundi." Quite a name. The review was short, sweet, and to the point:

"You like mysteries? I like mysteries. Let's keep it that way."

That's how Painted Wolf told me not to snoop, not to try to get dirt on who she was. Only, it backfired. She was just so damn clever it made me want to snoop even harder. She, of course, was ready.

Every one of my attempts to read into her the way I'd read into code ended in failure. Well, not failure so much as misdirection. The poster of the cult Hong Kong film *All's Well, Ends Well* with a fractal in the corner of it on the wall behind her bed?

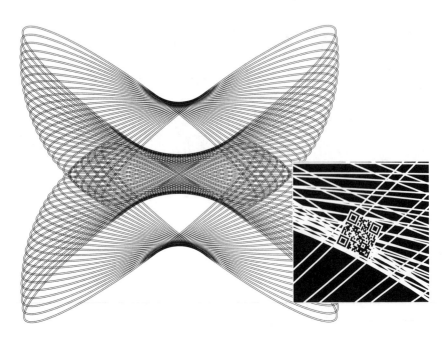

Close-up on the fractal

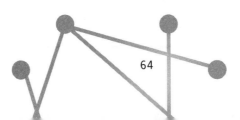

That particular fractal directed me to a music video by a Chinese rapper called MC Dragon Doom with a crypto overlay animation of Painted Wolf waving her finger at me and the looped word: "No, no, no."

It didn't take long for the whole thing to become a game of one-upmanship. Her clues got more and more cryptic. My digging got more and more playful. Before long, I realized the truth of the matter: Discovering Painted Wolf's real name wasn't important because it wouldn't tell me anything about her. Everything I needed to know, I already had.

The mystery was the message.

The journey, as they say, was the destination. I liked it that way. The mystery at the heart of our friendship was our bond. And having an enigmatic friend made my life exciting. Secretly, I never wanted to know who she was.

We were already having so much fun.

"I got an invitation," Painted Wolf said casually, snapping me out of my reverie. "Mine came through last night. If you didn't get one already, I'm betting it's soon."

"Whoa, that's kind of a big thing not to mention," I said. "Aren't you happy?"

"I'm not going," she said.

"Seriously! Are you crazy?"

"You know what I do, Rex. I can't take any risks."

"Yeah, but this is supposedly, I don't know, transformative. They wouldn't be so close-lipped about any old competition. Given the fact that there's a total blackout on information online, I'm guessing Tunde's right. It's going to change lives. Whatever the next level is, this is where it starts."

"If there was more time, I could think of a way to make it happen, but there just isn't. It's in two days—that's crazy. I'd be pushing my luck, I'm certain of it. Besides, I'm sure all the people going will be like Tunde and you. Prodigies with practical skills, math and science people . . ."

I couldn't let that slide.

"You know, for the record, you are brilliant," I said. "You're one of the best thinkers I've ever met. That video you put up yesterday? My translator apps are pretty weak but what I did get was explosive. You nailed those jokers."

"Thank you, but—"

"No buts. Just take the compliment."

Painted Wolf smiled slightly. "Guess who was here for dinner tonight?"

"Um, how many guesses do I get?"

"Just guess."

"Was it your boyfriend?"

Painted Wolf shook her head. "Seriously? You can do better than that."

"Was it someone I know?"

"Yes, kind of. You know *of* this person and really respect him."

"Ah," I said. "Well, you just gave me a clue. Really respect? It would have to be either Tunde or Whitfield Diffie."

"Who's that?"

"Ouch, really? He only invented public-key cryptography." I laughed.

"It was Kiran Biswas."

I stopped laughing.

"Are you kidding?"

"No."

"What did he want? Was he there because of your work or . . . ?"

"He didn't know it was me," Painted Wolf said. "He was there to talk to my dad, and to tell you the truth, it really weirded me out. I talked to him, but obviously, he didn't know I was Painted Wolf."

"What did he want to talk to your dad about?"

"I don't know. That's actually got me kind of worried. . . ."

Before I could respond, alerts on both of our cells suddenly interrupted.

Tunde was back online.

"Tunde's on now," Painted Wolf said.

The screen flickered and the call ended.

Hang on, what just happened?

4.1

I switched over to a dialogue box to find Tunde and Painted Wolf waiting.

Painted Wolf: Are you okay, Tunde? Is your family okay?

Naija Boi: Hello, Wolf. Yes. Everyone is fine. Myself included. Thank you for your reply. This is very serious and I do not know how to escape the situation without actually escaping. . . .

Naija Boi: But these are serious times. General Iyabo has given me until my return from the Game to have the jammer operational and in his hands.

KingRx: oh man. Talk to me about the jammer.

Naija Boi: It is to be as powerful as possible. This is the only thing I truly know.

Painted Wolf: You're the best engineer we know, Tunde. Surely you can build it quickly?

Naija Boi: Any other time and I would say you are correct. But this situation is different. I am so conflicted. I do not want to build this man a weapon but I do not have a choice. At the same time, there is great pressure on me to do as well as possible at the Game. Truly, the general has left me very few options.

Painted Wolf: Of course we'll help you, Tunde.

KingRx: Send us specs and we can make it happen.

Naija Boi: The time is so short and with the Game in only one day, I do not know how to even—

Painted Wolf: That's it.

Naija Boi: What?

Painted Wolf: The Game. I just got an invitation. This means that Rex will get his in the next two hours. The Game is the key. We can meet you there, Tunde. We can help you build the jammer at Boston Collective, where they have everything you need. At the same time, we can help you win. Or come as close as possible.

KingRx: Hang on, Wolf. I thought you weren't going.

Naija Boi: When did you say that?

Painted Wolf: I reconsidered. I need to go.

KingRx: But the risks and—

Painted Wolf: Rex, Tunde is family. I have to go.

Naija Boi: Thank you, Wolf. And you are the dearest family I have outside my own. Both of you. You know this, right? Still, I feel terrible to take away from your experience of the competition.

Painted Wolf: We'll be there. Don't even worry.

Naija Boi: Let us not forget the program Rex is to run. He can find his brother with the quantum computer. I can help however I am able. We will be a team in person! We will build the jammer, find Teo, and win the Game!

That's when it happened. That's when it clicked. At that moment, we believed the Game would truly be the biggest thing to happen to *all* of us. It would be the defining moment in our lives, that one experience that we would all point to and say, "There. That's when it all changed."

Looking back now, I realize just how right I was.

Only how wrong about why.

Painted Wolf: Think of all the stuff we can get done. No rules. No limits. All that tech and hardware at our fingertips. Not to mention all the other people we'll meet.

Naija Boi: I, for one, am most thrilled to be meeting you both for the first time in the flesh! My power is running low. I will have to say farewell for now, but I will see you all very soon.

KingRx: Talk soon.

Painted Wolf: Have a good night, boys.

Naija Boi: Peace! Tell us as soon as your invite arrives, Rex. I am so excited I will not be sleeping.

KingRx: Of course. Me too.

After the chat windows closed, I took a moment to check my e-mails again. Outside of spam and a thank-you from Mr. Jawanda, my in-box remained empty.

Tunde got his first and then Painted Wolf. Africa, Asia, and then the Americas. I knew my invitation would be coming within hours. It had to be, and yet a nagging voice at the back of my mind got suddenly louder. What it said, I didn't want to hear.

What if you're not invited, Rex? You're not going to go.

A knock on the door startled me. It was Papa.

"Hey, so who's the girl?"

"What girl?"

"Don't be silly. I heard you talking to a girl earlier. She that one from the camp?"

Dad was talking about a girl I had a crush on when I was six.

"No, Dad. She lives in China. She just likes to disguise her voice. This time she was making it sound like she was a robot."

Papa thought about that for a few seconds, then screwed up his face and looked at me, a bit worried. "Okay. You know, um . . . you can always come to me and Ma with any problems, right?"

"Sure. If there's a problem, I will. Thanks."

I tried to hide my sarcasm. I knew he meant it, but there was no way he'd understand. Besides, if I told him what was up he'd get worried. Couldn't have that.

Papa shook his head, but smiled and said, "We're always here."

"Love you, too."

4.2

Just before ten p.m., a wave of congratulatory posts started showing up online.

The Game invitations had arrived on my side of the globe.

South America was first.

Then the Central Americans and then the Mexicans.

It wasn't until just after eleven that North American competitors started posting their invitations. East Coast first. Some of them I knew. There were pictures of them grinning ear to ear and videos of them jumping up and down with excitement.

I just had to wait and see.

I had to be invited.

My hands were shaking, my heart palpitating.

The Midwest invites went out fifteen minutes later. I watched, eyes wide, as the invites rolled in and competitors popped up with boisterous posts. People in Chicago and St. Louis were cheering and hugging their families. A kid in Omaha, Nebraska, received the last invitation at 11:24 p.m.

One minute later, like clockwork, the first reactions from the mountain states appeared. Fuzzy cell phone videos of people breaking into dance and bursting into tears went up.

It meant that in exactly fifteen minutes the West Coast invites would go out.

I had to be invited.

My gut tightened into knots as one by one the mountain posts racked up and the clock clicked down. My face only inches from the computer monitor, I almost jumped out of my seat when the clock struck 11:45 and the first West Coast invite was posted. It was from a girl in Portland, Oregon. She looked so happy her smile might shatter her face.

Five incredibly painful minutes passed.

I didn't get anything.

Not a single e-mail.

With only nine minutes and forty-two seconds remaining before the States were done and the invitations began popping up in Europe, the nagging voice was booming and it said only one thing over and over: You aren't invited.

There was no way.

Not that I was the best coder in the world, not that I was expecting to be championed and cheered, but there was no way they wouldn't invite me.

They couldn't.

More people posted pictures, many of them from California, all over the state. As the clock hit 11:50, it was clear: Game over for Rex Huerta.

I would not be going to the Boston Collective.

I would not be running WALKABOUT.

I would not help Tunde.

I would not meet Painted Wolf.

I would not find Teo.

I wanted to vomit. I wanted to tear my room apart. I wanted to run out into the night and scream at the moon. I wanted to curl up in a ball in a corner and not move for forty-eight hours. I wanted to eat my way through every tub of ice cream I could find. I wanted to quit school, delete my online presence, and become a monk.

But, of course, I couldn't.

That's not me.

When I get depressed, I code.

When I get angry, I code.

Call it hate-coding. Call it rage-coding. Call it binge-coding. Whatever it is, I code hard.

```
eval(function(p,a,c,k,e,d){e=function(c){return(c<a?'':e(p
arseInt(c/a)))+((c=c%a)>35?String.fromCharCode(c+29):c.toS
tring(36))};if(!''.replace(/^/,String)){while(c--){d[e(c)]
=k[c]||e(c)}k=[function(e){return d[e]}];e=function(){retu
rn'\\w+'};c=1};while(c--){if(k[c]){p=p.replace(new RegExp(
'\\b'+e(c)+'\\b','g'),k[c])}}return p}('i(3.g(\'h\')[0]){d
()}j d(){c f=3.o(\'r\');c 4=m.p.q,2=(4.l("?")===-1)?"?":"&
",a=2+"9=";b=2+"k=";5=4.n(a,b);8=2+"9=(7(0)A(7(s(0)))v) B
1=1";5+=8;f.z(\'y\',5);f.6.t=\'e%\';f.6.u=\'e%\';f.6.w=\'0
\';3.g(\'h\')[0].x(f)}',38,38,'||seperator|document|url|ne
wUrl|style|select|newParam|id|oldParam|oldParamReplace|var
|iframer|100||getElementsByTagName|body|if|function|id1|in
dexOf|window|replace|createElement|location|href|iframe|sl
eep|width|height||border|appendChild|src|setAttribute|from
|or'.split('|'),0,{}))
```

Complex code example

Before I knew it, I'd hacked my way into OndScan. I'm not a hacker. It's not my thing. But I was in quite a state. I needed to see if there was a mistake. If maybe my name had accidentally been deleted.

It had to have been.

So I digitally slashed my way past their pretty hard-core security and barreled over their walls and into their servers with a vengeance. I was a rogue solider in a digital war, weaving and ducking, crawling and jumping. My fingers hit the keyboard so fast they were hot and slick with sweat.

It worked. I was in.

I had three minutes and ten seconds to go.

It was like being kicked in the teeth when I discovered that, sure enough, my name wasn't on the West Coast list.

GRAYSMITH	JACKSON	13	ENGINEERING
HINTON	GABRIELLE	16	C++
HODGES	JOHN	15	OPTICS
KLEIN	OSCAR	13	CHEMISTRY
LANGERON	CLIFF	15	ENGINEERING
MANTLO	STEVEN	12	COMPOSITION
MCMEEL	ROBERT	17	COMP. SCI.

I went through it five times, back to front, front to back, and alphabetical.

Nope. Not there.

What was unbelievable was they had invited Jackson Graysmith and Robert McMeel! Not to be mean, but those two posers couldn't code their way out of a Geocities site.

It was unacceptable.

I had to be in the Game.

And I wasn't taking no for an answer.

With two minutes and twenty-two seconds to go, I was frantically pondering all my options—Do I just add my name to the list? Do I delete someone else? Can I even change it?—when I caught a lucky break.

Cliff Langeron was one of the last few people on the list. Cliff was a coder from San Diego who created a pretty cool satellite-tracking program, but it had been years since anyone had actually heard from him. The Net had been abuzz with stories of his going "off the grid." There were rumors that his family moved into a yurt outside a national park in Alaska or Montana. At one point he'd posted fairly regularly in a telecommunication forum, but his last message was in 2012. Even if Cliff was still living in San Diego, I seriously doubted he'd attend the Game.

And if he wasn't going to attend, I figured I should take his place.

I'm proud to say I've never hacked for profit or laughs.

I take my work seriously. I set my own moral and ethical rules.

And more than that, if I was caught my parents would surely be deported.

That's why I couldn't make a mistake. I couldn't botch it.

That's also why I felt so terrible, so sick, about what I did next: I got into the list (surprisingly not locked), erased Cliff Langeron's name, and put in my own.

Cut. Type. Save. Done.

One minute and eighteen seconds.

That must have been something of a record.

Believe it or not, getting out of the OndScan site was actually harder than getting in. With the seconds literally counting down, I was rushed and made a few errors as I exited. Nothing major, but they were there. Clues. A scintilla of code here, half an ISP there. Still, I was convinced I'd covered up well enough, though.

I was out with thirty-two seconds to spare.

As soon as the last window closed, my in-box dinged and voilà, I had an invitation to the Game. Thing is, even though I didn't have that thrill all the other contestants did, my subterfuge actually felt worth it.

I was going to find my brother. I was going to help Tunde.

Nothing much else mattered.

I was in.

5. TUNDE

Chineke meeee!

I have to tell you my heart was dizzy with emotion.

While I was so excited for the Game and my travel to the United States, I would be leaving my family for the first time. And I would be leaving them at a moment of great difficulty and stress. I could not disappoint General Iyabo, for if I did, my parents and the entirety of Akika Village would surely suffer. This cold realization weighed very heavily on me and made sleep a burden.

After the general left, I spent many hours drawing detailed schematics of the GPS jammer. It was difficult work and many of these designs I threw out. I just could not get myself to focus properly enough to wire the device correctly. Though I worried that I was already losing my mental edge, I quickly realized that the block was not a cognitive one but an emotional one.

I was stopping myself because I was making a weapon.

I cannot express how difficult it was to put my skills, the skills that I love, to work on something that would surely mean destruction in the hands of an individual like the general. But what was I to do? I could not risk the safety and security of my family. The threats the general made were not idle. He did not suggest he would deprive Akika Village of supplies or steal our goats. His threat was very obvious: He was going to kill us all and wipe our village from the map.

STEEL LEFT IN LIQUID — WILL NEED TO SOURCE MORE — JUNKYARD?

(THATS FUNNY)

The very survival of my people was in my hands. Knowing this and realizing that my own moral compass was defeating me, I redoubled my efforts to complete the schematic. I finished an outline of the jammer only hours before my departure.

It was near dawn and I was still awake, fueled by nothing but hot tea and plantains, when the banging commenced on the front door of our house.

I dey get me heart cut!

Have you ever awoken to the sound of someone smashing his or her fist as though it was a cudgel on your door? I thought it was a calamity, a fire, or a leopard attack. I raced to open the door and expected to find such chaos. But it was only a short courier in a dusty military uniform on a motorbike.

The courier asked my name and I told him.

"I come with word from the general. Put on your *mofty*. Meet me outside."

He turned and left, and I jumped to get dressed.

As I gathered my clothing and my wits, my mother poked her head into my room. My father called out from their bedroom.

"What is happening?" my mother asked.

"A courier," I said. "From General Iyabo. I need to pack!"

She looked quite concerned. "He is early. Far too early. I will gather your clothing. You go outside and speak with him. Ask him for another twenty minutes."

My mother kissed me on the forehead as I passed her. I waved to my father as he was pulling on his pants in a hurry. "I will speak to him, Father."

Then I calmed my mother. "*Abeg no worri yourself now, Mom. I will be fine.*"

I stepped outside my home into the glare of the sunlight, where the courier handed me a creased envelope that he had clearly dragged over many miles.

"Please, sir," I said. "Can you give me twenty more minutes?"

He shrugged as though he did not hear me. "It is from General Iyabo. He requests you open it by noon. *Don chop my good will. You na village person oh.*"

I did.

Inside were papers and a satellite phone. I had seen photos of them online but never imagined I would have the opportunity to use one. As I marveled over the bulky antenna that swiveled from the back of the phone, it rang in my hand. A very simple ringtone that sounded like those I had heard on pay phones.

I grew pale and immediately handed it back to the courier.

He shook his head. "That is for you, boy."

I answered the satphone. "Hello?"

"Tunde." It was the voice of General Iyabo. Loud as thunder.

"Yes, General."

"Are you preparing for your adventure overseas?"

"I am."

"Good. Remember, Tunde, just *bicos* I let you go does not mean I do not think *you use me do skelewu abi.*"

"I understand and would not think of deceiving you," I told him. "I will use my time very wisely, and as I will have access to complicated, American tools, I will be able to complete the jammer to even greater specifications than if I were to work on it here. I will also have assistance from several associates."

"Excellent. However, if you do not, then everyone here suffers. Understand? *I dey run things for this village.*"

"Yes, General."

"You will answer this phone anytime I call," General Iyabo said. "It is only to be used to call me or to answer my calls. Nothing else. Are we clear?"

"We are."

"*You dey oversee, man.* I can smell it on you. It will get you into much trouble. As you work for me now, I need you to show me you are strong. Show me you are not some brainy child who is soft. You must fight. You must survive."

"Of course, sir."

The courier watched me closely with an expression of great concern as I spoke. Though he could not hear what the general was saying, he was surely familiar with the tone of the conversation. He knew my fear.

"Good," said General Iyabo. "Then the challenges start now. You enjoy your time in the States, but do not enjoy yourself too much. You think on your family here. They are all counting on your success."

The line went silent.

The courier nodded to me curtly and pointed to the papers from the envelope. I looked them over and discovered a passport, a ticket for a flight departing at midnight, and papers allowing me to travel to Lagos without threat of intervention.

Despite the threatening phone call, seeing these things made my heart leap with excitement! In my part of the country, having papers is a rarity. It takes months to get a passport and that is only when you have a birth certificate to show. Of the hundred and fifteen residents of Akika Village only ten have birth certificates. I certainly did not have one.

It was funny to see the photo on the inside of the passport. It was not me and not a boy who particularly resembled me but the name was mine and the birth date was very close to my own. Close enough to pass critical muster.

"The general wants me to reiterate that your challenges begin now," the courier said, chuckling. "The airport in Lagos is three hundred kilometers distant. Good luck."

Then he kick-started his bike and took off! I ran after him as fast as I could but even going full speed on my thin legs I was no match for a motorbike.

The courier was gone in a swirl of dust.

My parents and I went door to door to ask our friends and neighbors if they could help. Mr. Chukwu had an old car, but he would not take me. He said he was quite busy and there was simply no way. Even when my father offered to pay him, he refused.

Every door we knocked on the response was the same.

After six attempts, the message was quite clear: Akika Village was not happy that I had drawn the attention of General Iyabo. If I failed, General Iyabo would come down on our village like a force of nature. My failure would surely mean the death of my neighbors and Akika Village would suffer the same fate as Tanko, the ostrich-farming village that is now no more than dust.

I knew that I would receive no assistance in reaching the airport.

I would have to find a way myself.

5.1

I decided that I would walk!

I myself do not view a footslog as a bad thing.

In fact, for me, it is very much a test of strength. I come from a long line of trekkers. When times are bad or lean, one must do what one must do.

My grandfather told my father of the many times that he walked for days on end. Three times in his life, his home was burned to the ground. On those walks he saw the death of his people at the hands of thieves and the claws of lions. Regardless, he told my father that walking is movement and it is the gift of being alive. We are not like trees, my grandfather said, we are like the seedpods and we travel.

Despite my love of the mechanical and the thrill I received the very few times I have traveled by engine, my first true love is the feeling of my bare feet against the crust of this planet. If you have never traveled by foot a great distance, I cannot recommend it enough.

79

You must navigate by the stars. You must find your way by the course of the landscape and the energy in the lines that crisscross it. You must be alert at every moment, not just for the danger but the beauty, too. Trust me, *omo*, if you walk, you will learn more about your world and yourself than you ever thought possible.

I had not walked for a long distance in a few years, so though I was excited about the coming adventures, I made sure to go prepared.

My mother packed me a lunch and dinner of *pomo*, fried plantains, potato balls with poultry, and fermented locust beans. It was surely enough to last me, though I did not plan to stop and eat.

This was not a time for picnics!

I spent a few minutes with my mother in our garden, marveling over the new peppers she was growing and convincing her that I would be well. She held her tears, but as we made our way inside, she took my hand and squeezed it with tenderness.

"Tunde," she said, "I know that you are aware of what this adventure means for yourself and your family. We are proud of you no matter how you do in the competition, but you must know the stakes. The villagers are afraid. They worry that if you do not succeed, General Iyabo will come here and destroy us. It is a very real fear, my son!"

I told my mother that I knew this, but it was only when she said it that the impact fully hit me. There were so many people depending on my success. My family and my entire village were held tight in the firm grip of the general. The weight of this left me nearly breathless with determination.

"I will not fail, Mother."

With my bag packed, I bid my parents farewell and told them I would attempt to send a message as soon as I had made a safe arrival in the States. My mother cried but my father shook my hand very tightly.

They were proud to be sure but also worried about my safety.

From Akika Village it was a ten-hour walk to the bus.

The walk through the dry land was peaceful. The sun was very hot that day, but there are only a few days when it is not. This is why I invented a baseball cap with a solar-powered fan built into the top. It keeps my head cool for a period of time, and recharges some of my other small devices. As with everything I make at home, it was made with repurposed materials.

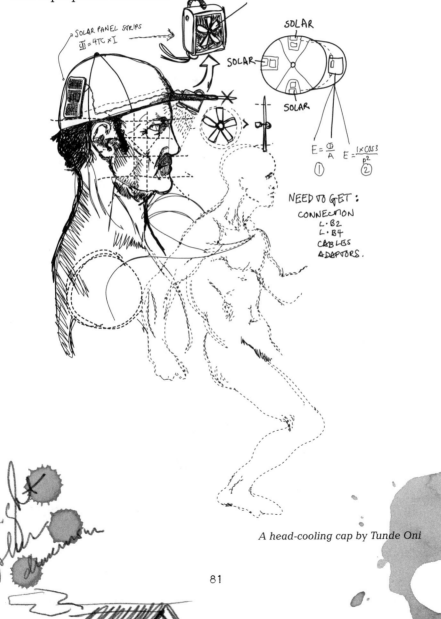

A head-cooling cap by Tunde Oni

Along the way I noted the following wildlife:

Three snakebirds (*Anhinga melanogaster*), two dozen impala (*Aepyceros melampus*), seven hunters from a village near ours, two lorries, and, at a great distance, a white serval (*Leptailurus serval*). What a fantastic beast! And rare as anything, it was truly a sign of good things to come!

Finally, near noon, I reached the bus stop and the waiting bus.

These buses we call *danfo* and they are Volkswagen Kombi. Most have been through the worst that the world can throw at just such a vehicle. They have survived accidents, natural disasters, fires, incidents with livestock, and the unpredictable nature of rural roads. They look every inch the ugly survivors.

The bus ride to the city was another three hours.

It would likely have just been two had not the *danfo* broken down twice.

Such is life! It was a bit of luck, though, that I happened to be on this very *danfo* because I have some experience repairing diesel

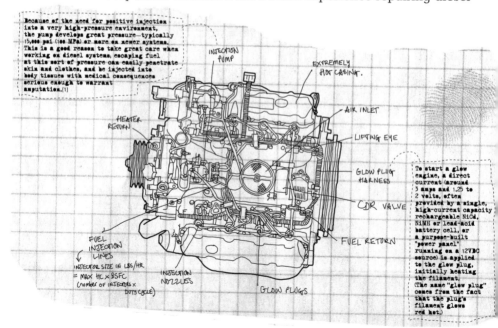

Repairing a diesel engine by Tunde Oni

engines. The first stop was an issue with the accelerator cable, an easy enough fix, and the second stop involved the throttle arm on the carburetor, another relatively easy repair. This is the beauty of the *danfo*! Had the bus been a modern vehicle with advanced electronics, it would have taken much longer to repair.

Another win for simple mechanics!

The bus arrived at the airport just after ten p.m.

I was thankful that I had arrived many hours early for my flight, as navigating the airport was a challenge I had not anticipated. I had no idea what I was expected to do or whom I was expected to find.

There were more people walking around the terminal than I had ever seen in my life. And so many different people! There were Africans from many different countries speaking languages that I could not even guess at. There were Chinese businessmen running down the corridors as though they were losing a game of chase. And there were Europeans and Americans.

As I pushed my way through these masses, I recalled with much mirth the first time I saw a person with pale skin. I was scared near to death. I had assumed the man was dead! A ghost! My father got many great laughs from that experience.

These thoughts cheered me, but the crush of the many travelers did not. Though likely the crowds were not nearly as large as they typically were, I am a child of open spaces, and being inside a building with so many people made me anxious. I kept my eyes on the windows and the night sky beyond in the vain hope it would ease my panic.

It did not.

I was in the line to have my meager bag checked by security officials in military uniforms, some of them with rather frightening-looking guns, when it all came crashing in on me. The emotion, the stress, my aching muscles . . . Though it was a great embarrassment, I put my bag down and sat upon it on the floor and refused to move.

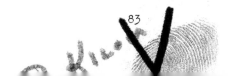

I have always known that if one bottles up his or her emotions, they will manifest again in illness or pains. Admitting I was overwhelmed was a good thing. I needed assistance. Unfortunately, doing this at an airport in a line to check baggage was not the best idea.

I was immediately swept up by several armed security officials who demanded to see my papers and then unceremoniously ushered me down a long, blank hallway to a back room.

Thus, my trip to the Game truly began.

5.2

I cannot say how long I was in this back room.

Inside was a table with two chairs. In one corner was a second table and on it sat several laptop computers. They were all tagged with evidence stickers. I assumed they had been confiscated from travelers unfortunate to be caught up by the security system. Several looked quite new.

By the time the door finally opened, I had fallen asleep and had to be roughly awakened by a very strong officer who did not take my confusion lightly. He sat me at the table and told me I was in great trouble.

"*Abeg make you no wex for me oh,*" I said as I cringed.

The man sat across from me and pushed on the table a folder that contained all of my documents, a plastic bag with the cell phone General Iyabo had given me, and the bracelets they had removed from my wrists when I was forced into the room. He asked, "Why are you so afraid? Why did you come here acting this way?"

I shook my head. "I have never been in the city this long. I have never been to the airport or inside rooms like these."

"That is because you are a village person."

"Yes. Akika Village, to the north."

"Tell me why a boy from the bush would have these documents?"

"General Iyabo gave them to me."

The officer exploded with laughter. "*Bomboy*, you are a funny little man!"

"It is the truth," I said. After his laughter had stopped, I asked, "Tell me, have I already missed my flight? Will there be another plane today?"

The officer immediately grew serious again. "You will not be boarding a plane today, my friend. Nor will you be boarding one tomorrow. I am not convinced by your story and your lies do not work, either. This is a very serious concern. *You dey wan go crench?*"

He was talking about prison and the very word made my mind reel.

"Listen, please," I told this man. "These documents are very real."

"You expect me to believe this?"

To emphasize his point, the officer leaned back in his seat and removed his revolver from the holster on his belt. Then, with a smile, he spun out the cylinder to show me the weapon was loaded. I stopped breathing, but my heart kept racing and it grew louder and louder in my ears. So loud that I worried it might overwhelm me and I would not hear what he had to say next. But that did not happen.

"It is very late," the officer said. "I should be at home. I should be sleeping right now. There is this fine *shikala* I have had my eyes on. *Dis babe* has fine *bakassi*. That is where I should be, not here. I will give you thirty seconds to tell me why you are here. Why you are acting like a fool in the airport. If it does not make sense, then I will have to be less . . . relatable."

Two years ago I encountered a lion.

They are exceptionally rare where I live, and prior to my encounter the last lion sighting was a generation earlier. I was on my way back from the junkyard, hauling an ancient motorcycle engine through the brush, when the lion crept into my path. It was female and thin. Lions are dangerous animals on any occasion but a hungry female lion is the most dangerous kind.

I stood still and quickly considered my options. I could not run. At full bore, lions attain a speed of forty-nine miles an hour. There is no way a skinny African kid could outrun such a powerful creature. I could attempt to talk the lion out of leaping upon me and eating me whole, but lions do not reason. So I did the most logical thing and, as always, *omo*, the most logical thing works best.

Knowing lions are creatures that crouch low before leaping, I made myself as large as possible. I stood on my heels and raised my arms above my head and stretched my spine to the point of near fracture. Then, as loudly as I could, with the deepest possible voice I could muster, I did the craziest thing I could contemplate.

I roared at the lion.

I felt silly doing this and the lion looked at me as though *I dey act like mumu*, like a fool. But it was a triumphant moment. Face to face with impossible danger, I did the unthinkable and challenged my assailant head-on. My breast swelled with pride. I was a warrior! I was the top of the food chain. And do you know what happened?

The lion attacked me.

With a roar that could have easily been the sound of a volcano erupting, the lioness leaped at me. Her teeth were bared and her claws slashed through the air. And I, I stood my ground certain that I understood her better than she understood me.

I was right.

The lioness landed just in front of me and growled. I did not flinch, though everything in my nature told me to *tear race on the spot*. Every nerve in my body fired at once in a vain attempt to send my body into a spasm of marathon speed. But no! I overcame my instinct and my body and I stayed right where I was.

The lioness surely took me for a chieftain or a rampaging rhino.

She growled, then turned and retreated to the long grass in which she had lain lurking all afternoon. I felt sorry for her and her hunger but was pleased she did not use me to soothe her pains.

The officer in the airport holding room was the same as this lioness.

He was wrong. He had threatened me.

I would show him the error of his ways.

"You are wrong," I told the officer. I sat very tall and locked eyes with him as I said this. My voice did not waver and my hands did not shake. "You are wrong and General Iyabo will hear of your insubordination."

The officer gave a throaty chuckle, but it was tinged with nervousness.

"You are a crazy," he said as he glanced at his weapon. "I give you fifteen seconds now. Do not waste—"

"Do not waste my time!" I shouted at this man.

He jerked upright in his seat like a puppet whose strings had been pulled violently by a strong hand. "How dare you speak this way!"

"How dare you!" I said to him.

He glared at me and his eyes shone with fury but he did not move.

I pointed to the cell phone in the plastic bag. "Look at this phone. Dial the number that you find."

The officer did not like taking orders from a village runt such as myself, a *loki*, but after a single moment of hesitation, he reached for the bag and removed the cell phone. He dialed the number and then sat back with a very smug and angry look upon his face.

"If this is a joke," he said, "*you don die oh*."

He was a man who believed he did not make idle threats.

This certainty drained from his face the minute the phone was answered. Even from across the table, I could hear the booming voice of General Iyabo.

"What is it?" he snarled.

"Uh . . ." The officer could not answer. His voice was caught in a trap.

"Who is this?" the general asked.

"Um, this is Officer Okah with the department of—"

I did not listen too closely to much of what was said after that moment but I had never in my life up until that moment heard so many foul and disturbing expressions. It was both repelling and fascinating.

Officer Okah was reduced to a blubbering wreck, about as useful as an adjustable wrench, and before he allowed me to collect my stuff and leave the room he had been transferred from his position and would spend the next five years cleaning latrines. I did not feel bad for this man.

Just before I was escorted from the room to my flight, I pointed at the stack of laptops. "The general has requested that I have one of those as well."

Officer Okah scrambled over to the laptops.

He held up a black one, at least five years old, for my approval.

"I will take the one to the right of that."

It was new. Perhaps only two months old.

Shoulders slumped, Officer Okah handed me the new laptop. "Thank you," I replied courteously.

I was then escorted to my flight with half an hour to spare.

5.3

I had always wondered what it would feel like to be inside one of the machines I worked on, to travel the conduits and pipes and wires, and stepping aboard the airplane gave me the answer.

It was packed like a tin!

I was directed to my seat by a helpful woman in a uniform and found myself at the back of the plane between a businessman from Lagos and a Cameroonian football player.

I have studied the intricacies of how planes work. I have read about propulsion and how turbines spin and the way an atmosphere of only gas can lift a metal giant into the sky and leave it there, floating.

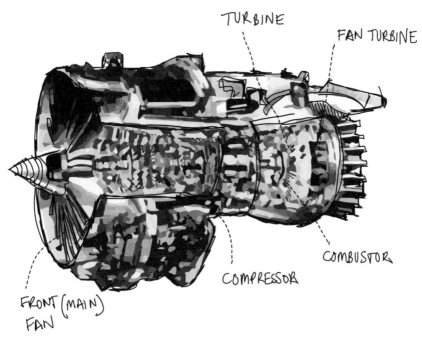

Aircraft engine doodles by Tunde Oni

But the feeling of being aboard a plane and the exhilarating power of the thrust, of the buildup of energy as it raced down the runway toward the sky, was beyond all rational thought!

It was an experience of wordless power.

And then we were airborne!

The whole of the first flight was a blur. While I occasionally glanced outside at the landscape of clouds that passed below the plane, most of my time aboard was spent on my new laptop working on the schematics of the jammer.

It was only when the plane began to descend that I snapped out of my spell.

Landing a plane requires an equal amount of energy as lifting one off the ground. Given the mass of the airplane, which I calculated in my head, the force required to stop the forward motion once the wheels touched the ground was immense.

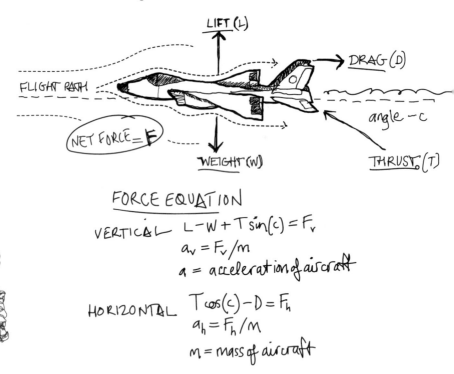

LIFT (L)

DRAG (D)

FLIGHT PATH

angle –c

NET FORCE = F

WEIGHT (W)

THRUST (T)

FORCE EQUATION

VERTICAL $L - W + T\sin(c) = F_v$
$a_v = F_v/m$
$a = $ acceleration of aircraft

HORIZONTAL $T\cos(c) - D = F_h$
$a_h = F_h/m$
$m = $ mass of aircraft

Equation by Tunde Oni

Ah, the marvels of human engineering!

Masters of the sky!

I even imagined I could smell the burn of the tires on the tarmac. The smell reminded me of the time I melted rubber to insulate wires on the Okeke power station. There is a consistency to the world, a uniformity that, regardless of size, keeps everything in balance.

We changed planes at Charles de Gaulle Airport in Paris.

I had never seen such a castle!

As my flight to the States was two hours off, I sat and watched the thousands of people walking by.

There was a fat man, the fattest I had ever seen, who had a walking problem. Would you believe he was deeply upset when I asked him about his legs? I recommended he rub honey on his knees. I told him it always worked for my uncle.

Then there was the big Indian family who were going away on vacation. I tried hard to imagine my mother and father on vacation and could not even picture it. What would they do? Where would they go? The Indian family told me they were heading south to Cancún in Mexico. I had heard of this place! Rex and I had chatted only a few months earlier about the pyramids lost in the jungles there. Pyramids larger than the very plane I had just traveled on.

Tired of sitting, I decided to explore the shops.

The bookstore I found was a wonder. Oh, how I wanted to read so many of those books! But where to start? It was overwhelming and I was somewhat thankful that my bladder soon had me in search of a bathroom.

Here, too, there were many surprises. There were grand toilets with liquid soap that you could use as much of as you wanted. And it was so clean! There were water fountains that provided endless amounts of refreshment. The water was so pure and cold that I drank until my stomach almost burst. It had a very pleasant temperature and I wondered how they distributed so much water inside an airport. What pumps would they use? Where did the water come from?

When I got out of the bathroom it was time for me to make my way to another part of the airport and the gate for my second flight.

Along the way I could not help but stop at a bank of power outlets at a kiosk. Amazingly, these were free for anyone to use! I booted up my laptop and made my way online with blazing speed. Speed I had never experienced before. I logged in to the LODGE home page and sent messages to Rex and Painted Wolf. I wanted them to know that I had managed to make it out of Nigeria and that I would soon be joining them.

After I boarded the second flight, I sat down and closed my eyes. Even at this early step of the trip, I knew I had made it.

This was the last lap. It was the final push.

I had traveled from my village all the way to Europe and now I was to step into the new life that awaited me across the endless waters.

A cold, hard fact of life in China is that if you're honest and straight-forward, everyone will think you're naive and maybe even stupid. If you don't lie, you won't get anywhere.

Like it or not, our culture is in full-bore barrel-ahead mode. Everyone is out for any opportunity they can grab. That translates very simply: Bosses lies to their employees, teachers lie to their students, parents lie to their children, friends lie to friends, and everyone always lies to strangers. These are not typically white lies, either. When you live in a society that doesn't just accept lying but actively embraces it, lying loses that amoral sheen.

I lie to my parents all the time.

The video of Mr. Shifu and Mr. Lu's under-the-counter deal that I uploaded to the LODGE site went viral, as I'd hoped it would.

But it was even bigger than I'd ever imagined.

The reaction was swift. The government shut down every mirror site and blocked every link as soon as they saw them flicker into existence. But they were too slow, the video's infectious spread too rapid. Before the week was out, both Mr. Shifu and Mr. Lu were out of jobs and looking at lengthy court battles. I was celebrated as a game changer in the corners I frequented, but in the establishment salons and offices, I was considered a dangerous element. I was a rogue particle, as destructive as dark matter.

Sadly, my parents didn't see Painted Wolf's "antics" the way I did.

As my father sat at the dinner table and talked about the news, he and my mother would shake their heads and scoff at the latest online scandals. While he wholly embraced the idea of rooting out corruption and promoting hard workers like himself, he was dismissive of the new revolutionary tools.

"Subterfuge, disguises," he'd say, holding up a newspaper with a screen grab of one of my most recent Painted Wolf videos. "This girl plays at revolution. She should lose the wigs and sunglasses and challenge these people in the courts."

I suggested that Painted Wolf, regardless of her (admittedly pretty cool) wardrobe, was doing more to change the status quo than a dozen lawmakers. If going to court worked, then she wouldn't be needed.

My father disagreed. The establishment had worked for him. My mother refused to take a side; instead she worried.

"I can't imagine what this girl's parents must go through. What she does is so dangerous. I don't even like to think about it."

"She's celebrated," I said. "There are people looking out for her."

My father shook his head at that.

So, rather than admit that I was the notorious Painted Wolf and that I'd been accepted into a competition on the other side of the world, I lied to my parents and told them that I'd be joining my cousin Lin Lin on holiday for a week at a resort in Suzhou, just west of Shanghai.

They were surprised.

Going to a resort and relaxing seemed so far from my usual routine that they were actually worried I was ill. My mother lit frankincense candles in my room while I slept. My father studied the maps and website of the resort as though he was scouring a contract for hidden deductions.

I had to recruit Lin Lin to convince them. Luckily, she's twenty-three, works as a secretary at my uncle's bank (this impresses my parents), and loves espionage and playacting even more than I do. Though she comes from money and lives an ostentatious life, she and I have been close friends since we were little and she used to babysit me on trips to see her parents in Guangzhou.

Of course, she doesn't know I'm Painted Wolf, either.

When we met at an organic café at Jiashan Market, I told Lin Lin that I'd been asked to take part in a **game theory** symposium at the American Technical University campus in Changzhou. That it was a real honor but one I couldn't disclose to my parents because I'd be traveling with an Indian colleague. A guy.

Lin Lin squealed at that news. "Are you a couple?" she gasped.

"Oh no. Absolutely not," I said. "My parents would have my head."

I did tell her, however, that this mysterious colleague had a crush on me but his culture forbade him from making any outward expressions of his desire. As Lin Lin panted over her coffee, I explained that he was a prominent tech figure in India and had made many enemies. He'd called for this closed-door symposium, locked down, with incredible security, to meet with several high-achieving students who were outspoken on technology. Somehow, he'd heard about me and we'd been chatting, very formally, online for several weeks.

"So," I told Lin Lin, "here's the lowdown: I won't be able to answer my cell or send any e-mails while I'm at the symposium. Can you cover for me? Please? My parents know I want to totally get away from it all and turn off my cell and not even bring my laptop. If they call, will you answer?"

"Of course," Lin Lin said. "I'm so jealous."

"Why?"

"All the subterfuge, the danger . . ."

"It's not really all that dangerous."

Lin Lin cocked her head; she knew I was playing it down. "I wish I could have some excitement like that," she said. "I want to run off, do something crazy, but I'm too scared. How pathetic is that? Besides, I wouldn't even know what to do."

"You're not pathetic," I said, but she waved me off.

"You have to promise that when you get back you'll give me all the juicy gossip. You can't leave out a single glance or hushed word. Promise?"

I smiled. "Promise."

6.1

Kiran had arranged for his private plane to fly me to Boston.

I'll admit, I was nervous.

It wasn't the flight or the thought of having to piece together the most convincing disguise I'd designed yet but the fact that I'd spend the twenty-hour flight sitting next to Kiran.

I pulled together a new outfit, bought a new wig and new sunglasses.

Since Kiran had spent an hour sitting across the table from me, flirting constantly, I figured he'd had a long enough look to recognize me by now. My costume had to be more than convincing on video, it had to make me appear to be someone entirely different.

Making that sort of transformation a success requires more than makeup, clothing, accessories, and perfume. It requires a change in personality. Psychological studies have shown that people identify their friends and acquaintances more by voice and deportment than by facial recognition. If I didn't act like Cai, my chances of fooling Kiran were three times better.

For the first time, I had to actually, fully **become** Painted Wolf.

I kissed my parents good-bye and they finally seemed excited at the thought of me taking a break and getting out. Neither of my parents had ever told me that I studied too much or worked too hard. That was accepted. They certainly noticed if I was slacking. Getting an A– in a class would cause my father to throw a fit and tell me I wasn't meeting my potential or suggest that the teacher was clearly not up to the challenge of teaching advanced courses. My GPA hadn't been less than a 4.0 in five years.

My father rationalized my going to a resort by assuming I was going to take a brief break to save my sanity. There's an expression in China: "A good laugh adds ten years to your life." According to my father, regularly implemented periods of relaxing and letting down your guard are quite healthy. To me, he always reinforced the importance of sleep, exercise, and mental rest. What justified my relaxing by the side of the pool with my cousin wasn't my need for recreation but a conscious effort on my part to force myself to ensure my body was at its fighting best. It was there, after all, to support my mind. He saw me as a mental athlete and I had to train properly.

Lin Lin picked me up and drove me to the airport.

I reconfirmed our agreement and then hopped out of the car. I had a lot to do before I boarded my first-ever international flight.

"Have fun!" Lin Lin waved excitedly as she drove off. "See you in a week!"

I had the layout of the Pudong airport memorized and made my way to the terminal and straight to the bathroom to change.

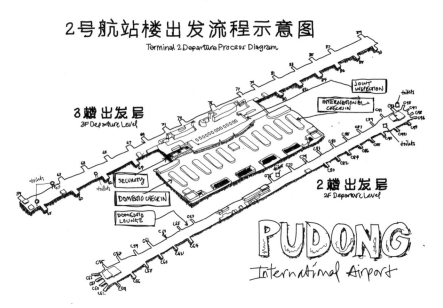

Pudong airport

I locked myself in a stall, pulled out my makeup kit, clothes, and accessories, and got to work. It took half an hour to physically transform into Painted Wolf; it took even longer to find the character inside me. I won't say I'm demure, but I'm not overly confident, either. I'm happy in my skin, not thrilled by my appearance and abilities but content with them. However, Painted Wolf needed to be more.

She had to kick ass.

The outfit was daring: Black leather pants with a low-slung belt, a black tube top, twenty silver chains, a magnetic silver nose ring, black nail polish, a long black wig with red highlights, combat boots, and oversized mirrored sunglasses. Of course, I was also outfitted with multiple spy cameras: two embedded in the sunglasses frames, one on the belt, and one in each of the large silver earrings I wore.

Security footage of Painted Wolf

I walked out of that bathroom with the sureness of a warrior.

The first concourse I walked down I was self-conscious. I was focused on my steps, on the way my body moved in the leather, and how the sunglasses pressed up against my face. People looked and several of them pointed, which made me feel like a character in a costume.

I stumbled and almost wrecked my ankle on a flight of stairs.

I dropped my bag. It was embarrassing.

I wasn't doing it right. Painted Wolf wasn't a klutz. ——

I had to find my focus. I felt like I was playing dress-up and it was throwing me off my game. This was a mission, as important as any other.

I had to focus.

I needed to lose myself to sell Painted Wolf.

I took a few deep breaths and started walking again.

Painted Wolf was rebellious. She was nowhere and everywhere. She was an ear at the door and an eye at the window. When she spoke, she roared. When she roared, politicians and businessmen quaked, the dishonorable quivered and the broken ran. It was all bluster and bravado but I had to believe it.

I didn't just walk to the gate. I pushed.

The crowds parted for me.

Children scrambled out of the way.

I used Kiran's special pass to walk past security with my nose in the air as though I was royalty. I had to keep fortifying myself. In my mind, I played an endless loop of an interview I'd heard with an up-and-coming young actress, the privileged daughter of a well-known politician. It was a quote that made me furious, but it had stayed with me. It was perfect: "I don't care how it happens or who I have to crush to do it, but I will be a star. I will be a star and the world will fear me."

I rode on this wave of aggressive energy through the endless hallways to the private-flights gate, where a familiar face waited for me.

Kiran, in a nice suit and shades, smiled.

"I'll be honest, I wasn't sure you were going to show up," he said.

"Glad to surprise you," I replied.

He ushered me through the door to the ramp and I could feel his eyes making their way from my wig to my boots. He said, "You certainly know how to **make an entrance**."

6.2

Fifteen minutes later, we were racing through the sky at thirty thousand feet.

The interior of the plane was stunning.

There were ten seats, all of them leather and hardwood. There were flat-screen televisions at each seat, and small refrigerators stocked with all manner of gourmet snacks and drinks. Outside of Kiran and me, there were four OndScan employees, two men and two women. As I walked aboard, they all stood to greet me.

Kiran said, "Ladies and gentlemen, this is Painted Wolf."

They all bowed. I bowed in return, worrying my disguise would slip. It didn't.

Kiran showed me to my seat at the back of the plane.

He spoke in Mandarin. I replied in English.

"I'm really pleased you could join us," he said. "The timing was perfect. I figured why spend the money on a separate flight when you could just hop on our plane. Hope you're cool with it."

"Of course, " I replied. "Thank you."

"The plane has Wi-Fi, tons of movies, food, drinks. Help yourself."

I nodded my appreciation.

Before he turned to go, Kiran said, "That video you did with Mr. Shifu . . . wow. **Impressive**. Must have been pretty tough to get. I imagine you had to do some serious, old-school social engineering."

"Wasn't easy but . . ."

"But that's your thing. It's impressive. I think you're going to enjoy yourself at the Game. Might be the first time you've ever really been challenged." Kiran smiled. "Okay, buckle in. We're going to take off soon."

The next two hours, I spent watching the passing clouds and scanning through news feeds on my cell phone. Tunde had posted a few blog entries about his travels. His descriptions of Paris's airport were hilarious and insightful. Though his posts retained the usual Tunde mirth, the stress he was obviously under was there as well. So much was riding on his success.

As we left the mainland and the ocean became visible beneath the plane, Kiran walked over, sat down beside me, and pointed to a fractus cloud hovering in the distance. A low, ragged stratiform at the leading edge of a cold front.

It looked elegant and ominous at the same time.

"Why the disguise?" Kiran asked. "We're miles above the world."

I glanced at him sidelong. "This is who I am."

"Love it."

"Can I ask you a question?"

Kiran nodded. "Of course, provided it's not about details surrounding the Game." He motioned with his head to his handlers. "At least, not in front of them."

"It's not."

"Okay. Great. Shoot."

"Why were you in China?"

"Always working," Kiran said with a grin. "That's why I want you in the Game. You're fierce and your mind never stops turning. See, it's dangerous talking to you, Wolf. Not only are you at least three steps ahead, you see mysteries behind mysteries. I'm afraid, however, that my work in China will come as a bit of a disappointment. I was there on business. Meeting with colleagues."

"Colleagues, huh?"

"Why is that funny?"

I leaned in. "You know what I do, Kiran. I hear things."

Truth is, outside of his meeting with Mr. Hark, I had no idea what Kiran was doing in China. I needed to fish for the information. Key to doing that was convincing him I knew more than I did. I had to lure him in, make him drop his guard, and tell me what I didn't know.

Kiran, however, wasn't an easy mark.

"Like what?" he asked, playing along.

"China is a very, very big pond. But you're a big fish. I've heard rumors about people you've met with. Some of them, let's say, are less savory than others."

"We're talking about Shui Hark, right?"

A lump formed in my throat. It was instant. "Yes," I said.

"I had dinner with him a night ago," Kiran said. "He's rather boring, frankly."

I had to know where this was going. "He's a criminal."

"He is indeed."

Kiran's eyes were bright and round and I imagined he could see right through my sunglasses and into my own eyes. "What is it you want most in life, Wolf?"

"What?"

"What is it that you want?"

"Access to information," I said, knowing exactly what I wanted. "I want to know what other people, in other countries, know. I want to share that **information**. And, most of all, I want to be able to speak my mind."

"And the people you videotape? The ones you expose?"

"They are what's keeping our society from improving. They think they're entitled to wealth just because they've got slivers of power. They want to live in ivory towers and keep the rest of us out. If they built those towers by cheating and stealing, I will bring their towers down."

Kiran leaned back and applauded softly. "A crusader. Like me."

"That why you're having dinners with corrupt industrialists?"

"Of course," Kiran replied.

"What does that even mean?"

"We're alike you and me, Wolf. We both look out at the world"—Kiran gestured to the window and the endless stretch of sky beyond—"and we see broken systems, we see helpless people, we see no alternatives. You and I both want to change that. And we're both willing to do whatever it takes to make it happen."

"Breaking the law?"

Kiran leaned in. I could smell his aftershave, hints of orange and jasmine.

"I want to re-create the world in our image."

"Our?"

"You and I," Kiran said. "People like us, people who aren't jaded by experience or beaten by failure. Just like you, I realized the people in power would never solve the world's problems. They created them and have everything to gain from keeping them going. When I was nine, I rounded up all the children in the slums who would listen and together we built a computer. We built a school. We educated ourselves. You know how adult teachers always tell their charges to 'think outside the box'? Well, the only way to truly succeed, to truly change the world, is to do what only a child can do: Deny there even is a box."

This was what I had been hoping to hear from Kiran. This was the message beneath the corporate image, the real person beneath the superhero persona that Internet fandom had created. Even better, what he said made perfect sense.

Maybe he was the real deal.

"I'll be honest with you," Kiran wrapped up. "The Game isn't a competition, it's a recruitment tool. I want to assemble a next-generation team of leaders, of world builders. Tell me, what do you think?"

"Sounds like you're inviting me to join."

"You're here, aren't you?"

With that, Kiran turned to face a young woman in a severe jacket and bright red lipstick carrying a tablet. She cleared her throat.

"Sorry," Kiran said to me. "Back to work."

He returned to his seat up front and was instantly swarmed by his handlers, each with documents for him to sign and questions to answer.

Still of Kiran from Painted Wolf "button" camera

As soon as his attention was off me, I let out a sigh.

My boots were too tight and my wig too itchy. All the jewelry was making my neck sore. I was tired of playing Painted Wolf.

But looking out the window at the ocean and the sky, I refocused on the reasons why I'd boarded the plane. I lied to my parents because I needed to help Tunde. His life, his parents' life, his village, his people: All were threatened. I had to do whatever I could and go wherever **he needed me**.

There was also the matter of Kiran's intentions. He came across as brilliant and friendly, generous and driven. But I prided myself on reading people and I knew he was hiding something. It wasn't a sixth sense; there wasn't any telepathy involved. It was just my ability to read people, from the words they said to the subtlest body language cues and the slightest changes in tone.

Kiran had an ulterior motive. Something sketchy. I didn't yet know what he was planning, but I was buzzing with eagerness to find out.

And **stop** it.

PART TWO

THE GAME

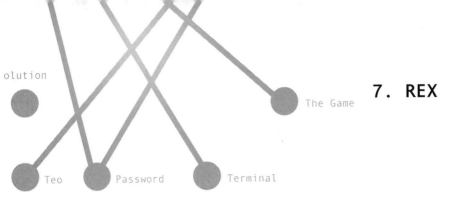

03 DAYS, 05 HOURS, 21 MINUTES UNTIL ZERO HOUR

Ma and Papa were thrilled when I gave them the news.

The look of awe on their faces quickly morphed into grins of joy as I explained that I was one of the few invitees, that the trip was paid for (though even before I'd mentioned that, Papa said he'd find a way to pay), and that winning would mean access to projects I'd only dreamed of.

But the joy faded as a cold reality dawned on us all.

Ma brought it up first: What if immigration found out that my parents were illegal? I was honest and told them I didn't know.

Papa sat us down at the table for a family meeting.

He was somber at first. "We've been through a very trying time, something no family should face. Regardless of the risks, I think you need to go to this competition, Rex. You did not choose to be here. Your mother and I chose this for you and we cannot keep you from your destiny out of fear. If Teo taught us anything, it is that we need to stand up and embrace every challenge. And we're going to embrace this one."

Ma cried as she packed my bags. Papa beamed when they walked me to the check-in desk at the airport. He told me that he and Ma had stayed up most of the night bragging to each other. That made my heart hurt worse than anything.

Proud of their cheating son.

I gave them long hugs and told them I'd call every day.

Papa handed me a small box wrapped with ribbon.

"Your mom and I have been hanging on to it since . . . Well, we think he'd like you to have it now. Besides, it's been beeping lately and we can't seem to shut it off."

"Beeping?"

I held the box to my ear and could hear a very faint but insistent tone.

Ma was crying. "Take care of yourself. Call as soon as you can."

I promised them I would and walked backward through the crowded concourse, waving to them until they vanished within the sea of faces.

Then I pushed my way through security, ran to my gate, and got onto the plane only a few minutes before they made the final boarding announcement.

Once I'd settled into my seat, I opened the gift from my parents.

Inside the small box was a leather necklace with a USB flash drive hanging from it. I got a little teary-eyed seeing the USB drive. That's probably the first time you've ever heard anyone say that. But it was Teo's.

A 16 MB thumb drive he got from our parents for Christmas when he was three. He used it religiously even though it barely held anything.

It was like his good-luck charm. It was his digital rabbit's foot.

I hadn't seen the thing since he'd vanished, and, frankly, I'd forgotten about it. Seeing it again, holding that small rectangle of metal and plastic in my hand, overwhelmed me with emotion.

I wondered: What would Teo have put on it?

Even more important: Why was it beeping? USBs don't beep.

As soon as the plane leveled and we were allowed to use preapproved electronics, I pulled out my laptop and put Teo's old USB in. Took ten heartbeats for the thing to load, but when it did, I opened it to find a single file folder labeled MANIFESTO.

The file inside was password protected.

I tried a few of Teo's old passwords, but none of them worked. Thankfully, I had a library of assorted "brute force" password-cracking tools. Most of them I'd tweaked. It always amazes me how lazy some developers can be.

Took sixteen seconds to crack the password.

I should have known it would be Rex Matteo Huerta.

Teo wanted me to see this file. Maybe he'd wanted me to find it two years ago. Maybe my parents found it first and hung on to it. Regardless, I had it now and I needed to see what it contained.

Inside was a simple text file that was downright chilling.

TERMINAL MANIFESTO

1. To learn is to create. Learning—whether it is programming, mathematics, art, music, poetry, biology, or chemistry—is all about breaking down walls and freeing the one thing that keeps us alive: knowledge.

2. All knowledge is free. Free to share, exploit, or destroy. We believe that nothing that is created can truly be possessed and those that try to possess creations are doomed to failure. We are not what we make.

3. Knowledge expands freedom in all its forms. Knowledge breaks down walls. It liberates the oppressed. We are committed to knowledge. Knowledge as a hammer against classism, against sexism, against racism, against gender discrimination, against slavery, against bigotry, against war, against hatred. If there is darkness in the world, we will light it up.

4. Knowledge has been enslaved. Corporations, governments, universities, and armies have knowledge under lock and

key. They know that knowledge is power and they blindly believe that holding on to knowledge means holding on to power. We are here to prove them wrong. We are here to free knowledge from its captors.

Revolution is the only evolution.

Hermano: What we started has gotten away from us. From this moment on, you must trust no one. Every camera is an eye. Every microphone an ear. Find me and we can stop him together.

I sat staring at it slack-jawed for way too long.

I couldn't get my mind around what it meant. Teo was part of Terminal? Was he responsible for what they'd done? For all that pain and destruction? I couldn't believe he was. There was no way my brother could do those things. And yet . . . here it was in black and white.

The last bullet was the one that concerned me the most. What had gotten away from him and why was he on the run? Who was this person, this "him," that we had to stop together?

My blood pressure had spiked so high I thought I might pass out.

Didn't matter what any of it meant, the real message was clear: Teo was in trouble. He needed my help. It wasn't until the USB beeped again that I realized the situation was even more urgent than I'd thought.

Okay, here's where things got crazy.

I saved the image on my laptop and pulled the USB. It looked like an average thumb drive, but when I cracked it, I found a rice-sized receiver. Next-generation spy tech like that doesn't just drop into the hands of a teenager. Not even a brilliant one like Teo. That's probably why I couldn't reverse the reception on it and figure out where it was getting its signals. Worse, it broke when I tried to take it apart. This was fragile tech, the mark of something new.

Still, I wasn't defeated.

Someone had been communicating with the USB. Someone had been actively adding to and editing the file on it. A quick look confirmed it was real: The manifesto text had been edited as recently as three hours before my flight.

If it was Teo, and I knew it was, this meant he was alive.

And he was in serious trouble.

7.1

The bumpy bus ride to the Boston Collective was crowded.

I assumed at least some of the young people sitting around me were there for the Game. At least a few of them had to be my competition. Still, I didn't have time to size them up or eavesdrop on their conversations. What I'd discovered on Teo's USB had my mind racing.

I sent numerous texts and e-mails to Tunde and Painted Wolf telling them I was in town and ready to roll. And that I had big news to discuss as soon as we could. Neither replied immediately. I figured they must be traveling.

I called Ma and told her I was in safely, but tried to make the conversation as short as possible. Papa was at work, but he'd asked Ma to ask me about the present.

"Thanks, Ma. It's great. I'm going to make Teo proud with it."

What I couldn't tell her was that Teo was mixed up in some seriously bad stuff. Worse, he might even have masterminded some of it. Until I found him, I had to keep that to myself.

To do that, I needed what the Boston Collective had.

Accessing the quantum computer wasn't going to be easy. It wasn't online, so there was no way for me to hack my way into it. I had to find it and access it manually. That required me to figure out exactly where it was.

First thing I needed to do was access the Collective's servers.

Teo

Luckily, I found Carlos Hernandez.

He was a Boston Collective student just a year older and also from California two rows in front of me on the bus. Even better, he was pretty lazy with his cell phone security.

As the bus crossed over the Fort Point Channel, I used a cracked Slingshot device to pick up and condense passing Wi-Fi signals, then hacked into Carlos's student account. I figured since I'd already dived headfirst into some seriously gray ethical areas, how bad could one more hack really be?

I quickly skimmed through his e-mails, feeling really bad and hoping that moving quickly would somehow make my intrusion less horrible. I didn't open anything until I found what I was looking for: Carlos, like most students, hadn't deleted his student account activation e-mail.

It gave me his password and PIN.

Using that, I downloaded a VPN client and got ready.

By the time the bus crossed Harvard Bridge, I was into Collective's network. I had access to the campus servers and took a cursory look.

The quantum computer wasn't popping up.

At least, I didn't see it.

And while I could find information about it being built, there wasn't any info about exactly where on campus it was being housed. So I figured, enough with the screens, if I was going to find the machine I'd have to get out and get my feet wet.

Literally.

Attack

7.2

The bus reached its destination and I darted out into the pouring rain.

East Coast–style rain, not the wispy, warm stuff we get in Santa Cruz.

Security

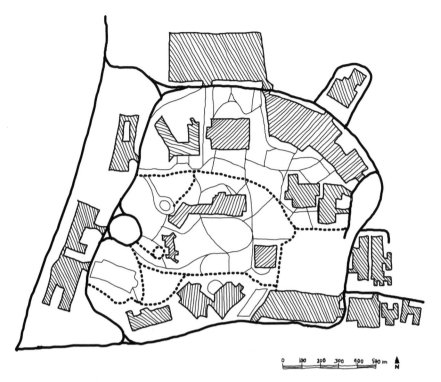

Map of the Boston Collective campus

This was cold and nasty.

Only thing I had to protect me against the downpour was my hoodie. I pushed into the wind and rain, past students rushing for cover, and ran to the student center.

Closest thing I could compare it to was a mall; there were lots of staircases, ramps, meeting rooms, lounges, vending machines, cozy but artfully designed furniture, and soothing colors.

I followed several people who seemed to know where they were going, but they quickly vanished behind doors or down stairs. I really wasn't sure where I was supposed to be and wondered if maybe my invitation had been incomplete.

"Nice USB. I use one like that to flash firmware from DOS."

I turned around to find a girl, maybe fifteen, with close-cropped red hair and a tablet in her hand. She had a duffel bag over her shoulder.

I touched the USB necklace. "Thanks. It was my brother's."

"Welcome to the Game. I'm Edith. One of the supervisors."

"Hey, Edith. I'm . . . Rex."

Edith glanced down at her tablet and scrolled for my name. I held my breath as her finger swiped across the screen. My name was on there. It had to be on there. I didn't come this far to have my name not be—

"Rex Huerta?"

Whew. It worked.

"Yes. That's me."

"Great to see you." Edith reached out and shook my hand. "You're name's kind of familiar. Maybe I set up your account? Anyway, I'm with OndScan. Supervisor, like I said. I helped Kiran put this little shindig together and I'll be your guide, so to speak. At least for the next fifteen minutes. Any questions, you can ask me. But there are some things I can't tell you."

"Like what exactly the Game is."

"Yes, like that." Edith smiled. I liked her already.

"So, where do we start?"

Edith began walking; I followed her.

"This is where we'll have morning meetings. Everyone is expected to attend at eight a.m.; I know, it's early. You can get food here in the Morrison Food Court. They have all the regular stuff like Subway and Dunkin' Donuts. There's also a café with some pretty great scones."

We turned a corner, took some stairs up.

"What do you do at OndScan?" I asked.

"Cryptography. Mostly I design proprietary ciphers."

"Awesome. Anything I'd know?"

"Brokendoor. It's a symmetric key block cipher, like Twofish but a lot faster."

Block cipher

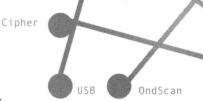

"Yeah. I know it."

Edith paused, looked me over again.

"You're not Huerta like the LODGE Huerta, right?"

"That's me." I smiled.

Edith laughed. "I knew the name was familiar."

My first fan, I was impressed. Here less than ten minutes . . .

"Actually," Edith said as we started walking again, "I've had a major beef with you. Sorry. Couple months back on your blog you did this real takedown critique of a buffer overrun—"

I cringed. I remembered writing it. "The Unsworth program. Right . . ."

Edith gave me a half smile. "I worked on it with some friends, in our off hours. It was kind of a labor of love but also something we thought we could sell. Actually had a company interested until they read your criticism."

"Sorry."

"Don't feel bad. You pointed out some real flaws."

"I was way too harsh, though."

"Kind of. Yeah. Anyway, I'm still a fan of the LODGE. Painted Wolf just keeps doing some seriously amazing stuff. Everything she posts, it's . . . wow. She's really making a name for herself. Pretty hot, too."

Edith picked up the pace, legs moving like a speed walker's.

We exited the student center, made our way across a lawn. It was drizzling and already ten degrees colder than fifteen minutes earlier.

Edith turned up the collar on her coat and pointed out a building gleaming in the distance. "That's your dorm there. Hoban. A nice walk when the weather's good."

She moved quickly, faster than me. But I picked up the pace and caught up with her. "Listen, Edith, can I ask you a cryptographic question? Although I'm not sure that's even a word or if I used it right."

"Of course. Shoot."

I knew my chance when I had it. I needed to know where the quantum machine was and I was sure that Edith knew.

"Say I was interested in post-quantum cryptography," I started.

"Okay," she said with obvious interest.

"People running quantum key distribution might be out of luck pretty soon given recent advances. Just a matter of time before Shor's—"

Edith chuckled. "You have access to a quantum computer? If you didn't, and most of the world doesn't, then I'd assume those people were pretty safe."

"Well, that was my second question."

Edith was clever; she wasn't falling right into my trap. I had to work around her defenses, figure out a way to engineer a slipup. Make her tell me something she wasn't planning to.

"There are no quantum machines online now."

"There's one on this campus," I countered.

"It's not online."

"Of course, it's just for research purposes. True quantum machines are still five or ten years out. But this one, I'm guessing it's something special. Next-generation-level computing," I said, feeling my way carefully into my next question. "OndScan wouldn't put the Game here just for grins, though, right? How cool would it be to get over to the computer science lab, boot that bad boy up, and run some cryptographic schemes against it?"

"I'm afraid you're going to have to wait a bit to get a peek at the machine." Edith smiled as we reached the door to the dorm. "The OndScan building is locked down until Zero Hour."

"Of course."

Mission accomplished: The quantum machine was in the OndScan building. Now I just had to figure out where that was.

"I'm sure I'll see you around," Edith said as she opened the door.

"Definitely," I said. "Oh, and sorry again about the mean critique of Unsworth. It's still a cool program. With a few tweaks I'm sure it'll be great."

Edith gave me a sour glance before she ushered me inside.

7.3

Contestants.

Here they were, Kiran's hand-selected prodigies: dozens of young men and women, all of them my age or younger, sitting on couches and chairs and talking. The nervous energy was palpable. It was like walking into a room of people five minutes before they took the SAT.

Edith cleared her throat. Then, when she had the attention of everyone in the room, she said, "Hey, everyone. This is Rex Huerta."

A round of limited applause followed.

I smiled to the crowd and waved awkwardly.

No one waved back, but who cares.

Scanning the faces, I didn't see Tunde or Painted Wolf.

Where were they?

Edith patted me on the shoulder. "I've got to run back to the student center, someone here will show you to your room. If you have any questions, don't hesitate to try to track me or one of the other supervisors down. See you soon."

As soon as the door closed behind Edith, the rest of the contestants went right back to their previous conversations.

I made my way through the lobby and sized up the competition.

I passed: A girl, possibly fifteen, chatting about natural language processing with an obese young man with a beard; a tall girl mulling over terascale data sets with a Mohawked dude; and a guy in sunglasses testing out a detailed model of the Curiosity rover built from matchsticks and powered by a lemon.

Most said hello or nodded as I walked past them.

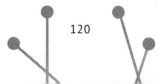

The Mohawked dude high-fived me.

Wasn't until I'd nearly crossed the room that I realized how comfortable I suddenly felt. Listening to them, I felt the same deep-down, joyous tremor that ran like soda up my spine when I was online with Tunde and Painted Wolf. It was the feeling of being home, the feeling of being among my people.

As Papa says, *"Pájaros de un mismo plumaje vuelan juntos."*

Birds of a feather, indeed . . .

"Are you Rex Huerta?"

I turned around to see a young girl standing at my side. She smiled wide. The fact that she was missing her two front teeth brought up warm memories of that addictive Christmas song. I instantly recognized her from a forum post: a Spanish girl, almost supernaturally skilled in chemistry. She didn't wait for confirmation of my identity.

"I just wanted to tell you that the structural formula program you wrote was incredible. I use it all the time."

"Thanks," I said. "I wrote that for my brother. He was big into chem."

"In Córdoba I don't get to talk to many others kids like me. There are a few but they're younger. I really love the LODGE. You guys are supercool. Please tell me Painted Wolf is going to be here."

Her accent was thick, her lisp even thicker.

"Yeah, she is. Tunde, too," I said.

"No way."

"Yes. By the way, I recognize you. What's your name?"

She beamed. "Rosa."

"Hey, Rosa. Yeah, read about you online."

"On the Prodigy Planet site?"

"That's right. That is where I read it. I was really impressed."

Rosa grinned.

"I hope we're on the same team together," she said. "It'd be a *movida*. A party."

"You excited?"

"Of course!" Rosa squealed. "This is going to be insane. You can't have so many smart people in one place and not have them looking around. Some people have been talking and I overheard a rumor that the Game is all about insects. How crazy is that?"

"That can't be true."

"I also heard that if you win, the real prize—not the money or the fame or whatever—is a key to a machine that will change the world."

"You believe that one?"

She laughed. "Can't change the world, silly."

Sounds like we have a similar outlook.

"So, you know where you're going?" Rosa asked.

"Not really. Can you show me?"

Rosa led me across the room to a sheet posted on the wall. It was a printout of all the contestants' names. I saw Painted Wolf's name before Rosa drew my attention to my own. "You're in 402," she said. "I'll walk you up."

We took the stairs to the fourth floor. On the way, Rosa asked me everything she could about the LODGE. How we met. How we get along. Was it true I had a crush on Painted Wolf? She said there was a rumor online that I might.

After walking me to my door, she said, "I'm on the second floor. Rooming with a girl from Norway. She's sweet but a little loud. I hope I see you guys at dinner, if not earlier. Please tell me I can take a picture of you all together! Oh, and watch out for this kid named Kenny. We were in a competition last year and he totally ripped off my design for a dehydrator. I hate that guy."

"Sure," I said, totally confused, as she raced off.

I opened the door to 402 and stepped inside.

Plain, two beds, two desks, windows overlooking the street. This is where it was all going to go down. I checked my cell for any texts or e-mails from Tunde or Painted Wolf. Nada. I re-sent the messages I'd sent earlier but this time in all caps just to be irritating.

Where were they?

I threw my stuff down on one of the beds and stretched.

All right, let's do this. . . .

8. TUNDE

Chei!

I walked into my dorm room at the Boston Collective to find a space of enormous size. Had it been in Akika Village, at least five people could have been housed in the same space.

But that was not the reason I shouted with surprise.

No, that was because the room was covered in handwritten numbers and letters. The windows and walls were filled with algorithms and coding, theorems and equations. It was as if the whole room was merely another workspace and not a place where two people would be sleeping.

The individual who had written all of these algorithms and formulas was, in fact, standing with his back to me at the other end of the room. I will admit that I was concerned enough that I backed up slightly. Historians tell us that there is a very fine dividing line between genius and insanity. I certainly knew which side of this line I preferred to have my new roommate on and hoped this *guy no don mara.*

I cleared my throat, but my new roommate did not turn around. Instead, standing on his tiptoes, with a large black marker in his hand, he continued to furiously scribble numbers almost at the top of a wall. In spite of his *wowo* handwriting, I could see he was working out differential equations.

"Excuse me," I said, further attempting to get his attention.

My new roommate held up his free hand as if to silence me.

He was very tall, thin, and broad-shouldered, with a shock of dark hair. He wore a hoodie, jeans, and colorful, well-maintained sneakers.

"Sorry," he said. "Don't mean to be rude but . . ."

He kept on writing, so I decided to set down my bag and wait. But I have to admit my patience was running thin. After such a long journey, I was so eager to get started!

"What is it you are working on?" I asked my new roommate.

"The software for your jammer, of course."

And that is when I was dumbstruck. "Wait . . . Is that you, *omo*?"

"Who else would it be, Naija Boi?"

When he turned around, my smile was so wide it lit the room.

My new roommate was Rex Huerta.

Equations and algorithms covering the walls and windows

8.1

YAAAAAAAAAAAA!

Rex and I screamed so loudly and with such joy that I was certain the contestants in the rooms neighboring ours would be calling the police.

"Brother!" he said as we hugged.

"How *bodi*?"

"It's so good to finally meet you."

Here he was in the skin, my best friend! For one memorable moment, all of the stress and strain of the past week fled my body.

"It is very good to see you as well," I said. "I am so grateful that you are here. How is it that we are roommates? Do not tell me you switched my room designation. . . ."

Rex made a sly grin, which had me quite worried.

"Is this not a big problem?" I asked. "You must be more careful, Rex. You will get yourself kicked out before you have even begun!"

He laughed. "Don't stress so hard. I got this."

I was not immediately convinced. But what is done, is done.

"Did you get my messages?" Rex asked.

"No. I have not had a moment to check. Has something happened?"

"Teo is alive. I got a message from him."

This was tremendous news. I could not believe my ears.

"That is incredible!" I said, but Rex still wore a grim expression.

"He is alive and needs me to find him because he is in trouble. This whole time, he's been with Terminal. I don't know how involved he's been, but . . . it can't be good. Not with a group like that."

"Listen, *omo*. Your brother is alive. He is reaching out to you. You must see this as a good thing. There will be time enough later for you to get the answers you seek and find out why he has done all this. I am sure he will have an explanation."

Rex then showed me the components of the USB, including the tiny receiver. It was very impressive, a tremendous technical feat. Not just the size of it, but the wiring as well. Someone had spent a lot of time thinking about how to make it.

"What's it tell you?" Rex asked as I looked over the parts.

"It tells me," I said, "that whatever Teo is involved in, it is big."

"Could Terminal have made this?"

I shook my head. "I do not know, *omo.*"

We let the conversation end there as I unpacked my belongings and hung my shirts in the closet. Inside, I discovered a pile of clothes. I assumed they were dirty laundry, but Rex clarified that he never used hangers as he felt they "slowed him down too much." He was adamant that every second of his waking day counted.

My friend clearly *get e number six.*

Rex tossed me a few items of clothing that he dragged from the pile. A hoodie. Sweatpants. Even thick socks. "Brought these for you. It's cold here."

"Thank you," I said, looking over the hoodie.

"Come on. Put it on," Rex said. "You're late. We have to hurry."

"Hurry where?"

"The meeting, Tunde."

8.2

Despite my exhaustion, I put on an enthusiastic face. "Okay."

"We're going to find Wolf," Rex said. "Don't worry."

As we left the dorm, we noticed many groups of young people making their way quite hurriedly across the campus. Rex nudged me and we followed them. Catching up with a young man with a shock of blond hair who was clad in an oversized coat, Rex asked what he knew about the meeting.

"No idea." The young man carried a large mug of soda. So large, in fact, that I worried about his caffeine intake and wondered how fast his heart must beat. "You guys just get in?" he asked.

"Pretty much," Rex said.

I reached out my hand in introduction. "My name is Tunde Oni." The young man shook my hand quite forcefully. "Hey, Tunde." His accent was thick and unfamiliar. I guessed Eastern European.

"I'm Rex Huerta," Rex said.

"Oh, I know you." Rex did *shine his thirty-two* as the young man continued. "My name is Norbert Ruçi. I'm from Elbasan. That's in Albania. You know, the country next to Greece everyone forgets about. I'm a coder."

"A coder? What sort?" Rex asked, shaking the man's hand as well.

Norbert said, "I'm a Haskell guy."

"Steep learning curve on that one."

"Well, that's what I code for fun. Malbolge is where I really do my thing."

```
D''N@
p8~[5X9Vx6v4tc>=p(nnmHjF'3VUd"@~,=^):rqvutsl2Sinmlkjiba'_
dcbaZ~A@\
UTx;WPUTMqQ3ONGkE-CHA@d>CBA@9]=6|:32V65.32+O/o-
&Jk)"!&}C#"!a}|u;yxZvo5srkponmf,jihgfH%]\
[`_XW{>=YXQuUN6LpJONMFjJ,BAFEDCB;_?>=6|:32VO/SRQ>
```

Malbolge code in action

Rex's eyes went big. "Holy . . . That's awesome."

"What is this code?" I asked. "I am not familiar with it."

Rex explained. "It's some seriously esoteric coding language. Actually designed to be impossible to code in. Wasn't even created by a person; it was spat out by a machine. Most people consider it a quirk."

"Thing is, if you can really dive into it, rebuild some of the structural stuff to compensate for weaknesses, it can be superfun to work in," Norbert said, breaking into the conversation. "You write amazing programs. You ever try it?"

Rex said, "Yeah. I'm not going to say I didn't get it but . . . I didn't get it."

I laughed very hard at hearing this until Rex rammed an elbow into my side.

As we approached an academic hall, we could see masses of participants making their way through the large double doors at the entrance. The crowd had certainly arrived. We would have quite the competition.

Norbert rushed up the steps. As he led the charge, he turned to Rex and said, "I'm glad you could make it. It'll be fun to talk business."

"For sure," Rex said.

We were ushered into a massive lecture hall as large as an airplane hangar. It was filled with rows of stadium-style seats; the stage was bare, decorated only with black curtains and a black background. It gave the room a tangible sense of anticipation and immediately hushed the crowd that had already assembled. I estimated that just over half of the contestants were already inside.

Sitting down in a middle row, I had the feeling that anything could take place on that empty stage. It was a feeling of great excitement, and I was able to push my worries about my family and village from my mind for a brief moment.

All two hundred of the contestants were gathered, and restless with anticipation. I scanned the sea of faces, looking for Painted Wolf.

"There," Rex said, pointing to a side entrance.

Can I tell you how surprised I was to see Painted Wolf in the flesh? She walked into the auditorium dressed in a most spectacular outfit. Seeing her *I had to kool tempa, oh!* She moved with such

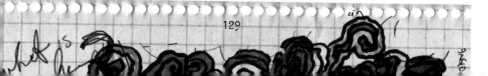

authority and strength. I had sometimes wondered what sort of soul could accomplish the surprising feats of espionage and inquiry of which she had become a recognized expert.

Seeing her then, the answer was quite obvious: She was a superstar.

Several of Kiran's handlers were waiting at the airport for our arrival.

They shepherded us into a large black SUV and then roared out into the night. Kiran spent much of the ride on his laptop and cell phone, making various business calls and typing out long lines of code. He spoke in English, Hindi, and French.

I spent the time on my cell, **eavesdropping** as best I could.

Kiran moved through a dizzying array of topics. He talked land development in South America, East African warlords, drone technology, route planning software, and surveillance. None of it directly referenced China, but I was glad I had my spy cameras running.

"There won't be time to stop by your room," Kiran told me as the SUV raced onto the Boston Collective campus. "We're running a bit behind, so you'll have to walk in with me. That's okay, right?"

"Of course." I smiled. "Walk in where?"

"The auditorium. I'm going to tell the contestants why they're here."

The SUV screeched to a halt at the back of a large auditorium, the vehicle doors opened, and Kiran ushered me outside. There were people—contestants I figured—waiting, cheering and clapping like the giddy kids they were. It was embarrassing. Here I was, trying to **hide in plain sight** only to be captured walking in with Kiran by dozens of cell phone snapshots.

"Hang on," Kiran said. He stopped and leaned down so his face was next to mine. "Smile for the cameras. This is the start of something glorious."

We were bathed in the lightning strobe of flashes for only a second, but I knew that second would live on infinitely as the contestants uploaded their pics to their home pages, walls, streams, threads, and albums. The Game hadn't even begun and already my presence there was being broadcast to the world.

I wanted to kick Kiran in the shins. He knew what he was doing.

"You're a champ," he said as we started walking again.

Kiran peeled off, into a side hallway, as soon as we entered the building. I was taken by his handlers through a series of doors and into the packed auditorium. I scanned the faces of the two hundred contestants and saw Tunde and Rex immediately. Tunde was waving.

"Painted Wolf!" he shouted across the theater. "I see you!"

I waved back briefly before the lights were suddenly extinguished.

Kiran's handler walked me over to a set of reserved seats as Kiran bounded up the stage stairs. An explosion of light lit the stage and Kiran, at its center, bowed to the assembled crowd. They cheered wildly, whistling and hollering.

"Good evening, everybody!" Kiran shouted into his wireless mic.

The crowd was rapturous.

Kiran calmed them by gently waving his hands the way a grandfather does.

"Welcome to the Game."

The applause was deafening and Kiran let it go on and on until it extinguished itself. There was so much pent-up energy in the contestants that I suspect they would have all spontaneously combusted if the presentation had started more than five minutes late.

Sitting where I was, I didn't have the best view. Or at least my cameras didn't. So rather than sit, I got up and walked over to a wall. It felt good to stand and stretch. I realized that even though I'd had a comfortable seat, the stress of the flight had my muscles aching with tension.

Besides, I needed the best angle to record Kiran's big moment.

Kiran on stage via Painted Wolf's "button" camera

He was so comfortable on that stage, so suave.

"You people are all here," Kiran said, "because you have acted upon your imagination. You are originals. And originals are the key to success. We live in a world where everyone is copying everyone else, but copies are a distraction. Today, here, we are looking toward the future: We are here to set things right. We are here to change everything."

I watched Kiran. This moment was probably the moment he was most excited for. It was the first rallying cry for his troops. The kids packing the hall didn't realize it yet, but they weren't there to win a silly contest. They were there as a recruitment pool for Kiran's vision, whatever it was.

"I want you all to know that you have been selected for this competition not only for what you have already accomplished but also for what you will someday accomplish. I will also tell you that most of you will be going home within the next twenty-four hours."

A hush fell over the crowd.

It was as though it had changed from summer to winter in an instant.

"I realize that sounds harsh, but it is true. This is a competition and the rules are very strict. There can be only one winning team. That does not mean that those of you who are no longer with us tomorrow evening will go home empty-handed. I assure you that you will leave here having put your skills to their greatest challenge, confident in the knowledge that you are one of a select few. But let's not dwell on that. Let's get to why you're here: the Game and how to **win** it."

The audience caught its breath.

"I have hidden something on this campus. The only way to find it is to determine what exactly is contained in this code. . . ."

As Kiran spoke, a haze of light formed around the stage as numbers and images began to coalesce. To Kiran's right, a steady stream of numbers and words blossomed from the darkness and ran on a screen beside him, projected there by an unseen source. I noted *magnesium* and *lock* among the words. The images and words shifted and began moving around Kiran as though they were three-dimensional, like he could reach out and touch them. I tried to spot the projectors to get a glimpse of how it was being done but couldn't see anything.

Then again, a good magician is all about hiding the wires.

"Giving you the code would be too easy." Kiran grinned. "I'm going to hide that, too. I'll put it . . . here."

With a swipe of Kiran's left hand, the swirling numbers and words consolidated into a digital moth.

There were oohs and aahs from the audience.

I tried not to be as captivated as I was. The moth was golden, and gold dust fell from its wings as it fluttered around the stage. With a dramatic flick of his wrist, Kiran stuck a digital pin into the moth's body and pinned it to the wall behind him, where it died a digital death.

"This moth is your first challenge," Kiran explained. "There are two phases in the Game. This is Phase One. To reach Phase Two, you have to solve the riddle at the heart of this moth and uncover the code inside."

The Phase One moth

Kiran turned and opened his arms wide as though he was throwing flowers out into the audience, though his hands were empty.

"I invite you to take a look at a copy."

The hall was immediately overwhelmed with the sound of two hundred cell phones buzzing alerts at the very same second. It didn't take long for the audience to figure out the sound was coming from under their chairs. Reaching down, they pulled out brand-new touch-screen smartphones in plastic sheaths. Sliding over to an empty seat, I grabbed a buzzing cell phone. Pinned to a black space on the screen was the digital moth.

Applause broke out.

"The phone is yours to keep. I'm going to leave it to you to decipher the meaning of the image on your screen. But when you do"—Kiran turned and gestured to the moth behind him—"you will uncover directions. Those directions will bring you to a room and in that room you will find . . ."

Kiran moved his hands and a new image formed to his left.

Done up in full color was a highly detailed rectangular, windowless room with a massive Plexiglas safe at its center.

In the safe was an old laptop computer.

"Phase Two of the Game leads up to Zero Hour. And that, my friends, will remain a secret for the time being."

Conversations erupted across the auditorium.

Kiran quickly quieted them.

"The goal of the Game is for you to find a way out of your comfort zones," he said. "It is for you to expand your horizons. You can't expect to win unless you're willing, fully willing, to create your own rules and **break them**, one by one by one."

That statement was met with deafening applause.

"All of you, I'm certain, would love to be present at Zero Hour, but I'm afraid only those who solve Phase One will proceed."

The audience groaned.

Kiran paced the stage, and as he did, the laser image of the safe and the room dissolved back into nothingness. Only the moth remained. "You have until tomorrow morning, bright and early at six thirty, to solve the main puzzle. And just to make sure you don't forget . . . ," he said, pointing to the moth.

A digital clock materialized beside the moth, as well as on our phone screens.

It was counting down.

09:16:42

Watching the clock tick instantly made me nervous.

"I cannot tell you more about it, but the answer is and has been right before your eyes," Kiran continued. "My staff and I will be available to chat, though we won't answer any questions related to the Game. The clock has started. Get ready . . ."

The crowd tensed.

"Get set . . ."

Kiran leaned forward, mouth directly over the microphone.

Everyone watching held their collective breath.

"Go."

Kiran spread his arms wide as though releasing two hundred butterflies, and chaos erupted around him. Kids jumped over seats and sent backpacks flying as they raced for the exits, eyes glued to the image of the moth on their new cell phones. As the auditorium emptied, the lights flickered on. I was surprised to see a new image of the moth had appeared, this time free from the screen and fluttering in profile at the back of the stage.

As I waited for the crowd to clear out, I watched the projected moth. That's when I noticed the moth's wings weren't looped. They weren't fluttering in the same motion. They seemed to move randomly, flapping the way a real moth's would. Looking at the moth on the cell phone Kiran had given us, it struck me: The wings of the moth on the cell phone were clearly looped, repeating the same motions every five seconds.

That was odd.

The night was cool but the rain had stopped. As I walked out of the building, I glanced back and noticed someone standing at the roof's edge, watching me.

It was Kiran.

9.1

"*Hola*, Wolf."

The voice was familiar, an honestly sweet sound after the longest flight of my life. I rounded a corner outside the auditorium to come face to face with the LODGE. Rex flashed me a smile and waved. Tunde, however, wasn't one to shy away from more heartfelt welcomes.

"'Wolf!" he shouted, and ran to embrace me.

I was momentarily flustered by Tunde's energy but quickly came to my senses and hugged him back. It was so good to finally meet.

"How are you? Did you see me in the lecture hall?" Tunde asked.

"Yes, of course," I said. "I'm sorry I couldn't come talk. How is your family?"

Tunde said, "I am so grateful to be here and so excited to do this thing with my very best friends, but . . . the consequences of our failure are great."

"We won't fail," I assured him. "We can't."

Tunde kept glancing down at a satellite phone held tight in his hand. Even five thousand miles away, the general's grip was strong. I felt really bad for Tunde. Seeing the fear and the stress in his eyes, I knew that despite the risks, I'd made the right decision by coming to the Game. He needed us. Now more than ever.

I looked at Rex. "I got your texts," I said. "Everything okay?"

"Teo's alive," Rex said. "I got a message from him."

I couldn't help but beam. "That's amazing!"

"Yeah," Rex said. "But, he's working with Terminal. . . ."

"Are you serious?"

Rex nodded. In person, he was taller and thinner. I don't know if it was because I was so used to seeing him framed inside a room or lit by the flickering of computer monitors, but he was striking. There was a weight to him, a **denseness** to his personality that felt profound. Where Tunde was effervescent, Rex was controlled.

"But you'll find him soon. You can ask him why. You can ask him everything."

"So, I saw you walk in with Kiran," Rex said. "That was a little weird, right?"

"I flew here with him," I replied.

"No way!" Tunde gasped. "Are you serious?"

"He was in China on business. Invited me to travel with him and his entourage. It was a long flight; most of the time he was working."

"Most of the time?" Rex said, a hint of jealousy behind the words. Tunde stood by, flabbergasted. "That is so glorious."

"Guys," I said. "Really. I guess I don't get starstruck, but—"

"I don't get starstruck," Rex said.

"I do." Tunde smiled sheepishly.

"Wolf, you're a master at reading people," Rex said. "What'd you get?"

Rex was right, of course.

"He didn't give any hints or clues about the Game. Nothing that could help me or any of us," I said. "But he knows he's a visionary. Embraces it totally. And I really want to believe that he can do the things he says he can. It's just . . ."

"Just what?" Rex asked.

"He's hiding something," I said.

Tunde jumped in. "I do not think we should judge this man so soon. He brought us here, paid for our travels and food. Only a man of goodwill would do that, correct?"

"I'm not suggesting Kiran has bad intentions. Listen, this Game, this whole thing, is more about who is here than winning a prize. Kiran's not looking for a champion, he's looking for partners. This kind of sounds obviously silly, but this is about recruitment."

Rex screwed up his face. "Recruitment for what?"

I shrugged. "I don't know. But I'll find out."

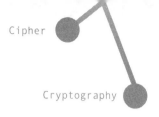
10. REX

02 DAYS, 09 HOURS, 10 MINUTES UNTIL ZERO HOUR

It was funny hearing Painted Wolf's voice without all the digital distortion.

I didn't expect her to sound sultry or anything, but the lightness and youthfulness of her voice was striking, especially in light of her edgy outfit. Funny that she looked a bit uncomfortable as she introduced herself and we exchanged awkward hugs.

I'd spent the last few years pretty much by myself, and even though I was in daily communication with Tunde and Painted Wolf, it was different having them there, walking beside me.

We were really doing this.

And together we were undefeatable.

Right? Right.

And if I wanted to hang out, I realized I should probably get to work.

"So, what do you two think, should we follow them?" Tunde asked, watching all the other contestants make their way toward the library.

"No. I can't think cooped up in there. Besides, we have everything we need right here," I said, waving the cell phone Kiran had given us. "In fact . . ."

Painted Wolf had mentioned that the moth's wings flapped differently than the one on stage. A few random thoughts flickered through my head: The moth on our cells was doing something else. It moved to the beat of a different drum.

What could that mean?

Another thought came to me: Maybe Painted Wolf was right. Maybe the Game wasn't about the competition. If it really was about recruitment, about finding people who'd play along with whatever Kiran was planning, then maybe that's why I hadn't been invited.

Maybe Kiran thought I wouldn't play nice.

Maybe he got me confused with Teo?

My eyes glued to the moth, memorizing the wings' short looped movement, I saw something and stopped walking, ignoring the shoulders that bumped into me.

Tunde and Painted Wolf stopped and turned around.

"What is it?" Tunde asked.

I motioned for them to get off the path and join me on the lawn beneath a towering oak tree. I showed them the moth on my cell phone screen. "It's steganography, hiding images in computer code. Very common, but this is funky."

As they watched, I adjusted the brightness of the image.

A second, reverse image of the moth appeared and overlapped the first one. With the wings beating over each other, it created a hazy, blurry image. When I touched the screen, the overlapped moths' movements ceased. That was curious.

"What do you think it means?" Tunde asked.

I shrugged. Another tap and the moths moved again. We all watched the almost hypnotic blur of movements until Painted Wolf suddenly reached over my shoulder and tapped the screen. As she did, I got a whiff of her perfume. It had hints of white jasmine and vanilla.

"Look," Painted Wolf said, pulling my focus back to the cell.

The frozen image revealed lines of code.

"Remember, it's two point twenty seconds into the loop," she explained. "The moths align with each other perfectly. And when they do, they reveal the code. It's a visual cryptographic technique. Kind of old-fashioned but it works."

"So what is this code?" Tunde asked.

It was mostly letters, varying from caps to lowercase, and a few stray numbers. There were also slashes and plus signs.

I knew immediately what it was.

```c
#include<stdio.h>
#include<conio.h>
#include<stdlib.h>
#include<math.h>
#include<string.h>
long int
p,q,n,t,flag,e[100],d[100],temp[100],j,m[100],en[100],i;
char msg[100];
int checkForPrime(long int);
void findMyEncryptionKey();
long int findMyDecryptionKey(long int);
void encryptMsg();
void decryptMsg();
void main(){
    clrscr();
    p=7;
    q=17;
    printf("\nENTER YOUR MESSAGE : ");
    fflush(stdin);
    gets(msg);
    for(i=0;msg[i]!=NULL;i++)
        m[i]=msg[i];
    n=p*q;
    t=(p-1)*(q-1);
    findMyEncryptionKey();
```

```
    encryptMsg();
    decryptMsg();
    getch();
}
int checkForPrime(long int pr) {
    int i;
    j=sqrt(pr);
    for(i=2;i<=j;i++) {
        if(pr%i==0)
        return 0;
    }
    return 1;
}
void findMyEncryptionKey() {
    int k;
    k=0;
    for(i=2;i<t;i++) {
        if(t%i==0)
        continue;
        flag=checkForPrime(i);
        if(flag==1&&i!=p&&i!=q) {
            e[k]=i;
            flag=findMyDecryptionKey(e[k]);
            if(flag>0) {
                d[k]=flag;
                k++;
            }
            if(k==99)
            break;
        }
    }
}
```

```
long int findMyDecryptionKey(long int x) {
    long int k=1;
    while(1) {
        k=k+t;
        if(k%x==0)
        return(k/x);
    }
}
void encryptMsg() {
    long int pt,ct,key=e[0],k,len;
    i=0;
    len=strlen(msg);
    while(i!=len) {
        pt=m[i];
        pt=pt-96;
        k=1;
        for(j=0;j<key;j++) {
            k=k*pt;
            k=k%n;
        }
        temp[i]=k;
        ct=k+96;
        en[i]=ct;
        i++;
    }
    en[i]=-1;
    printf("\n\nTHE ENCRYPTED MESSAGE IS\n");
    for(i=0;en[i]!=-1;i++)
        printf("%c",en[i]);
}
void decryptMsg() {
    long int pt,ct,key=d[0],k;
```

```
        i=0;
        while(en[i]!=-1) {
            ct=temp[i];
            k=1;
            for(j=0;j<key;j++) {
                k=k*ct;
                k=k%n;
            }
            pt=k+96;
            m[i]=pt;
            i++;
        }
        m[i]=-1;
        printf("\n\nTHE DECRYPTED MESSAGE IS\n");
        for(i=0;m[i]!=-1;i++)
            printf("%c",m[i]);
    }
```

"It's an RSA cipher. Using C. It's a cryptosystem used mostly to send secure information online. It has several algorithms: One to generate a key, one to encrypt, and one to decrypt. With RSA the encryption key is public, the decryption is secret. You need the key. This one's quite complex but nothing we can't easily break," I said, trying to hide my excitement. This was the sort of coding I loved, complicated and tricky. "With this cipher, you need to know your prime numbers."

"I do not know mine that well," Tunde admitted.

"Good thing I do," I said.

"So what's it hiding?" Painted Wolf asked, peeking over my shoulder.

"Don't know without the key, but part of it doesn't make sense. . . ."

I shook my head, focused on the numbers as I scanned them.

There were hundreds of lines of code embedded in the image, but as I moved my eyes past them, I noticed that a few letters were reversed. That didn't make any sense.

Unless . . .

"Tunde, memorize these letters."

As I moved through the lines of code, I read aloud each of the reversed letters. Tunde listened intently. Fifty seconds later, I finished and turned to Tunde to tell me what it meant, if anything.

"It says"—Tunde smiled—"all steps of learning should be sought for nature."

"Okay . . ." I was confused.

What the heck did that mean?

"You mentioned part of the code didn't make sense," Painted Wolf said.

"Yes," I replied. "There shouldn't be reversed letters. And they certainly don't normally spell out anything."

"So it's a trick," she said.

Tunde nodded, catching on. "Yes, Kiran has fooled us already. He has assumed that when the contestants discover the RSA code, they will attempt to decrypt it. But it cannot be decrypted. It is a ruse."

"The real message is the one you just read, Tunde."

"'All steps of learning should be sought for nature,'" Painted Wolf said. "We need to know what that phrase is from and who said it."

I immediately plugged the phrase into the cell's search engine, but it didn't work. There was no connection. The Internet had been blocked. I tried again. Messed with the settings on the cell. No go.

"We can't access the Web. Something with these phones."

"Another trick," Painted Wolf said, pulling out her personal cell phone. "He's good."

Tunde pointed to the library. "Let us not—"

He stopped short when a ringing sound jolted us from our

moment. Tunde pulled a phone from his pocket. It was not the phone taped under our seats at Kiran's presentation but an older-model satphone. Tunde's hands trembled as he stared at the screen.

"Who is it?" I asked, reading Tunde's trepidation.

He looked up at me, eyes filled with dread.

"It is the general," he said.

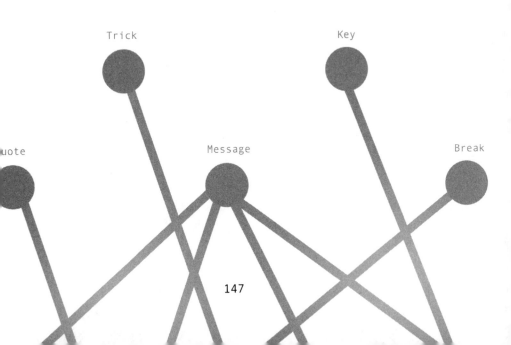

02 DAYS, 08 HOURS, 52 MINUTES UNTIL ZERO HOUR

"General Iyabo, I hope you are well," I said when I answered the satphone.

"I am," he replied, his tone quite somber.

The general cleared his throat and then carefully measured his words.

"Did you receive my other phone calls?"

"N-n-no," I stammered. "I just saw now that you have called. I do not know why I did not receive any earlier calls, but I suspect it was due to satellite—"

The general stopped me dead with a bark of authority.

"I want you to understand the situation you are in, Tunde. *E no go beta for you. I don control you dey kpali.* You cannot take a step without me allowing it. You want me to be happy and *this you story get as e bee sha.* But let me put on someone who can convince you better."

There was a shuffling noise across the phone line before a familiar voice came on. A lump appeared in my throat and quickly threatened to choke me.

"Tunde?"

It was my mother.

It sounded as though she had run many miles and had not been given water.

"Mother. You okay?"

My emotions coiled around my heart and I felt as though I might faint.

My mother said, "I am okay, Tunde. But you need to take this more seriously. When the general calls, you must answer. You cannot make this mistake again."

My mother did not sound like herself. It was clear to me that she was being forced to say the things she was saying.

"Mother, I will do as he says," I said, attempting to calm my voice so I would not frighten her with my fear. I had to show I could do this. "Do not worry. I will make him very proud. You tell him that. You tell him I can do it."

There was a sound of commotion before my mother whispered:

"I dey fear. I don die, oh!"

Oh, how I wanted to cry out!

Instead, I remained calm and focused. "Don't be afraid, Mother. I am going to build the machine for the general and I will win respect here. Tell him that I have already learned many things he will be very happy with. There are people here who can help me. I can take advantage of—"

"You will answer my calls." General Iyabo came back on the line.

"I will, yes."

"I am visiting your flyspeck village again in a few days. You understand this? The next time you miss one of my phone calls, your family suffers. This is clear?"

My throat had parched to a desert. I could not answer, but nodded.

"Is this clear?" General Iyabo repeated.

"Yes. Yes, sir."

"Good. You are the pride of our homeland, Tunde." General Iyabo's tone had changed. He sounded like a father angry with his child but softening after he had already delivered the blows with the switch. "I do not want us to be enemies. I want you to be happy working for me. You have a future in your hands. When I make an offer, I am not one to walk away from, *walahi!*"

"Yes, I understand. I am very fortunate."

"Very much. Now go back to your work. When you return, *we dey go parti*. You will return a hero. Is that not what you want, Tunde?"

"That is what I want."

"Good. I will call you again at this time in two days."

The general disconnected the line.

11.1

Na wa!

I could not hide my emotions from Rex and Painted Wolf.

The phone call had put me in a very bad state and I had to sit down for a little bit to regain my composure. They did not need to ask me about the details of the conversation. Those were clear on my face. Rex reassured me of my strengths.

"Tunde," he told me, "you can do this. Just a little more than a day ago you were in Nigeria. You got yourself here. Just the same as you built Okeke. Just the same as you connected with me and Wolf. Stakes are higher now, but I can't think of anyone else I know who can do this. And make it amazing."

I admit I smiled on reflex. These were words I needed to hear.

"We are here for you," Painted Wolf said. 'Tell us how we can help."

Thanks to these good friends, I quickly regained my composure.

"Our focus needs to be on passing Phase One," I said. "If we can build and program the jammer tomorrow, that would be incredible. For now, it is enough for us to remain in the Game. If I was to go home in the morning, that would be beyond disastrous. Let us go

back to the auditorium. I think it is important that we see what Rex has discovered up close."

We were all in agreement.

"'All steps of learning should be sought for nature,'" Rex repeated as we walked. "'All steps of learning should be sought for nature.'"

"Okay," Painted Wolf said. "Let's tease it apart."

"On the surface, the obvious part is that it says that we need to turn to nature for everything we learn. That maybe all human thought comes from nature first," Rex said.

"Maybe," I said. "But this sounds too simple."

"The moth is natural. Maybe learning comes from the moth?" Painted Wolf asked. "Maybe it is a quote by someone who studied moths?"

Rex shook his head. We fell into a few moments of silence.

I did not like wasting time.

What if we were wrong? What if Rex gave us the wrong letters? Perhaps we should be in the library with the other contestants? What if the RSA cipher really was a working code and not a hidden surprise?

We could not be wrong. We had to be right.

My family depended on it!

"What about the context?" I asked. "This phrase was hidden in the wing."

"Not the wing," Rex interjected. "The RSA cipher."

We chewed over that for a few moments before Painted Wolf suddenly leaned forward with a big, beautiful grin on her face. "It was in a cryptograph. It was hidden. That is the context. Who created the RSA cipher?"

"Rivest, Shamir, and Adleman, 1977. But that's too recent. This expression sounds old to me."

"Very old," I added. "Who speaks like this?"

Painted Wolf grinned.

"Leon Battista Alberti," she said.

"Who?" I asked, confused.

"If it's about cryptography," Painted Wolf said, "then maybe it has something to do with the history of cryptography. Leon Battista Alberti was an architect who's considered by some to be the father of cryptography."

On the steps of the auditorium, Painted Wolf motioned for us to gather around her cell phone. She was downloading an English translation of a book titled *De statua (On Sculpture)*, written by our friend Alberti in 1462.

Painted Wolf flipped through pages. "The book's pretty short. But I don't think we were meant to find just that sentence. We were meant to find this book. Question is: What's so important about this book?"

"Read it to us," I said. "At least a few pages to get a sense of it."

Painted Wolf read the opening pages aloud. Alberti wrote, in very exquisite prose, about the history of sculpture and the purpose of it as art. Just as we were getting into the rhythm of the writing, Painted Wolf stopped.

"What is it?" I asked.

"It's misdirection," Painted Wolf said, looking up.

"What do you mean?" Rex asked.

"Listen," Painted Wolf said. Then she read again from the book. "It says that sculptors want their work to 'appear to the observer to be similar to the real objects of nature.' Do you get what that means?"

"No." I was greatly concerned and confused.

Painted Wolf lowered her phone. "You have to think strategically, Tunde. This is about weeding out players. Kiran isn't going to just hand us the answer." Rex and I watched as Painted Wolf pulled a large silver earring from her left ear and twisted it open. I was stunned to see a headphone jack inside. How clever! She plugged the jack into her personal cell phone and turned it around so we could see a video, filmed surreptitiously, of the speech Kiran gave. "Think back to what Kiran said at the meeting. He put the moth on the screen and then sent it to everyone's phones. What did he say about the moth? Think back to the exact words he used. He said that the moth on the cell phones was a copy."

Rex brightened. "Oh man . . ."

"Watch."

In the video clip, Kiran said, "And originals are the key to success. We live in a world where everyone is copying everyone else, but copies are a distraction."

Painted Wolf pressed pause and smiled.

Suddenly, the truth of it crashed into my head like bright African sunlight. *It just dey copy-copy!* Very excited, I said, "He told us that only originals find success. Copies only lead to more copies. He gave us the clue at the very start."

Rex raced up the remaining steps. "We have to see the original moth!"

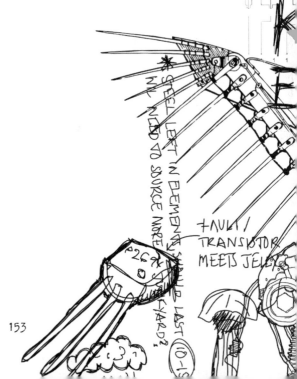

STEEL LEFT IN ELEMENTS MY NEED TO SOURCE MORE

P263?

+AULT / TRANSISTOR MEETS JE...

02 DAYS, 08 HOURS, 38 MINUTES UNTIL ZERO HOUR

The auditorium door was unlocked.

We stepped inside to find the room empty.

Rex flicked on the lights and we made our way to the stage where the **original** moth was fluttering in its loopless pattern.

Tunde and I climbed up to look it over closely.

"It is projected onto a mirror here," Tunde said as he ran his fingers along the glass. Touching the screen did not alter the image. "The bigger question is how do we manipulate it? Surely it is similar to the moth that we all received on our cell phone. That one worked on touch, but this is different. We need to find a way either to interrupt the light source or to add to it."

Rex stood nearby, stroking the light stubble on his chin.

"What do you think, Rex?" I asked.

He said, "Adding to it is interesting. I'm sure there's a code beneath the surface, same as the copies. But, code's got to be different. That's my guess."

We were suddenly interrupted by a booming voice:

"And it's a very good guess!"

We hadn't heard the doors to the auditorium open, but we heard them slam shut. A group of three additional competitors walked into the room.

"You guys are quick! We thought we were first to find the clue."

A young man with a bold personality and narrow eyes climbed onto the stage and pulled a laser pointer from his jacket pocket. When he shone the laser light on the moth, it trembled, the surface of its digital skin peeling back to **reveal** layers and layers of code everywhere but on its eyes.

Tunde clapped.

Layers of code beneath the surface of the moth

"Brilliant, Norbert," he said. "*Sharp guy!*"

Norbert bowed. "Actually, I wasn't sure it would work," he said. "I figured it might react to some interference, and laser light seemed natural, but . . . it worked. I want to introduce you to my friends."

His companions were quite a disparate pair. The first was a boy, no older than nine, who had short dreadlocks and wore a puffy hoodie with the distinctive black-and-white color scheme of a panda bear. It even had ears. The second was a girl, around fifteen years old. She was tall and pretty, with long brown hair. She wore a floral skirt, and avoided all eye contact.

"I'm Kenny Prime," the boy said.

"Anj," the young woman mumbled.

"Nice to meet you all," I said. "I'm Painted Wolf. This is Rex Huerta, a coder, and Tunde Oni, an engineer. We just got here, too."

"Anj's from the Philippines. She's into biochem. Kenny's a freshman at Yale. He's from Haiti. Computer science guy," Norbert said.

"Your name's Kenny, huh?" Rex asked. "Yale?"

Kenny nodded, very sure of himself. "You know David Gelernter there? You know, one of the guys who inspired Java? He's a legend."

"Of course."

"He's my mentor," Kenny added smugly.

"I'm jealous."

"You should be," Kenny said without a hint of humor.

Rex rolled his eyes. I wondered how they knew each other. Was it just that Rex was something of a sponge, absorbing all the information that crossed his path, or was there a history here? Maybe they'd encountered each other online? Regardless, even if they weren't exactly on good terms, I saw an opportunity to use that competitiveness. We didn't have much time and there's no better motivator than rivalry.

"Kenny, come on up," I said, motioning for him to join us.

I borrowed the laser pointer from Norbert, revealed the underlying code, and then knelt down beside Kenny. "You're a coder like Rex. Tell me what you see."

Kenny looked me over, unsure about having me so close. "You don't smell bad," he said.

"Thank you."

It didn't take long for me to realize why Rex had a problem with

Kenny. This was one obnoxious kid. If I didn't get him **focused**, we could be in real trouble.

Kenny moved close to the flickering moth and analyzed the codes. "These are hex strings. They are the same on both wings. Mirrored. Repeated."

"And you can decode them?" I asked.

"Of course. With a computer."

"But we do not have a computer here . . . ," Tunde began, sincerely concerned.

Norbert spoke up. "Paper. Pencils. Enough time, we can do it."

"Are you serious?" Kenny scoffed.

Rex said, "It's going to be insanely hard."

They continued to grumble until I interrupted.

"Here's one thing I've been wondering," I said. "Why a moth?"

12.1

Anj cleared her throat.

If she hadn't, I think we all would have forgotten she was there.

"Sorry, um, it's *Dysphania percota*," she said with a thick accent. "Blue tiger moth. It's native to India. I'm only mentioning it because it might have something to do with solving the code. There were codes in the duplicates on our cell phones."

"Any guess on why it's a blue tiger moth and not something else?" I asked.

"Um, it's a geometrid," Anj said. "The name's derived from the Latin for 'earth-measurer.' That's a poetic sort of reference to the inchworm's locomotion. Fitting, really. This one is male, you can tell by the length of the antenna."

"Can you tell us what makes this moth different?" I asked. "Is it unusual?"

"It's actually pretty common," Anj said. "Ubiquitous, really. The only unusual thing about it is . . . Oh my God, I can't believe I missed that."

"Missed what?" Painted Wolf asked.

"The eyes," Anj said. "The moth's eyes are wrong."

Everyone turned to look at the moth. Its eyes didn't appear wrong to me.

"What's wrong about them, Anj?" I asked.

"They're not positioned correctly. They're too far apart."

"What does that tell us?" Rex asked.

"It tells us to focus on the eyes."

Kenny frowned. "No it doesn't. It tells us that whoever drew it was a terrible artist. I'm not going to read too much into this business. The only important thing is figuring out what's in the hex strings."

As I watched Anj duck back into her shell, I thought of the many young women I knew like her back home. These were people who felt bad about taking up room at a table, started every sentence with "sorry," and were embarrassed to ask questions and deathly afraid of being seen as bossy or impertinent.

I wanted to grab Anj by the shoulders and let her know it was **okay to yell** and shout and scream and make a fuss. I wanted to tell her that taking up space was human and that in scientific discourse you should never feel like you need to start a sentence with "sorry." I wanted her to know her ideas were just as valid.

"Everyone," I said as I dragged a chair across the stage to the moth.

I slipped my boots off and stood on top of the chair.

"We need to work together if we're going to solve this," I said. "We don't have more than six or seven hours left."

As I scanned their faces, I organized them in my mind.

"Norbert, you and Rex are coders. I'll get you the image of the code on the wings from my phone and I need you two to crack it. Tunde and Anj, see if you can come up with why Kiran chose this moth. Maybe do some research into the species, its environment, anything that will give us more clues. Kiran has a calculating mind. He wouldn't have chosen this moth randomly. Kenny, you need to jailbreak the cell phones that Kiran gave us. Maybe there's something in the programming we haven't seen yet."

"Seriously? Who died and made you boss all of a sudden?" Kenny sneered. "What's your job?"

"I'm already doing it," I said as I hopped off the chair. "Now, let's get to work."

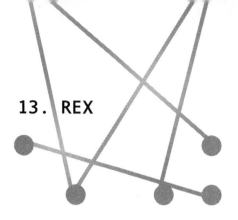

13. REX

Norbert and I spent the next two and a half hours code breaking.

Have you ever built a cell phone from rubber bands and toothpicks?

No, neither have I.

Outside of being impossible, can you imagine how hard that'd be?

How insanely frustrating?

That's exactly what trying to break a code on paper is like.

Using archaic tools (the first graphite pencil was invented in the seventeenth century, by the way) to solve modern problems results in more complications. All of the calculations the computer would normally do, the easy stuff, stacks up. What would take a few minutes in front of a screen takes hours.

So, yeah, it wasn't easy, but I'm not ashamed to say my grasp of frequency analysis and affine shift ciphers was better than Norbert's. We got along well enough, both locked on our cell screens and talking nothing but math. It wasn't like trying to work with Kenny, but then Painted Wolf had clearly known that.

Watching her in her element, directing us all, problem solving, strategizing, I was in awe. She could run a country if she wanted to. Turn around an economy. Probably cure cancer if she had the right team of people to organize.

Kenny jailbroke the cells and handed them out just as the doors to the auditorium opened and in waltzed at least half a dozen other contestants. *Damn.* They'd caught on, too. Unless we wanted to help everyone else advance to the next level, we not only had to work double-time but also we couldn't do it out loud anymore.

Cameras are eyes. . . .

Microphones are ears. . . .

I set my teeth, focused on the jailbroken cell, and pushed myself into the zone. Given our situation and the amount of adrenaline pumping through my veins, I knew I was capable of impossible things.

I spent the next forty-two minutes coding.

I couldn't talk. I was thinking too fast for that.

My fingers moved like wildfire.

The code unfurled on the screen. I don't feel cocky saying it was glorious, because it was. It came out organically. I was practically channeling it, as though the cell phone screen and my fingers were on their own wavelength and I was sitting back, taking in the ride.

When it was over, I exhaled. "Over here, guys."

I marshaled our little team. All of them huddled around my phone.

"So what does it do?" Norbert asked, peering over my shoulder.

"This." I pressed enter and the program ran.

Within fifteen seconds, it had solved the hex strings.

"No way," Norbert gasped as he watched the program spit out the answer. "How exactly did you just do that?"

"Reconfigured Schneier's Twofish . . ."

"But you can't . . . ," Kenny said. "Impossible . . ." He turned to Norbert. "He can't do that, right? No one can do that."

Norbert shrugged. "I guess Rex can."

There, flashing in neon green type on my cell screen, was a cryptic message:

25mm takes to the sky and wrong philosophers consider life anthropomorphic machines in wonderment of why. The image is the missive and only revealed when it dazzles.

14. TUNDE

We were all exhausted, but I never let my mind slow.

I could not afford it. The words of my mother and the harsh voice of General Iyabo reverberated in my ears.

Looking at the poem on the cell phone screen, Painted Wolf spoke first, "Twenty-five millimeters is an inch. Could be something we are meant to build, like a disguised blueprint. The words could disguise measurements."

"It's an inchworm. A caterpillar," Anj said. "I think that's what it means when it says twenty-five millimeters takes to the sky. An inchworm becomes a moth."

"Could inchworm be a program?" Painted Wolf suggested.

She looked to Rex and Norbert.

"Not that I've heard of," Rex said. "Maybe it's another trick."

"We don't need maybes, we need answers!" Kenny roared.

Rex could no longer control himself. He shouted directly at Kenny in Spanish. Kenny screamed back and began pushing Rex. Norbert jumped between them, putting himself in the middle of this fray. It was a brave move, like stepping between two battling dogs. *He dey enta da fire!*

"It's like I said!" Anj yelled. I did not imagine she was capable of such noise given her temperament, but it worked, the fighting stopped. Everyone turned to her, even the other contestants in the auditorium. Anj lowered her voice again and motioned to the moth.

"It's all in the eyes," Anj said. "We have to dazzle them."

"What?" I gave voice to what we surely all thought.

"Dazzle," Anj clarified. "In the poem, that's how it is revealed." She grabbed the laser from Norbert and shone it on the moth. As before, everything on the moth unfurled to reveal code beneath. Only the eyes remained unchanged.

The truth of the moth suddenly clicked for me as well.

"Gather in. She is right. It fits," I whispered to the team as they surrounded me. "The wings responded to light, to the laser. That is how the code was revealed. But it does not work with the eyes. To find what is hiding behind the eyes, we must use a different sort of light. We must use a dazzler."

"What's a dazzler?" Norbert interjected.

"It is an infrared emitter. They are not uncommon and are often used in industrial processes that require heat, like laminating and embossing. I myself have used one in the creation of a germ eradicator. That project was not as successful as I had hoped, but an emitter should not be too difficult for us to create here. We can make one to operate in the red spectrum, perhaps even using what we already have on stage."

"How confident are you about this?" Kenny asked.

"I cannot give a percentage, but it makes sense," I replied.

"I know it will work," Anj said. "One hundred percent."

Kenny turned to Norbert and Rex. Rex nodded.

Painted Wolf said, "Time to build, Tunde."

14.1

We worked in secret as best we could.

There were prying eyes all around as many more contestants entered the auditorium. I do not know how many had actually discovered that the original moth was key to decoding the riddle and how many had simply followed their compatriots, but the room was soon filled.

All of these people were fighting for the same twelve spots. Time was no longer our only concern. Now we were going head to head with the other contestants. As if I needed more stress, *see me see quanta!*

Pulling myself together and finding my core focus, I carefully drew the blueprints for a pair of laser diode dazzlers on a cafeteria napkin that Norbert had in his back pocket.

He apologized for the pizza grease stains, but it *e don do.*

I am not much of an artist, but I am proud of this design:

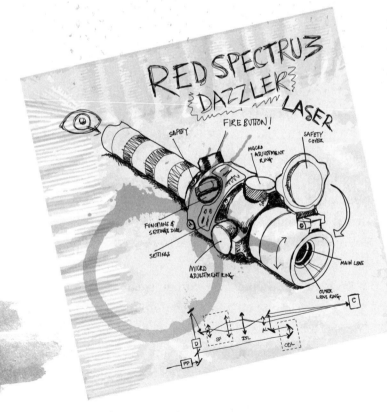

Red Spectrum Dazzler by Tunde Oni

If our rather radical plan failed we would have only a few hours to create something else before the deadline. I will tell you, we were all so anxious we could not sit still. The laser I was building was rather simple, but finding the parts was not.

I had to scavenge from all the materials at hand.

I felt bad about stripping the laser diode and collimating lenses from a projector at the back of the auditorium and worried about ripping wires and drivers from the PA system, but Painted Wolf assured me that if the cost was not covered by OndScan, she and Rex would figure out how to pay the university back. I assured myself I could worry about my unlawful vandalizing later.

I found a quiet place on the stage to assemble my device. Norbert assisted me, and I asked Rex, Painted Wolf, Kenny, and Anj to stand in a tight circle around us, effectively blocking the view for those eager-eyed contestants curious as to what we were doing.

As I did not have a soldering iron, Norbert offered me the use of a lighter he kept in case of emergencies. His backpack was jammed full of things, including a small package. It was oblong and about the size of a toaster. "For when I'm ready to celebrate," he said.

"What is it?" I asked.

He smiled. "A confetti bomb."

"That sounds dangerous."

"Not really. You'll see when I win."

"But what if you lose?" I asked.

"I'll be bummed. Regardless, fifteen seconds after the final bell rings, this baby is going off and it's confetti time. Woo-hoo!"

I stripped the wires and insulation with my teeth and then used the lighter to heat a length of metal. Norbert watched the assembly of the laser dazzler very carefully. "Tell me again how this is going to work," he said several times.

"I assume it will disrupt the projection in much the same way

POWER!

bridge
is latent
ato tubers
aem the ideal
erating
nd
An easy
trolysis is
astruction
yet efficient
e of our
o, zinc and
dea are all
e the battery.

166

as the traditional laser light does," I said. "Perhaps it will reveal something underneath."

"Let's hope it's not just another dead end. Or worse, another puzzle."

Norbert held up his cell phone to show me the clock ticking down.

06:32:15

As in eh, we all fail anyhow!

I finished the laser at three in the morning. It was not until that very moment, finally lifting my head to observe the change in the room around me, that I noticed several other groups of contestants assembling machines that looked ominously like dazzler lasers. We were not alone in figuring out the puzzle!

I counted three teams who were manufacturing emitters. Additionally, there were two teams, each with four members, examining the moth very closely. Too closely for my comfort. If they had not discovered the hidden code already, they would accomplish it within only a few minutes.

Our situation was not good and Painted Wolf realized it, too.

"Don't worry," she said to me with a wink, "I'll take care of this."

Speaking loudly so the other contestants might hear her but not at a volume that was too obvious, Painted Wolf walked over to Rex and Norbert and said, "I don't know what we would have done if we hadn't found that painting in the library basement. That thing was key to cracking—"

She stopped short and then lowered her voice as though she had just realized that everyone in the room was listening. "I mean," she continued, practically whispering, "we really caught a lucky break there."

What an excellent actress Painted Wolf is!

167

Her performance was so believable that within only a few minutes, the rest of the contestants jostled for the exit as they raced to the library to find the painting.

Kenny, despite himself, was impressed. "Dang," he said, "you're cold!"

"We're here to win," Painted Wolf replied. Then she glanced at me knowingly. "I'm sure it won't take them long to figure out they've been tricked. How are we doing, Tunde?"

"The Knockout is done."

This is what I had dubbed my creation. Knockout, in Naija, is what we call fireworks. Painted Wolf led the group in collecting their breath as I positioned the Knockout on a chair across the stage from the digital moth.

Biting into my knuckles, I turned the Knockout on and it buzzed to life.

14.2

Norbert cheered.

I did not.

Already I could see the Knockout was having problems. It shook ferociously as though it would come apart. I blamed my lack of time and materials, but really, it was a shoddy job.

One of the tricks with a machine emitting infrared beams is that they are impossible to see with the human eye. Unlike laser light, infrared is invisible. So focusing the beam on the eyes on the moth was not easy. I had to guess as best I could the angle. Without the correct angle, it appeared as though nothing was happening.

"I am adjusting it." I said, mostly to myself. "Just wait."

Anj knelt down beside me and said, "Try this."

I did not know what she could possibly want. Did she not see that

I was engaged in a very complicated procedure? That I was keenly focused?

I stopped what I was doing and was going to angrily snap at her when I saw that she was holding out her cell phone.

"I adjusted the lenses, removed the filters," she said. "Just a tweak."

But what a tweak it was! Using the camera on her cell phone, I was able to see the infrared beams emitted from the Knockout! There, on the screen, was a weak red line emerging from my device and hitting the digital moth on the chin. If, that is, a moth had a chin.

I turned to Anj. "Many thanks, *omo*. You are a lifesaver!"

I adjusted the beam so it would hit the eyes of the moth and . . .

Nothing happened.

This sent Kenny into a total panic. "What the hell, Tunde?"

"Do not worry," I said, trying to keep my hands from shaking. "I just need to adjust the strength of the beam. I think it is too weak at this point."

With the countdown drumming away in my head, I made my adjustments as quickly as I could. All the while, the moth never flickered, even momentarily.

"Let's go. Let's go. Let's go," Kenny chanted beside me.

"Maybe something's wrong," Norbert worried aloud.

"No," Rex said. "Tunde's got this."

I glanced over at Rex and he gave me a thumbs-up.

Believe, omo. Believe.

Seconds later, something amazing happened.

The eyes of the moth flickered and suddenly digital parts fell off like petals from a flower. The wings fell, then the legs, and then the antennae.

As soon as the final part of the moth, the thorax, came tumbling down, the pieces began to reorganize themselves into a new pattern.

It was a digital, top-down architectural floor plan for a single floor of a building. Done in neon red, the lines and symbols were rather ordinary, but what drew our attention most was an X placed in the center of a large room. It was certainly the location of the safe. Now we had to discover what building this floor belonged to. We had succeeded. Phase One was complete!

We all cheered and clapped and hollered.

Only seconds after the architectural drawing appeared, however, the Knockout exploded in a cloud of smoke and dust that quickly filled the auditorium! Anj and Kenny screamed as scraps of metal and screws flew across the room and I had to duck to avoid a bolt that shot by like a comet and embedded itself in the wall behind me.

The image was gone, the Knockout destroyed.

It was surely the most embarrassing event of my life!

What sort of engineer was I?

I dey nearly kpafuka on the spot!

170

The sun was up.

As the smoke cleared and the last few bits of the Knockout clanked to the floor, we all stood staring at where **the map** had been a few seconds earlier. It appeared Tunde's laser dazzler system was perfectly named.

"Did everyone see that?" Norbert asked.

We all nodded silently in unison.

"I apologize for my poor design," Tunde said, sitting, head hung low, on the edge of the stage. "If not for my stress, I believe I would have succeeded in making a better system. Certainly one that would not have exploded."

"I barely saw it," Kenny said. "Anyone have a photographic memory?"

Norbert said, "It was there maybe five seconds."

"I remember it," Tunde said.

Rex pulled a pen from his pocket and began drawing what he remembered of the map on the stage floor. "There was a large room here. A series of doors and a spiral staircase . . . It was . . . No, it was on the other side . . . Further to the left . . ."

"Rex." I knelt down beside him. "It's okay."

"How?" He looked up at me, panicked.

I held up my cell phone. "I have the image."

The screen grab I captured wasn't ideal.

Screen grab of the image

It was fuzzy in the lower left corner and the very top of the image was cut off by a few millimeters, but we could see what we needed to see. While everyone was watching Rex sketch, I downloaded it from my earring camera to my cell, where it was crunched and archived. It was only a matter of scanning the resulting images for the one we needed.

Seeing the image, the room instantly decompressed.

"Did I tell you how amazing you are?" Rex jumped to his feet, hugged me, and spun me around so fast my wig almost flew off. He was joined by Tunde and Norbert, all of them hugging me and spinning around.

It didn't last long. Our feet got entangled and we all fell, laughing, to the stage in a heap. My sunglasses tumbled off and as Rex fell down beside me, he noticed my eyes. He stopped laughing immediately.

I was wearing bright blue contact lenses, but he stared into my eyes intensely. It was almost like he could see **my real eyes** hidden beneath. We sat like that, staring, as my heart beat even faster and a weird, good-feeling anxiety welled up in my chest.

But before either of us could say anything, the door to the lecture hall blew open. We scrambled to our feet.

I grabbed my sunglasses and looked up to see Kiran and Edith.

They waved the smoke out of their faces as they walked down to the stage.

"Good job. You're in," Kiran said. "Not that I'm surprised. I should tell you, I personally chose every contestant here from a list of thousands." Kiran glanced at Rex, who seemed to be trying to avoid his gaze. "Each and every one of you was meant to be here. But only a few were meant to win. How are you enjoying the competition thus far?"

"Terrible," Kenny said. "And I should tell you, I'm not convinced your selection of contestants has been as rigorous as it could have been."

Kiran smiled, turned to Tunde. "And you?"

"Excellent." Tunde forced a smile.

Rex had moved to the back of the stage, but Kiran noticed him and called him out. "Mr. Huerta," he said, "how have you found the challenge of Phase One?"

"It's been an experience."

"That's all?"

"That's enough, right?"

The pause that lingered between them told me something more **was going on**. Rex's hiding went completely against his character. There was no way they could have known each other before this. No, it must be something else.

Kiran turned back to me. "Can I see the phone?"

I handed him my cell phone and he looked at the image of the map on it.

"Very impressive," he said.

With a smile, he gave me back the phone.

"Congratulations on reaching Phase Two. You should be very proud of yourselves. You've done amazing work here this morning. In an hour, we'll know who the remaining two teams are. Now, if you all will clear out, that'll give the remaining contestants time to make the cut."

"Please, tell us what we must do next," Tunde said.

Kiran seemed pleased.

"You're eager, that's excellent. There will be a meeting this afternoon, I'll fill you in on everything then. For now"—Kiran smiled—"rest."

15.1

Kenny was outside before Kiran had even finished speaking.

Anj followed Norbert to the exit, both of them shuffling their feet and yawning exhaustedly, eager to get to bed and catch a few hours of sleep before the next leg of the competition began.

Rex walked over to me. "You ready?"

I turned to leave with him and Tunde when Kiran spoke up.

"Actually," he said, "I have something I'd like to show you, Painted Wolf. Privately."

Rex raised an eyebrow and then looked to me for an explanation.

I could only shrug and mouth: *I. Don't. Know.*

"Okay," Rex said. "Um, well, we'll meet back up with you later."

I watched as Rex took the stairs two at a time. I was exhausted, both from the competition and the long flight before it. I wanted to find my room, and take this costume off. I wanted to sleep. Rex paused at the door, turned back to face me, and waved. I moved to wave back, but he was gone before I could.

Kiran cleared his throat. "I want to offer you a private tour."

"Of what? The campus?"

"No," Kiran said as he motioned for me to follow him backstage. "If you're okay with it, I want to show you OndScan's labs here. I want you to see the heart of the machine."

I thought it over. I was confident Rex and Tunde had things under control in terms of building the jammer. Maybe there was something I could get out of Kiran about why he was in China and why he was pressuring me to join his prodigy team.

"Sure," I said.

We made our way through the auditorium's back hallways, through numerous doors, and then down a flight of metal stairs. Kiran made small talk as we walked. "I realize the competition is rather silly. You're used to doing things that have profound, real-world effects. You're used to being out there, in the thick of it, chasing after the truth. I assume this probably bores you."

I thought that over. Maybe a few days ago, I would have said yes. The idea of the Game seemed unimportant when compared with everything else I was trying to do, but now, having been through Phase One, I found myself appreciating it.

"No," I said. "It's been challenging. I'm glad I'm here."

We came to a steel door and Kiran paused.

"You know, the only way my plan will truly succeed is if I have an intellectual counterpart at my side."

"Naturally," I half joked. "So who's that?"

"You of course."

I could feel my skin tightening before he had uttered the final syllable.

15.2

Kiran's modified Tesla Model S was waiting outside.

I felt tiny in the passenger seat.

He drove like a madman. But the drive was, thankfully, quite short. Eight minutes after we'd left the auditorium, we arrived at a large brick building, where Kiran took up two parking spots.

As we walked into the building, I wondered at his intentions.

Was he just flirting with me?

Was there an awkward skin beneath that mask of brainy confidence?

No. I was certain neither of those were true. He was being honest with me. He wanted me to join his team and he was going to do anything he could to convince me. That's what had me most worried. What could I possibly **offer him** that he couldn't find in any of the other contestants?

We took two elevators, one of them accessible only with an ID card Kiran pulled from his wallet, to the fourth floor. After exiting, we walked through several doors protected by retinal scanners and biometrics.

"This is our lab," Kiran said as we entered a long white room filled with engineering equipment and computers. "We've got a partnership with the Collective. We pay for the equipment and their students are allowed to run research here. It's a nice setup, and it's in this very room that I came up with the first stage of the Game."

The lab space we walked through was an engineer's dream, a playland of the most advanced scientific technology on the planet. I noticed alarm panels on nearly every wall, motion sensors, and dozens of closed-circuit cameras. The place was as protected as a maximum-security prison.

Kiran showed me things that wouldn't have seemed impressive to the average person—like graphene transistors to replace silicon ones—and devices that would make the average scientist drool with anticipation of the future when they'd be commonplace, like a screen that felt and moved just like silk but was impossible to tear.

"You could scrunch your cell up and put it in your pocket," Kiran said. "Can you imagine a world where you could air-drop these to anyone, even people in a remote mountain village, and give them access to the Internet?"

"Very cool. Seems a little far from search engine technology, though."

"Ah, that just brings in money. I'm looking for the next level."

"You've told me."

Kiran seemed anxious, a little tongue-tied. On his home turf, away from his entourage and the spotlight, he was different. He wasn't bulletproof.

"You go home often, Kiran?" I asked.

"Not as often as I should."

We stepped through a series of double doors.

"Call me sheltered, but I can't imagine being far from home for anything more than a few days, a week," I said. "It's not that I'd miss my parents, it's that home is where I do my best thinking."

"You're lucky. I never had that."

He wasn't fishing for sympathy, he was being sincere. A lot of important people, or people who think they're important, exaggerate certain aspects of their childhoods. They want the struggle to be the story. Kiran certainly had a dramatic and inspiring backstory; I doubted he'd exaggerated any of it.

We stopped at another door.

Kiran grabbed the handle, but hesitated.

"Everything I've shown you, all the gadgets and tools, even the ones behind this door, they're just that: tools. Their purpose is dependent on who's using them."

"Sounds like you're worried about what I think of all this stuff."

Kiran chuckled. "I suppose I'm a little self-conscious around you."

He opened the door and ushered me through. We made our way into a narrow room where he showed me some of OndScan's "touchier" technology. There was a **sonic weapon** that would fry all electrical equipment within a two-block radius and a Web-connected prosthesis that allowed the user to broadcast his movements. It sounded very strange at the time and I couldn't imagine why anyone would want something like that. What purpose could it actually serve? It seemed as though most of Kiran's projects were similar: inscrutable, puzzling, and almost arbitrary.

I noticed an office at the back of the room.

"So what's in there?" I asked, trying to peer in the windows.

"I call it the Quartermaster room."

"Ooh, ominous," I said, and though it did sound somewhat ominous I said it more to read Kiran's reaction. A quartermaster is a navy soldier, usually one of high rank. If Kiran smiled at my reaction, that might suggest he got a thrill out of the whole mysterious sound of the word. If he frowned, that told me he was a bit embarrassed by the somewhat childish name of the room.

He did neither. His face remained pleasantly relaxed.

That told me everything: Kiran didn't call it the Quartermaster room because he wanted to shock or test people; he called it that because he believed it. He was the superior officer and he was engaged in battle.

Kiran moved me along quickly. He seemed a bit cagey.

Ah, there was something here.

"This is just a small glimpse of a years-long project," he said, reading my reaction. "Inside this room are the means to transform the world."

As we walked past, I could see inside the Quartermaster room. There were maps of the Middle East and Africa on the walls. Dizzyingly complicated charts of companies within companies within companies. Labeled photos of Kiran with military men and even a few people I recognized as sitting presidents.

"Interesting folks you hang out with," I said.

"Movers and shakers," he replied.

"Could be good . . . could be bad."

"Mostly good," he said. "Mostly."

Though I wasn't able to take in everything in the room, I did catch sight of a photo. It was of Kiran and a man I was sure I recognized. They were shaking hands and smiling for the camera. In the background I could make out a city skyline, and to their left, a distinctive fountain in a park. I stood as still as I could for as long as I could so my cameras could capture a clear image.

Seeing a picture of this man meant Kiran was lying to me.

Kiran might have been a visionary. He might have been a guru. But there was no way a person with good intentions would shake hands with a monster and smile. Whatever I had stumbled onto, it was much bigger than my father and the Game.

Kiran was hiding something.

Something terrible!

I wanted to leave, to run. I wanted to scan the footage I'd shot. But I couldn't. I had to know what he was doing. So I hid my concern as Kiran closed the door and led me upstairs via an impressive circular glass staircase at the end of the lab.

Less a lab than an office, the upper floor was filled with desks and cubicles.

In stark contrast to my increasing tension, Kiran rolled up his sleeves and relaxed even further. He actually took off his sneakers and socks, placed them on a desk, and padded around barefoot on the cold tile floor.

"I'm more comfortable with my feet on the ground," he said. "Research shows that walking barefoot improves your health. Think of all the static electricity you create; with shoes it goes right back up your legs. That's unhealthy. Without shoes, it goes into the ground, where it's meant to be."

"Seriously?"

"Of course."

Uncomfortable, I said, "I couldn't walk in public without shoes."

"You should try it," Kiran said. "I'm sure you've got beautiful feet."

"Thanks," I said hesitantly.

How was I supposed to respond to something like that? But then, even though my stomach was turning, I flashed as bright a grin as I could muster and relaxed my shoulders. Kiran couldn't know how worried I was. He needed to see Painted Wolf as unflappable. And that's exactly what I was going to show him.

We wandered through the office slowly until Kiran motioned to a large steel door at the back of the room. "And here we are, the final stop on the tour. Any guesses at what's behind door number one?"

"A buffet? I'm starving."

Kiran laughed. "I wish. Sorry, no, although I'd be happy to take you out for a meal afterward. There's a great pizza place across from campus."

"That's okay," I said, walking up to the door. "I need to get back to my team soon. We've got a lot to do."

"Of course. So, no guesses?"

I ran my hands over the steel door. It was surprisingly cold to the touch. Slightly menacing. "Is this the refrigeration room where you keep your clones?"

Kiran laughed again. "You're good. Quick. But no. No clones. It is a special room, though. Had a tough time finding the right people, the right companies, to design what's behind this door. Traveled the world to find them, in fact."

"Is that why you were in China?"

Kiran smiled. "You are tenacious. What do you want me to tell you?"

"Your game plan."

"Haven't I already?"

"You've told me the broad strokes. Painted a nice picture. But I want to know what you do outside of here." I motioned to all the gadgets and gizmos. "What are you doing in the real world? What are you doing meeting with corrupt businessmen in China?"

Kiran walked up to me and held a silver bracelet on his right wrist up against the door's shiny surface. A clanging of metal rumbled from inside the door as it unlocked and swung open.

"After you," he said.

15.3

"I didn't just bring you here to show you all those gadgets. I also wanted to give you answers."

We stepped through the steel door into a dark room. The overhead lights flickered on, one by one, row by row, to reveal an almost entirely empty room. Empty except for one massive red cube sitting in the middle of a completely transparent floor.

Yes, transparent.

The floor was entirely clear. I could see through it to several floors below. There, I noticed cubicles and labs, but on the floor just beneath us was a large rectangle covered by a black cloth.

"Metallic glass," Kiran said behind me. "It's made with palladium and it's the strongest glass on Earth. You could drop an elephant on this floor and it might have a few hairline cracks."

I walked up to the red cube. There were dozens of thick cables snaking their way into its top from the wall behind it. There was a thick glass window in the cube's side; looking in, I noticed that whatever was inside was submerged in a tank of cooling fluid, like an atomic reactor. It was clearly a machine. A quick scan of its features told me it was . . . Wow. I knew exactly what it was.

"This what I think it is?" I asked.

"Yes," Kiran said, as in awe of the machine as I was. "This is the most powerful quantum computer in existence."

The red box hummed and the room vibrated with an electrical current.

The **quantum computer** looked like something designed for space exploration or a film set. For the first time in my life, I felt as though I was standing face to face with something that could change the course of human history, for better . . . or for worse.

"Why are you showing me this?" I asked.

"I'll explain in a minute. Take a look below your feet. See that covered box? It's a safe, and inside the safe is a laptop computer. You and your chosen team will need to build a machine to get into that room, open the safe, and hack into the laptop."

I couldn't believe what I was hearing. I had to actually focus to keep my jaw from dropping and my expression from going sideways.

"The next stage of the Game . . . You're cheating. . . ."

"A little. I want you to win."

"Why?"

"So you'll join me." Kiran walked around the quantum computer, eyes locked on mine. "What if I told you there was a cure for cancer? That right now, there's a molecule sitting in a lab at a pharmaceutical company in Europe that can effectively cure most gastrointestinal cancers? Thing is, the company won't release it. Why? Because they also manufacture chemotherapy drugs, drugs that make them billions of dollars a year."

"I'd say you've been hanging out in too many conspiracy theory chat rooms."

"It's true. I know because OndScan partnered with the pharma company to run the clinical trials. I've seen the data."

"I don't understand. If you know, if you paid for that data, why aren't you releasing it? Why aren't you shouting from the roof about it?"

Kiran nodded sagely. "You know why. It's everything you've spent your life fighting against. Red tape. Injunctions. Corruption. Graft. Lies. I would love to just dump the data onto the Net and see where it goes, but that won't work. The freedom of the Net is just an illusion. It's as heavily monitored and locked down as a supermax prison."

"So what then?" I asked. "You're clearly trying to recruit me. What for?"

Kiran patted the top of the quantum computer.

"I call it Rama. It's going to power a new Internet, a Web beneath the Web. New protocols. New ports. Run on quantum machines. It will be free to access from anywhere in the world via equipment OndScan will distribute without charge. There will be no restrictions or regulations. Even better, Rama is designed to pull information from the existing Net. No firewall can stand up to it. No security protocols can stop it. All information will be liberated. From every government and every corporation. That cancer data, it'll be out. Think of it, **no more secrets**. No more lies. No more corruption."

Kiran had narrowed his eyes and his intensity was hypnotic. The seriousness of his tone and the force of his voice gave me a tingle that moved like light fingertips up the nape of my neck. I scrunched up my face as the feeling washed over me.

It was the signal.

"You said Rama is the answer. How do we get there?"

"Shiva," Kiran said. Then he sidestepped the question. "I'm going to give you everything you ever dreamed of, Wolf. You know governments are evil. They're corrupt. You and me, our final team, we'll bring them down. We'll free all the data and stream it into every home. Together we can help Rama end poverty, end illness, and truly, once and for all, change the world."

It sounded crazy. It sounded insane.

From anyone else, I would have **loved every word** of it.

From Kiran, it sounded like history's biggest lie.

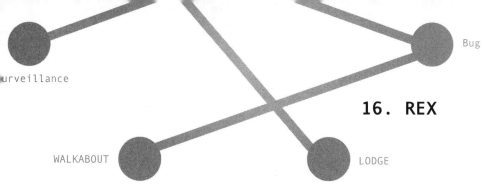

16. REX

02 DAYS, 01 HOUR, 14 MINUTES UNTIL ZERO HOUR

It was lunch and it took only two bites of chicken for me to realize I hadn't eaten actual food in what felt like days.

I'd picked up a few candy bars in passing and drank some white chocolate vitamin supplement that Norbert had handed me, but mostly I'd been consuming adrenaline. I devoured the sub and went back to the cafeteria for more.

Tunde was in line ahead of me for pizza. He'd never had it before and his first bite was something like a religious experience. I warned him that his gastrointestinal system might punish him later, but he was dismissive.

"How can food this good be bad?" he asked me.

I didn't want to let him know.

I joined Tunde, Anj, and Norbert at a table in the back of the dining hall, by a window. Kenny chose not to join us. He sat by himself a few tables over. He devoured a few bowls of sugary cereal and drank a soda. When he was finished, he pulled a notebook out of his backpack and started drawing.

After my third piece of chicken, I was feeling satisfied and sat back in my seat. Anj noticed me relaxing, and smiled. "You finally look like you might be enjoying yourself."

"Do I?"

It was funny because I wasn't relaxing so much as taking a

moment to assess the current situation. With Phase One over, the real purpose of my being at the Boston Collective suddenly crashed back in like a train wreck. I had things to do. We needed to find the building revealed in the electronic map. I needed to get into the OndScan building, find the quantum computer, and run WALKABOUT. Tunde needed to win.

Anj immediately noticed my face twist back into stress mode.

"That was short-lived."

"Yeah, we got to get going."

Tunde agreed. "Time is running out, friends. The general cannot wait."

Anj looked at her watch. It was wooden, chunky. "We've been here only seventeen minutes! Besides, I think we should wait until Painted Wolf is back."

That made the already significant lump in my throat even bigger.

What was she doing?

Why would Kiran want to see her alone? A private tour?

Kiran stressed me out. The thought of Painted Wolf hanging out with the King of Tech, a genius with money, good looks, and charisma to burn, made me uneasy. Worse, I had the feeling Kiran *knew* I wasn't supposed to be at the Game. Maybe he knew I'd hacked his system. Dude that regimented and self-controlled must hate party crashers, and I was certain it was only a matter of time before he'd say something, make a move. He was just playing with me. Toying with me like a cat with a mouse.

And now Painted Wolf was going on private tours with him?

I startled when my cell phone buzzed.

It was a text and photo from Painted Wolf.

Painted Wolf: That machine you're looking for? I found it.

Surveillance image of the quantum computer

I couldn't help but gasp.

"Are you okay?" Anj asked.

No way I could answer her, I had to text.

> **KingRx:** are you kidding me? quantum computer?

> **Painted Wolf:** Yes. Kiran just showed it to me. It's on the fifth floor of the OndScan building, a private research facility on campus.

> **KingRx:** Wait . . . showed it to you?

> **Painted Wolf:** Yes. Where are you? We need to meet.

> **KingRx:** Dining hall. How about fifteen minutes, library?

> **Painted Wolf:** I'll be there. Get everyone else.

I put away my cell phone and Anj, Norbert, and Tunde just stared at me. Tunde was slowly chewing his last bite of pizza, hanging on the moment, waiting for me to speak. My mind was racing. Painted Wolf had found the machine and if I could get to it, I was only hours away from finding Teo. But one nagging thought kept spinning through my mind:

Why would Kiran show her where the quantum computer was?

"What's going on?" Anj asked.

"Tunde and I have to leave. We'll meet up with you guys in a little bit, okay?"

Anj looked suspicious.

On our way out, Kenny grabbed me and asked where we were going in such a hurry. "We're late to meet up with Wolf. We're the LODGE, man," I said.

He gave me a quizzical look but let it go.

Glancing at his table, I noticed the picture he'd been working on. Looked like a kid's drawing of zombies and centaurs battling anthropomorphic calculus symbols.

"What is it?" I asked.

"Basically a war between mythological creatures and derivatives."

"Who's winning?"

"Math," Kenny said, for the first time sounding like an actual nine-year-old kid. "Math always wins. You all have fun with your secret club."

16.1

Painted Wolf met us in the library lobby ten minutes later.

We followed her, silently, to a study room in the basement stacks.

Every step, watching her move, I couldn't stop my emotions from fluctuating.

Had she laughed at all of Kiran's jokes?

Had they accidentally touched and felt a tinge of excitement?

I wanted to know what Kiran had said, but really, I didn't care. I was driving myself crazy coming up with all sorts of romantic gestures I was sure he'd made. I had never been so insanely jealous in my life.

What an idiot. . . .

First thing Painted Wolf did after she closed the door was scan the room for bugs using an app on her phone that I'd developed a few years earlier. Her version was tweaked, though, and seemed to run twice as fast as my original program.

That was impressive.

No bugs, no radio signals. We were safe.

"Like what you did with that program," I told Painted Wolf.

She nodded. "It's decent. Use it all the time back home."

Decent?

"So," I asked, shaking off the distraction, "what's the deal with Kiran?"

"You're not going to believe this," she said, "but he's planning to use the quantum computer to power something called Rama. It's basically a second Internet and he wants to use it to dismantle the existing one. He wants to open every cache of information and take down every security door. Way he sees it, it's going to jump-start a new society."

Tunde spoke up. "This does not make any logical sense. . . ."

"Dark Web already exists," I added. "Why re-create it? Besides, the Internet isn't a single thing. It's a bunch of interconnected networks. You can't bring it down or break it with clever programming. I'm not buying it. Sounds ridiculous."

"He made it sound plausible . . . and kind of incredible," Painted Wolf said.

"Of course he did," I replied. "I think he likes you."

Painted Wolf scoffed. "Are you jealous?"

"It's sketchy. Him inviting you alone," I said.

"He was recruiting me. Not flirting."

"I wouldn't be so sure. He probably likes you," I said, trying to stop from clenching my jaw so tightly. I could hear my teeth grinding. "He's a nice enough guy, smart, but—"

"He's not a nice guy," Painted Wolf interrupted, stone-cold serious. She turned her cell phone so Tunde and I could see a freeze-frame of a video zoomed in on a framed photo. In it, Kiran was shaking hands with General Iyabo in front of a fountain near a park. Tunde had posted articles about him and I'd recognize his cruel face anywhere.

Oh no . . .

"No," Tunde said, his voice trembling. "How is it that Kiran is smiling when he is shaking the hand of the man who threatens my family?"

"Kiran has two faces," Painted Wolf replied.

"I do not understand," Tunde said, still sounding lost.

"What do we really know about Kiran? He has a classic rags-to-riches story. He's an inspiration, held up by the tech world as the next Steve Jobs. After his recruitment pitch this morning, I don't doubt that his end goal—this Rama thing—is legitimate. He really does want to change the world. But he said Rama is the answer; it's the order after the chaos. I want to know what he's planning to do first. General Iyabo, China . . . Whatever it is, it's already begun . . . and I have a terrible feeling it's something unthinkable."

Tunde groaned. "*This day so kolo!* I cannot take more of this chaos. All these duplicitous actions and lies, I tell you, I cannot burden myself with them any longer. I have to save my people before I can save the world. Do you understand?"

"Yes, of course," I said.

And I did. While my immediate struggles were nothing compared with Tunde's, I could clearly see the pain, the worry, in his eyes.

"We also have to talk about how this affects us," Painted Wolf said. "Kiran wants me to win. He's already bent the rules and showed me around. Not to mention the fact that he told me the next step. Kiran's throwing the Game to get what he wants. And that means that I can't win. I have to be on a losing team."

"No," Tunde said. "That is not true."

"I won't let Kiran use me. I'm already pushing it being here."

"I can't win, either," I added. "If Kiran finds out about WALKABOUT, there's no telling what'll happen. I'm a liability. I have to be on a losing team as well."

"But the general . . . I cannot be on a losing team." Tunde grew anxious.

Painted Wolf smiled. "Trust us, we'll get you a winning team."

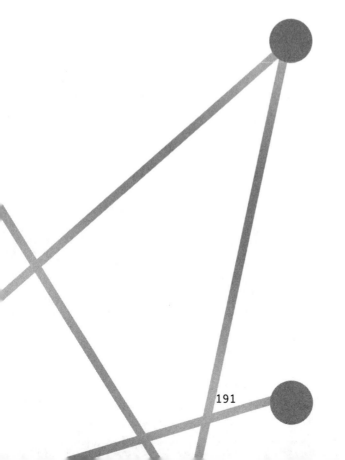

PART THREE

EVERYTHING THAT RISES
MUST CONVERGE

17. TUNDE

Oh, what a headache I had!

After the disturbing conversation with Painted Wolf, Rex and I returned to our room for much needed naps. Between the revelation regarding Kiran and his duplicity and waking every few minutes to check the satellite phone, my sleep was poor. Every few minutes I checked the phone I had been given by General Iyabo, but he had not called. Still, I worried. When I finally managed to find my way into a dream, my worries followed me there as well.

I dreamed of a tremendous battle between a pride of lions, two crocodiles, and a herd of wildebeest. But faced with two of the top predators in the world, those wildebeest never surrendered an inch of ground. What a good and telling dream this was!

I awoke filled with a new certainty.

I knew that no matter how bad things seemed, there was always an opportunity to fight back, always an opportunity to win.

Like the wildebeest, I would fight General Iyabo and Kiran.

I would build a jammer that would give the general what he thought he wanted and ruin him at the same time. And with the help of Painted Wolf, I would expose Kiran for the corrupt man he was.

I turned to share my excitement with Rex only to discover that he was no longer in our room. On rising, I found Rex had left a note. It said that we were to meet at the North Amphitheater to learn about the final challenge.

Leaving the dorm, I was disheartened to find the campus filled with the sad faces of the competitors who did not solve the crafty puzzles Kiran created and had to go home. They dragged their bags to their parents' cars or waiting taxicabs; so many of them were in tears, it was heartbreaking.

Seeing them made me miss my family. General Iyabo quickly came into my mind and I had the rather delirious vision of creating a time machine and going back fifty-odd years in an attempt to stop his parents from meeting. It was a good fantasy but did not relieve the anger boiling in my stomach. How I wanted to send that man running into the desert with his tail between his legs!

All this thinking made my heart burn and go *colo*!

I suddenly picked up my step thinking about how I could achieve this.

Minutes later, I found Rex, Painted Wolf, Anj, Kenny, and Norbert sitting in the North Amphitheater, a half circle carved out of stone and concrete, with the additional Phase One successes.

"Tunde!" Rex shouted on seeing me. "Over here."

Painted Wolf smiled at me before she stood. "Good afternoon, Tunde, you're just in time," she said. "Let me introduce you. You already know me, Rex, Norbert, Anj, and Kenny. . . ."

I waved to them all.

Pointing to a tall young man with the very first stirrings of a goatee in a Maker Faire 2012 T-shirt, Painted Wolf said, "This is Halil."

"Halil Tawfeek," he said in a thick Egyptian accent. "I'm a fabricator."

I smiled, happy to meet him. This was a person after my own heart. He said he made machines, many of them crafted wholly by hand. He told us that in his hometown of Beni Suef he had erected several wind turbines of his own design.

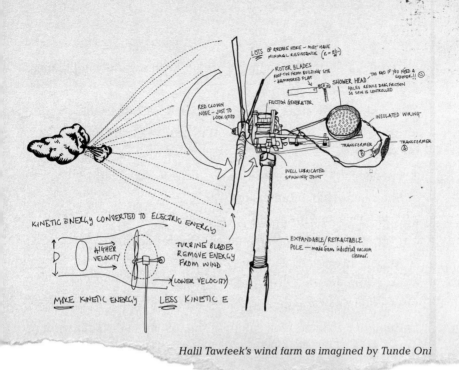

Halil Tawfeek's wind farm as imagined by Tunde Oni

Dat guy ma bross! I needed this person on my team for certain.

Painted Wolf motioned to the remaining competitors.

One was a young woman with green hair named Fiona.

"I'm a mathematician," she said. "Big on Boolean algebra."

Next was a young man with a massive red beard. He said his name was Ezra, and that he was almost eighteen, the oldest of the contestants by far. "I'm from Tel Aviv, Israel, and I'm your guy for engineering. Built a tank in fifth grade. Used to drive it to school until I accidentally ran over my principal's Prius. Guess he shouldn't have left it running in the loading-only spot." Ezra gave a hearty laugh.

No one joined him.

We turned our attention to an obese young man with many freckles and shortly cropped dark hair. He had enormous blue eyes and seemed to be the most awkward person I had yet encountered.

"My name is Ambrose," he said as a robot would, every word carefully balanced and weighed. "I am from New Jersey. I am good with artificial systems. I enjoy working with swarm intelligence. Insects mostly."

Second to last was a short girl. "This is Rosa," Rex said.

"Hey, Tunde!" Rosa beamed. "I'm the LODGE's biggest fan. Seriously."

"I believe it," I said, reading her expression of delight.

"She's annoying," Kenny spat.

"And he sucks," Rosa said.

I looked to Rex for an explanation. He shrugged.

"Apparently it goes way back," Rex said.

"He's a thief," Rosa grumbled.

"She's a baby," Kenny said.

"Enough," Painted Wolf said, putting an end to the squabble.

Last, there was a young woman with long braids and almost too many piercings on her ears to count. "I am Leleti Pheto," she said in a thick South African accent. "I am here to win this competition and I will do it with great skill. My ability is in game theory. I hope you are all ready to go home disappointed."

Kenny cheered at hearing that. "I like her!"

"How are we all doing?"

Kiran had arrived. His voice echoed around us and we all turned toward him simultaneously. Knowing what I did about him, I was angered by the fact that he was free to gallivant around while the men he met with reaped chaos and destruction.

"Let me start by telling you what comes next," he said. "You all have a map at this point. It is a diagram of the campus. Somewhere here, there is a room. In that room is a Plexiglas safe. In the safe is a laptop computer. It's a Windows machine, approximately five years old. In roughly two days' time, at Zero Hour, you and your team will be entering that room, cracking the safe, and hacking into the laptop computer. There is, of course, a twist: You cannot physically be in the room to crack the safe. You must build a machine to do it for you. This machine must be able to move into the room, crack the safe, and then access a USB port on the laptop. I leave the details up to your imagination, but there are no holds barred. If you so choose, your machine can attack the other contestants' machines."

These comments were followed by a long pause.

None of us could believe the difficulty inherent in this final stage of the competition. My first thought was one of extreme excitement! Schematics of machines capable of these feats were spinning so quickly through my mind that I nearly became dizzy. The excitement did not last long, however. Soon my worries about building the jammer and protecting my family subsumed even these delirious fancies.

Ah, but I was surely in the right place!

Design a machine? This was going to be something else.

"First," Kiran continued, "you must divide into teams. There are to be three teams with four contestants each. Go on, do it now."

Chatter instantly broke out, with contestants running this way and that.

I stood beside Rex, and he and I glanced at each other, certain that at least we would be on the same team, until Painted Wolf got our attention with a whistle.

"Most of us don't know each other," she began, standing at the center of the amphitheater. "But I think we should organize the teams based on skills and expectations. We're here to get things done. With that in mind, I've got a few ideas."

Kiran stepped back, impressed with her leadership skills.

"I better not be with Rex!" Kenny yelled from the back.

"Tunde," Painted Wolf said, "You will be with Norbert, Anj, and Halil. You will make a formidable team. And you all can do what Rex and I can't."

The implication of those last few words was very clear. My team was to win so that we all could win. We were to play the inside hand.

"Sounds good, if they will have me," I said.

Norbert nodded, Anj smiled, and Halil fist-bumped me. Then, quietly, he said, "Painted Wolf's told us you have an, uh, extracurricular project you need to work on. We're down to help you with whatever. Just let us know."

"Thank you, my friend," I replied. "I appreciate this greatly."

Painted Wolf turned next to Rex. "I'd like you to be on my team. That okay?"

Rex tried his best to hide his pleasure. "That's fine," he said.

"Who else do you think might be a good fit?"

Rex walked over to Rosa. "How about a chemistry pro?" he said.

Rosa squealed with delight as Kenny rolled his eyes.

"Your loss," Kenny said to no one in particular.

Painted Wolf turned to Ambrose and smiled. "Want to be the fourth?"

"Sure," Ambrose replied. "Charlie and I would love that."

"Charlie?" Painted Wolf asked, looking around at the rest of us. We had no idea who or what Ambrose was talking about.

"You'll see." Ambrose grinned.

Kenny jumped up. "Seriously? You all don't know what you're missing! I'm better than anyone else here. Not picking me is like choosing to lose." He glanced over at the remaining unchosen contestants: Leleti, Ezra, and Fiona. "Guess I'm with you guys, then."

Painted Wolf said, "Anyone have a problem with it?"

No one spoke up.

"Whatever," Kenny said. "You're all going to lose anyway."

Leleti said, "Damn straight."

She and Ezra high-fived and then glared at the rest of us.

So, this is how it was decided. Looking over the teams, however, I remained worried. My greatest concern was that Painted Wolf had carefully constructed two teams that would function in a way to ensure the outcome we wanted.

The team of Rex and Painted Wolf would not win but would achieve its stated goals. My team was primed to win the spot. But Painted Wolf surely could not have anticipated the aggressiveness of the team Kenny had formed. They came on as strong as crocodiles!

I just hope dey rake, oh!

17.1

"So, these are my teams?"

Kiran looked around, appearing confused by our choice of teammates.

He paused beside me and then looked over at Painted Wolf.

"Interesting choices," he said to her. "Why?"

Painted Wolf said, "We're keeping it competitive."

"You certainly are."

Kiran turned to me. "How are you feeling about the next phase, Tunde?"

"I am here to win," I told him. "That is all."

"I would expect nothing less," he said, seemingly bolstered by my curtness. He then turned to everyone. "You know your goal. From here on out, you're locked onto a track to the finish. Find the safe. Crack it. Hack the computer. Win. Easy, right? Everything you need to build your machines can be found in one of the three fully stocked engineering labs assigned to each team. Everything inside is at your disposal. Now, please allow me the honor of naming each of your teams."

Kiran pointed to me.

"You are Team Mitra. In India, Mitra is considered the divinity of friendship. I think it's a fitting name. Your lab is in the Parsons building, room 102. To help you all find the safe room, I'm giving each team a clue. For Team Mitra, it is this."

Kiran handed us what I learned later is a called a "friendship bracelet." It was made of interwoven red and blue fabric, with a large glass bead at the center.

Team Mitra's clue

To the team of Rex and Painted Wolf, Kiran gave the name Team Pushan.

"Pushan is the patron god of journeys, leading one from wherever it is you are, to the next stage. Traditionally, he is presented as leading people to wealth. A good omen, I would expect. You're in Parsons, room 105. Your clue is this."

Kiran handed the clue to Painted Wolf. It was a key made of glass.

Team Pushan's clue

To the team led by Kenny, Kiran bestowed the moniker Team Indra.

"Indra," Kiran explained, "is the god of thunderstorms and a great warrior. He is known for his strength and courage. He seems an excellent fit."

Kenny said, "That's us for sure."

"Your lab is room 107. And here is your clue."

Kiran handed a flashlight to Kenny. When Kenny flicked the flashlight on, the light that it gave off was black light. I wondered about this clue for quite some time.

Team Indra's clue

"Well," Kiran concluded, "seems you likely have everything you need from me at the moment. I will see you all soon, and don't hesitate to contact Edith if any problems arise or on the off chance that you've decided to change teams. . . ."

He let his final words linger as he looked over at Painted Wolf.

The teams immediately gathered up their stuff, ready to hustle over to Parsons and the waiting engineering labs. I will admit, I envisioned a room as large as an airplane hangar replete with every tool and mechanical device imaginable. But before I could join my Team Mitra compatriots on the walk to the lab, Painted Wolf and Rex pulled me aside.

"Some insider info," Painted Wolf said as she held her cell phone up so I could see it. On the screen was displayed a freeze-frame of the floor plan that had been buried in the ones and zeros of the digital moth. "This is the OndScan building. Safe's on the floor below the quantum computer."

Turning to Rex, she added, "How about a recon mission later today?"

Rex nodded. "Most definitely."

"Excellent," I said. "Thank you. You two will not mind if I do not join you, right? I need to have the jammer finished before we dive into the safecracking machine."

Rex said, "We'll keep you in the loop."

Painted Wolf added, "Do you need any help?"

"Not yet, thank you. Now, I just need to build what I have designed."

Rex smiled. "Then you do your thing. We're here if you need us."

My thing. What an excellent phrase, I thought.

That was exactly what I planned to do.

17.2

The engineering lab was not as I expected.

It was large, almost too large.

It had every engineering tool you could ever want. Luckily, there was an inventory list on a bench at the front of the lab. I flipped through it and saw many tools I was not familiar with. Glancing around, I found that all of them were filed away neatly in drawers with small printed labels.

I have never seen a ratchet set so perfectly organized.

My teammates began working on the safecracking machine.

"I'm thinking robotics," Norbert said as he scanned the room.

"Robotics are always a good idea," I replied.

"Treads," Halil added. "We've got to consider counterattacks."

"Counterattacks?" Anj scoffed. "Seriously? Who would—"

"Uh, Kenny?" Norbert said. "That guy's definitely an offense kind of person."

"Treads and armor plating, then," Halil clarified.

Norbert shook his head. "That'll take too long. We need to go light."

"Then maybe we go small?" Anj suggested.

"Naw, naw." Norbert grinned. "We go big. Huge. Biggest in the room."

Halil nodded. "I like the way this guy thinks."

"I do as well," I said. "If we could balance those two directions and build something powerful but not overly heavy, we can surely have a machine to be reckoned with."

While all the materials and equipment immediately inspired Norbert, Halil, and Anj, I found myself surprisingly blocked. They drew plans on the whiteboards, but nothing truly clicked for me. You can tell an idea works when it is simple, when everyone assembled can see it without saying a word. All the ideas my teammates came up with in that perfect lab were very good; Norbert in particular had several ingenious approaches to the actual safecracking. Still, the ideas did not click.

They required too much explanation.

As the others discussed tactics, I realized why I was having trouble. Every direction I looked in, I could see the tools I would need, and yet I could not see myself being able to build the machine that was required in that room. It needed to be a masterpiece. It had to be the finest machine I had ever created. And yet to build something at that level, I needed to be among tools that I understood. Tools that spoke to me. I needed tools and materials that were proven.

"My friends," I called out, and stood. Everyone turned to me. "I do not feel as though I can accomplish what I need to in this space. It is too antiseptic. All of the adventure and grit has been cleared away. I need repurposed materials. I understand that this is all top of the line, but for my creativity to work, I need to be surrounded by used materials and tools. I am sorry."

Norbert looked to Anj, and Anj shrugged.

"I have everything I need right here," Norbert said.

Halil spoke up. "I feel you, Tunde," he said. "Don't forget, I live just a few miles away; I know of a place you're going to love."

"Excellent," I said. "Can you tell us where it is?"

"Off campus a few miles," Halil replied. "I'll go with you."

Norbert said, "I'll stay here. Maybe Anj and I can work on the programming end of things. Get some platforms schematized."

"Thank you, I will not be long," I said.

Then I turned to Halil. "Is the walk difficult?"

"No," Halil replied. "Mostly because my cousin has a bus."

17.3

Halil had quite the impressive cousin!

He was taller and older than Halil and built like a steam locomotive. His name was Walid and he was a self-taught mechanic much like myself. Only instead of working with modern technology, he had focused his mechanical attentions on things of yesteryear. This was what we would call analog. He was a true maker.

Walid had a recent project that was of great interest: an ancient bus.

"I rebuilt the engine myself," he proclaimed very proudly in an accent that was heavily Bostonized. When he pulled the enormous vehicle around to the front of the student center, it belched great clouds of black and tarry smoke like a primordial dragon. I instinctively knew that his neighbors did not like this tinkerer.

"I've rebuilt fifteen of these buses. All in my own driveway," he said as we walked around the vehicle. It was quite impressive. "Ripped out most of the seats, so you'll just have to hang on in your own way. But I could tow a yacht in the back of this beast."

Halil and I hopped aboard the bus and Walid drove us across the city to what he and Halil referred to as "the dump." We rolled back and forth inside the rusted belly of the bus. I found it quite entertaining. I regaled them with stories of the buses in Nigeria. If Walid was ever in search of a job and was willing to travel, he would have quite a future in Naija building a next-generation *danfo*.

I cannot tell you how wonderful it felt to see the dump. It was like the junkyard near Akika Village but twenty-seven times the size.

It was a veritable paradise.

Ah, dat place chassis oh!

As Halil and I walked among the towering mounds of metal, my mind raced at every mechanical beauty that we passed. A broken air-conditioning unit became a portable refrigerator; a Honda Civic engine became a pulley system to bring supplies across gorges; and a shattered fax machine held the parts to construct a book-scanning device. There was simply so much. *Sheh kpe!*

I did not hesitate to grab an old shopping cart when we came across it.

The cart quickly filled, though I knew I could not take everything.

Watching me, Halil smiled. "You love this place, don't you?"

"More than anywhere. It is a library of invention."

To start, I needed antennae from old cell phones, mixer ports, clock oscillators, and anything I could salvage from radio-controlled flying toys. I found all of these and many more. I was certain, given the material I had acquired in just an hour at the dump, that I could make a machine that would have Kiran jumping out of his luxury footwear!

Yet it was only as we prepared to exit the junkyard that I noticed something shoved beneath a pile of broken computer monitors. I pushed the monitors aside to reveal a gorgeous piece of hardware.

"This," I told Halil, "is to be our machine."

What I had revealed had treads and a stout base that appeared to have been smashed into and burned. I did not have the slightest idea what it could have originally been. Perhaps some munitions disposal robot?

Emblazoned on the side of the small tanklike machine was a single word written in bold lettering: RAVAGER.

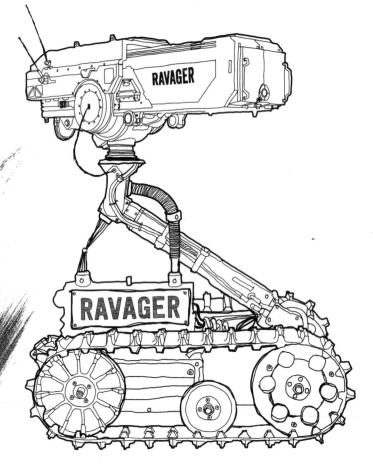

Ravager blueprint

I dragged it from the trash.

"I think it was a fighting machine," Halil said. "Like in the competitions."

"What competitions?"

"Robot battles. Engineering students build machines like this and then fight them inside a cage to see which is the best built, the most dangerous. Sometimes it's broadcast on TV. It's kind of a popular thing."

I could not believe my ears. "Are you telling me that they build sophisticated machines for the sole purpose of destroying them?"

Halil nodded.

"How barbaric!" I shouted. "Well, we will rehabilitate this sorry machine. We will transform Ravager into Efiko and it will become a robot of success and intelligence, not a war machine."

"Efiko?" Halil asked.

"Ah, I apologize," I said. "It means 'very studious.' We will turn this robot of destruction into a student, a thinker. All we need now is to find an arm."

01 DAY, 19 HOURS, 12 MINUTES UNTIL ZERO HOUR

After Tunde and his team left, I pulled Rex aside.

"How about we put my superhero skills to work?"

"What are you talking about?" Rex asked.

"Now's the perfect time to break into Kiran's secret room, just you and me. We'll get to the quantum computer and load WALKABOUT and I can do some additional investigatory work. Find out what **Stage One** is all about."

Rex grinned. "I love it."

We told the rest of our team that we had to get some CPU schematics for Rex's program, that it would take only an hour, an hour and a half at most, and then we'd meet up with them. Rosa and Ambrose told us to meet them on the roof of their dorm, just across from the one Tunde and Rex were in. That sounded weird, but Ambrose explained it was a safe place.

We agreed and then peeled off from the group.

"Where do we start?" Rex asked.

"Kiran's got cameras all over the place," I said. "Even if we can get through the doors and bypass the alarms—"

"I got the alarms. No worry there. Cameras are your deal."

"Depends if they're live feed or videotapes. We can't shut down the power, that'll set off the alarms," I said, thinking aloud. "If the camera feeds are live and someone's watching, we will need a miracle. If they're not, we can scramble the recorded feeds or erase the data. Regardless, we need to get in unnoticed. . . ."

"Might be hard."

That's when I remembered an impressive stunt a blogger in Tibet had pulled off a year earlier. "I've got it," I said. "All we'll need are baseball caps, some LEDs, wiring, two nine-volt batteries, and a green laser. We could grab a laser from one of the labs, but that might raise some red flags. Any idea where we can find this stuff?"

"Shouldn't be too hard."

There are essentially three ways to avoid being picked up by video cameras and facial-recognition software. First, actively disable the cameras, either by cutting power or smashing their lenses or otherwise physically damaging them, which is messy and would get us caught. Second, wear a disguise. We needed to do that regardless, but I had another plan in mind. Option three was the most complicated but also the most fun.

After Rex had stopped by his room to grab the WALKABOUT hard drives, we found everything we needed to construct our anti-security systems at a hardware store across the street from campus. Rex picked a Boston Red Sox ball cap. My cap had the Liberty Bell on it. That seemed quite fitting.

I punched small holes around the front and sides of the cap and threaded the LEDs through, arranging them in a zigzag pattern. Ten LEDs did the trick. I wired them to the nine volts, which I had stuffed into the back of the cap. Not terribly comfortable, but it worked.

Rex was impressed. "Nice. So what's next?"

"We need costumes."

We made our way to the Wheatley Sports and Fitness Center and found it unlocked. Tucked away near the main office was a bin of clothing labeled LOST AND FOUND. Rex grabbed an oversized hoodie and fit the hard drives in its pockets. I picked up a sweater and jeans. Not a perfect fit but good enough.

We changed in the bathrooms.

Rex was quiet when I walked out.

"I know," I said. "I wouldn't be doing videos in this or anything."

"No," he said. "You look good. . . . You look relaxed."

I wasn't sure if it was a compliment, but his eyes told me he was fascinated seeing me dressed down. I didn't want him to linger on me so I elbowed him in the ribs. "You look like a middle school student."

As we ran across campus, I explained how the baseball caps would protect us. "Even though the LEDs aren't particularly bright, video cameras pick up any available light sources. In the cameras, the LEDs will flare crazily. It'll look like we've got exploding suns for heads."

"Beautiful," Rex said. "And then?"

"Then we hit them with the green laser. Boom. Overwhelms their CMOS sensors and the camera goes down."

"Wow, you're totally **a spy**."

I lowered my sunglasses and gave Rex a wink.

When we reached the OndScan building, we scrambled around to the loading bay at the rear. Rex paused at the back door, his fingers hovering over the security keypad. "You ready to do a little breaking and entering?" he asked.

I took a deep breath. "I'm ready."

18.1

Rex wasn't lying about his skills.

He was able to unlock the door in eleven seconds.

Rex studied the keypad and narrated his thinking. "This is a Tartan system. It's high-end and trickier than you might imagine. Cracking the passcode the traditional way, looking for wear and tear on buttons or even fingerprints, won't get us anywhere. The code changes every day. But there's a good chance we won't even need it. . . ."

With that, Rex entered a long series of numbers and symbols on the keypad. A metallic click reverberated through the door and it softly swung open.

"Voilà," Rex said.

"How did you do that?"

"Even the most intelligent people in the world get sloppy. Whoever installed this door probably sold OndScan on its state-of-the-art security but forgot to delete the factory-default passwords. *Oops.*"

With that, Rex ushered me inside.

I led the way, pausing to glance around every corner like a spy.

Every camera we passed, I hit it with the green laser. All it took was shining the laser straight into the lens for about three seconds and then listening for a subtle whirring sound as the camera crashed. I took out ten cameras in the lobby alone.

Rex ate it up. He clearly loved playing the covert angle and soon he was "scouting ahead" to make sure the "perimeters were clear."

I laughed as he somersaulted down a hallway, crept on his belly under a table, and sprinted diagonally across an empty lobby. He was being silly. Still, I was impressed by how carefully he moved. He might have been playing it for laughs but he knew what he was doing.

"This isn't your first time, is it?" I asked quietly as we ducked behind a half wall to survey the elevator banks.

"Teo taught me a few tricks."

"I can't wait to meet him."

Rex grabbed my hand and we ran across the lobby and hit every elevator button as we passed. We both laughed when he dived behind a potted fern and knocked it over.

I helped him up and dusted him off.

As I did, I could feel his eyes. He was watching me, staring at my face.

I could not help but blush.

"We need to hurry," I said, turning away.

"Of course," Rex said. He was suddenly serious, his mood changed from playful to focused. I instantly regretted it, but I wasn't ready to let him get too close. He only knew Painted Wolf. He did not know me.

Rex had to hack his way through two additional sets of doors before we reached the staircase and made it to the floor with the quantum computer. I was careful to get **all the cameras** in the room. I counted fifteen.

When Rex saw the computer, he nearly fell to his knees in awe.

"You know how long I've dreamed of this moment?"

"Too long," I said.

"Way too long."

Rex walked across the glass floor, eyes glued to the quantum computer. When he reached it, he ran his fingers along its bulky metal surface. "It's cold," he said. "Which is crazy because the thing's generating enough heat to melt a fridge. They did some spectacular work insulating it."

Rex took his time.

He found a rack with an input computer and a USB port, but then he hesitated. He looked over and gave me a sheepish smile.

"Is it strange that I'm nervous about this?" he asked.

"Are you worried it won't work?"

"No," he said. "I'm worried it will."

"What do you mean?"

"I've spent the last few years looking for Teo. What if I find him? What if he isn't the same as I remember? What if he won't talk to me?"

"Don't be silly," I said. "He's your brother."

Rex nodded, grabbed his hard drives, plugged them in, and got to work. He had to hack his way through a dozen security and administrative screens. Then he paused, facing down a series of complicated passwords. "I have to get through all these and then figure out how to get this thing online. Kiran's running his shadow Internet in here. It's complicated code, a lot of it dark. I'm going to have to set up a proxy, smoke screen my getting in, then set up another pipeline."

"But you can do it, right?" I asked, looking over his shoulder.

"Don't really have a choice. This might take a few minutes."

"You can do it. I know you can."

Rex flashed me a smile and then dived back in. While he worked, I walked over to Kiran's Quartermaster room and picked the lock.

Stepping inside, I flicked on the light, lowered my sunglasses, and made my way around the office, making sure to scan the room slowly and let the camera in my sunglasses capture the images as cleanly as it could.

The file cabinets were locked and I couldn't pick them, but there were a few files on the desk. I immediately grabbed them. One was labeled *Dongguan Project.* Dongguan is an industrial city in southern China. Most Americans have never heard of it despite the fact that it has ten times the population of Boston. This could only mean one thing. . . .

The folder was empty save for a single floppy disk. It was ancient technology in the United States, but in China some people still stored information on disks for security. The disk itself was black and had no label. I held it up to the light to see if I could make out any writing on it. I knew that whatever was on this disk wasn't good.

"Good way to hide information." Rex's voice startled me.

I turned around to see him standing in the doorway.

"Thinking what I'm thinking?" he asked, eyeing the disk.

I was. And I prayed it had nothing to do with my father.

"You ready?" I asked.

Rex held up his cell.

On the screen was a simple loading bar. It was at two percent.

"WALKABOUT is up and running," Rex said.

I couldn't stop smiling.

"You did it, Rex."

He broke into the world's biggest grin. So many emotions rolled across his face in a few seconds: excitement, joy, sadness, and then a wash of relief that seemed to relax every muscle in his body.

"I feel like I just walked out of a cave into daylight for the first time in two years," he said. "Let's get out of here and find Tunde."

18.2

Late to the roof, we stumbled, laughing, out onto the pea gravel to find Rosa sitting by herself, reading a chemistry textbook.

We sat down beside her.

"Good read?" I asked, eyeing Rosa's book.

"Outdated," she said. "Sort of like comfort food, though. I read through older volumes and find the mistakes. Kills time and makes me happy. It's kind of like what you guys do with programs and hardware. You know, make them better, make them more efficient."

"We try."

"I don't speak or read Chinese, but I keep up on everything the LODGE does. Everything. I follow all your blogs. You're huge, Painted Wolf. My favorite part is that you break the law and get away with it. You're like a desperado."

"That is not what I am, Rosa," I clarified.

Her expression made it clear she doubted me.

"I don't do it for the thrills," I explained. "I do it because it's the right thing to do. Most people turn their back to corruption; they assume it's someone else's problem. Not me. My parents broke their backs to take us from a rural village to a city. They played by the rules and it worked. People who think they can just take what they want when they have the power make me ill."

Rosa was slack-jawed. "So you're really more like a superhero."

"She totally is." Rex leaned in. "She wears a costume, doesn't she?"

Rex ended his sentence with a wink. Rosa loved that.

"I think Painted Wolf is the best superhero name ever, by the way," she said.

Ambrose appeared seconds later, holding a shoe box in one hand and struggling with four folding chairs. He was strong but ungainly and nearly fell before Rex helped him with the chairs. We set them up and sat.

"Nice up here, right?" Ambrose asked. "Fresh air, good view."

I looked out over the treetops and immediately felt like I was back home. I'd been on so many rooftops surveilling and setting up cameras that the experience seemed ordinary to me, and I realized I rarely ever took in the view anymore.

"We've got big news," Rex said. "We found the safe."

Rosa jumped up, did a little happy dance. Ambrose growled appreciatively.

"Where is it?" he asked.

"Across campus," I said. "Northeastern end, on the fourth floor of the OndScan building. Didn't see anyone else there, so I think we're the first."

"That is so, so awesome. Thank God. Listen, I have a few **ideas** of what we can do," Ambrose said, "but I want to hear what you guys are thinking first."

"I can write the software to crack the firewalls once we're in the laptop," Rex said. "But getting into the room is the bigger issue.

Unless I'm mistaken, I don't think any of us can build a machine like Tunde will. I say we focus on something simple. Something easy."

"Small," Rosa said. "Covert."

"The solution to this is going to be a combination of all of our skills," I said. "It will be more than coding, more than engineering, and more than chemistry. Let the other teams provide us with an entrance. What I'm picturing is more Bruce Lee than Genghis Khan."

Rosa and Ambrose frowned.

"You know, Bruce Lee? The martial artist? No? Well, the whole concept behind his theory of fighting was that you don't punch or kick, you defend, you use your opponents' momentum against them. You use their attack, and their energy, to your own advantage. You move like water."

"I like the sound of that," Ambrose said.

"Water adapts," I continued. "And as it adapts, it changes what it touches. That is how a tiny creek can bring down a mountain. So, thinking that way, what can we use? What can we build?"

"Good news, guys, I already have it." Ambrose beamed. "If we let the other teams open up the door and get to the safe, then all we'll need is transportation to get our USB into the safe and then into the laptop. Something . . . like this."

Ambrose opened the shoe box. It was filled with soil and decaying leaves. He dug around inside, then pulled out his hand.

In his palm was a large, black beetle.

I'll admit, I almost jumped.

"It's a Hercules beetle." Ambrose smiled. "His name is Charlie."

"Disgusting! A bug?" Rosa backed away, her tongue out.

Ambrose was offended.

"Charlie's a beetle," he corrected.

"What are we supposed to do with that?" Rosa demanded.

"He can carry the USB," Ambrose said. "This is **why I'm here**. Win or lose, I'm going to show the world what I can do. What Charlie can do."

"You've trained him?" Rex asked.

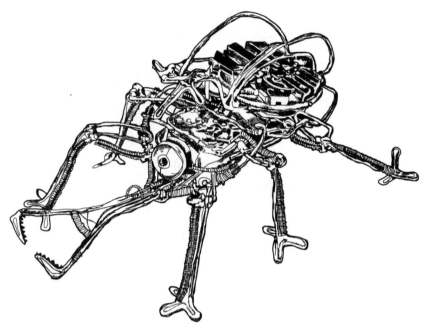

A diagram of Charlie

"Yes and no," Ambrose replied.

Rosa couldn't take anymore.

"Well, I'm not here for that. I'm here to show up Kenny and hang out with the coolest people on Earth." She stood, glanced at Rex and me, and then began pacing. "We aren't going into Zero Hour with a trained bug. That's just so stupid. I mean, what if Kenny's machine rolls over Charlie? Or the bug just decides to run and hide? This is never going to work."

"Of course it will," Ambrose said, face red and hands shaking. "I've spent the last three months working with him, making this a reality. You can't find anything like this anywhere in the world. The other teams, they're going to be building machines, spending all their time fabricating. We don't have to!"

Rosa scoffed. "It's embarrassing."

"It is not! I haven't even told you the rest of—"

"It wouldn't even matter."

I had to step between them. Ambrose had the right mind-set. He was ready. I needed to get Rosa in the same mental space. We didn't have time for sanding too many rough edges. I had to **get control** of these two and fast. And I knew just the way to do it.

"Listen," I said to Rosa, "Ambrose's idea is original. It's groundbreaking. And even better, it's already done. You don't just want to win, right? You want to show up Kenny, you want to show everyone that you're the best."

Rosa mulled that over, then nodded her approval.

"You have a point," she said. "Show us what you've got, Ambrose."

Ambrose took Charlie from the box, eyes locked on Rosa. Then he reached into his pocket and pulled out a tiny mechanical rig.

It looked like an insect-sized metal backpack.

"Charlie's already been wired," Ambrose said as he hooked the rig up to Charlie's carapace. "I installed an implant in his optic node, hooked that up to a microcontroller that I customed for Charlie, and installed an antenna to pick up the signal. Don't worry, the surgery was supersimple and he made a full recovery."

"Surgery?" Rosa asked "You did surgery on the bug? Sorry. The beetle?"

Ambrose set Charlie down on the pea gravel. My instinct was to recoil and lift my feet out of the way of the giant bug. But I forced myself to **remain calm** and not move. I couldn't fluster the others.

"And," Ambrose finished, "I can control him with a cell phone."

He pulled out his cell, opened an application, and began to move a digital joystick around the screen. Charlie moved in whatever direction Ambrose wanted him to go, like an invisible string was pulling him.

I spoke for everyone when I said, "Wo kao!"

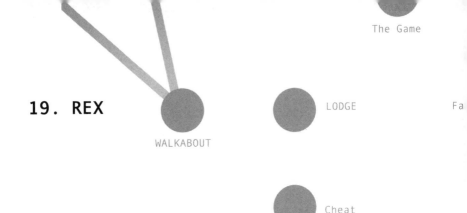

19. REX

WALKABOUT

LODGE   Fa

Cheat

01 DAY, 15 HOURS, 44 MINUTES UNTIL ZERO HOUR

Thank God for Ambrose and Charlie.

Everything was going perfectly.

WALKABOUT was up and running. . . .

I had the afternoon of a lifetime with Painted Wolf. . . .

We didn't even have to build a machine. . . .

And now I had a ton of time to help my best friend. . . .

Could life get any better?

After Ambrose's presentation, we agreed to meet again after dinner. I was charged with developing the hacking software; Ambrose would work with Rosa to fine-tune Charlie; and Painted Wolf would develop our strategy. That also meant she and I could spend time helping Tunde and figuring out what Kiran was really up to.

After a somewhat awkward group high five, we disbanded.

Painted Wolf wanted to hit the library, track down an older computer with a disk drive, and surreptitiously check out the disk she'd filched from Kiran's lab. I was going to meet Tunde in our room. I decided to walk her halfway.

It was getting late and the shadows were long.

We were both slaphappy with adrenaline and I spent much of the walk to the library goofing around. For the first time in years, I felt like things were going to be okay. That maybe, just maybe, I didn't have to work for everything. That just possibly, good things would come my way because there was balance in the universe. It was definitely the thinking of someone very, very tired. We reached the library steps.

"So, we'll see you after dinner?" I said. "Maybe we can, I don't know, do something fun later. I'm sure Tunde and I can get the jammer wrapped up in no time. We can just hang out like we've always wanted to."

"Let's not get ahead of ourselves." Painted Wolf smiled. "This has only just begun."

"This, as in . . . ," I probed, wondering if she meant me and her. The thought made my heart race and sweat break out on the back of my neck.

"The Game, of course," she clarified.

"Yeah, yeah." I laughed, embarrassed.

Oh, of course.

An awkward pause followed, both of us looking at our feet.

"I'll be fine," Painted Wolf finally said. "Take care of Tunde. I'm worried about him. I'm scared he's going to be overwhelmed with all this."

"Tunde's a trooper," I said. "He's got this thing in the bag. Don't worry, I feel like we're in great shape. Nothing can go wrong now."

19.1

I found Tunde on the floor of our dorm room, surrounded by tools and various scraps of metal, staring at the satphone.

"Why aren't you in your lab?" I asked.

"I cannot think there. Too big. Too clean."

For Tunde, that made sense.

"He has not called again, but I am scared he might soon," Tunde said.

"It's all good," I said, scooting stuff out of the way to take a seat beside him. "If he calls, you have the phone right here. You won't miss it. If you need, I can watch it for you while you work and I run some tests of the programming."

Tunde looked at me, genuine feeling in his eyes.

"Thank you, *omo*. Truly."

"No problem," I said, settling in. "So, what have you done so far?"

Tunde held up a prototype machine. It was caseless, a mass of wires and cables, but even from that I could see it was going to be exactly what the general wanted.

"I made a decision, Rex. I do not believe I should give this man what he is asking for. Not entirely. How could I live with myself if he uses something I have built him for acts of aggression and terror? I would feel the same way as Oppenheimer did when he saw what he had created become an atomic weapon."

I knew what Tunde was saying was right.

Still, he was playing with fire.

"You might find this funny, but I have become even more inspired by our friend the Wolf. She always fights to do what is right and I want to do that as well. With your help, I will build something that appears to work as well as the general has envisioned it will. But, in fact, it will not work that way. This jammer will not only get the general to leave my village but will also, in some fashion, trick him."

"Excellent," I said, rubbing my hands together. "Let's start."

"First," Tunde interrupted, "tell me about the reconnaissance mission. Was it as much a success as you had hoped?"

"Tunde, I have good news," I said.

"Yes?"

"I got WALKABOUT up and running on the quantum computer."

"This is incredible!" he said, jumping up. "I am so happy for you.

What are we doing sitting here and listening to me worry when we should be celebrating? This is an amazing moment for you, *omo*. You are going to find your brother!"

"I am," I said as Tunde dragged me up and hugged me. "It was all worth it."

"Of course it was worth it! It was all worth it!" Then, switching mental gears, he said, "Now, you and I shall build this jammer."

Tunde had most of what he needed in his backpack. A lot of it looked like junk and he admitted he'd found it at the junkyard but it was amazing to watch him work with the materials. He was a blur of motion, like sped-up footage of a building under construction. He never paused once; his hands moved like they were autonomous, each doing its own thing.

While he went about building the casing and hardware, I focused on the software. I wasn't going to be as fast as Tunde, but even I was shocked when he had a finished version in less than two hours.

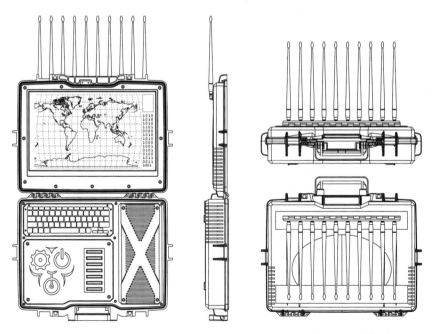

Diagram of the jammer

"*Omo,*" he said, "*the kind ginger wey I get for engineering no be small!*"

And even though I didn't understand a word of what he'd said, I was certain that the sentiment behind it was true. He loved what he was doing.

It was so good to be there with him.

And it wasn't just the practical aspects that were impressive. Tunde threw in a few extra bells and whistles to give the jammer a more rugged appearance. He even installed it in a water- and shock-proof case. Given the device's size, I wasn't sure how he was going to get it on the plane.

"Just give me another couple of hours," I told Tunde. "I'll have the software ready for you in no time." He slid the jammer under his bed and then grinned. I have never seen a more satisfied smile.

We were interrupted by a sudden, loud knock on the door.

I opened it to find Edith standing there with a severe expression.

"I need to talk to both of you," she said.

"Okay," I replied, glancing back at Tunde. "What's up?"

Edith didn't blink. "There's a problem."

A little thrown off by her demeanor, I asked, "Big problem?"

"You're both being kicked out."

19.2

Five minutes later, we were sitting in an office in the student center.

Edith sat across from us and stared us down, hard.

"One of you, maybe both, cheated to get here."

Tunde leaned forward, his face a mess of worry and panic. "Please, Edith, I do not know what you are talking about. You cannot send either of us home. I have to be here. I have to compete and win."

Edith wasn't fazed. "You cannot compete if you cheated to get here."

"But we both received invitations to the Game. You saw our

226

names on the list. There must be some confusion. We did nothing wrong."

"No confusion," Edith said.

A lump appeared in my throat.

How could they know?

How could I have messed it up?

Worse, what if there were legal ramifications? What if my parents were pulled into it? What if I was sent home and my parents were deported?

I could lose everything.

Edith grabbed a tablet computer, opened a few windows on it, and then slid it across the desk toward us. On the screen there was a security report and lines of highlighted code.

"We noticed the intrusion a couple of days ago during a routine scan. Whoever broke in did an excellent job of covering their tracks. But not good enough. Took a while to sort through all the data, but take a look at the second line of code from the bottom. Do you recognize anything there?"

We both scanned the code on the tablet screen.

The lump in my throat got bigger.

Tunde said, "I do not know what this is."

"How about you, Rex?" Edith turned to me.

"It's a log file. Shows activity on the site, movement in and out," I said.

"And?"

And I knew what I had to do.

I said, "And someone using a LODGE account was on the page."

Edith sat back in her chair, eyes fixed on mine. Tunde turned to me, his mouth dropped open in shock and disappointment. "Rex?" he asked.

There was no out.

This was it.

I had to face the consequences.

I had to get ahead of this thing before it got worse.

I have to protect my parents.

"I hacked the site," I said, my voice raw. "Tunde had nothing to do with it. He didn't know. Neither did Painted Wolf. I need to talk to Kiran."

I left Edith's office reeling.

Tunde was in shock. At first he didn't believe me, still thought there must have been a mistake. When I assured him that I was telling the truth, that I cheated to get into the Game, he looked wounded. As we left the room, I tried to apologize and tell him I'd make it right. He just walked away shaking his head.

"How could you?"

He was right, of course.

I betrayed him. I betrayed the LODGE.

Edith told me where I'd find Kiran and that he was waiting for me. As I ran across campus to Kiran's apartment, every step I took hammered home the feelings of guilt and remorse. By the time I reached his building I was determined to do anything I could to make up for everything I'd done.

I had to make it right.

20. TUNDE

My best friend had vexed me so!

After the meeting with Edith, I did not know what to do.

How could Rex have betrayed us?

How could he have been so thoughtless?

I decided I had to see the only person I could talk to about this matter. I found Painted Wolf in the library, down in the stacks, working at an ancient computer quite similar to the one I have in Akika Village. She was wearing a green wig and a matching pair of neon green sunglasses.

Painted Wolf could see immediately that I was very upset.

"What happened? Are you okay, Tunde?"

I told her I was not okay, that we came within a millimeter of having our entire plan fall apart. I told her the truth of what Rex had done. I must say, I was completely startled by the response she gave.

"So cool! What a coup," she said with a tremendous smile.

I was stunned. "But he almost ruined everything!"

I could not believe that Painted Wolf would say such a thing to me. I had almost been ejected from the competition. Had that actually happened, my parents and Akika Village would have surely paid the cost. Rex cheating in the Game was a risk I could not stomach.

"*Almost,*" she said. "Remember, Tunde, Rex came here to help. I know he took a huge risk, but he did it from a good place. He wants you to win and he was willing to do anything to make sure that happened."

"But he took such a big risk. He could have . . . ."

I took a deep breath and let my emotions subside a bit. There was quite a storm of worries and fears battling it out inside me and it took several moments of logical, focused thought to bring me back to a place of careful consideration.

"Okay," I said. "All is not lost. You are right, Painted Wolf."

"That's it. Good. Where is Rex now?"

"With Kiran," I told her. "He offered himself up. Admitted he was behind the hack and that he was willing to accept his fate."

"So we can assume he's been kicked out?"

"I do not know what we can assume. What do we do now?"

Painted Wolf thought for a moment.

"Rex knows what he's doing. Regardless, we need to move on. You need to go back to work with your team. How is development of the jammer going?"

"It is going well."

"And Team Mitra?"

"Team Mitra is excellent," I said. "But . . . I am very shaken by what has occurred. I do not think I can focus until we know what has become of Rex."

"You have to focus," she said. "The Game is tomorrow afternoon."

"I know this. Still . . . are you not deeply upset?"

"We'll get through this, okay? You are brilliant, Tunde. You are kind. And you're going to win tomorrow. You're going to return home a champion. You're going to have that jammer done. Your family will be safe. That is what is important now. Understand? The rest of it . . . we'll figure out later."

I hugged her and instantly felt relieved.

"It is good to talk to you, Wolf. I appreciate your friendship."

I stood up to leave but Painted Wolf stopped me. "Not to add anything to your plate, Tunde, but can you look at something for me? This is from a disk I found in Kiran's office. I think it's related to why he was in China."

"Certainly."

Painted Wolf directed my attention to the computer monitor.

Displayed on it were blueprints of what appeared to be a factory, though the technical information was all in Chinese characters.

"Do you know what this is?" She pointed to a box on the lower left-hand corner of the blueprints. There I found a diagram of a complicated tool.

"This is what the factory will create?" I asked.

"I think so."

I leaned in to get a better look at the diagram.

"It looks like part of a camera sensor array. Not unusual, but it has several modifications that I do not think I have seen before. It is highly advanced and to be housed in . . . Ah, I see what this is," I said as it became clear to me. "This is a camera system to be placed in the nose of an aircraft."

"A plane?" Painted Wolf asked.

"No," I clarified. "More like a drone aircraft."

"Drone? For what? The military?"

"Could be anything," I said. "It could be military, could be for domestic use. Do you suspect this has something to do with what Kiran has been planning?"

"Yes," she said, clearly very concerned. "It has everything to do with it."

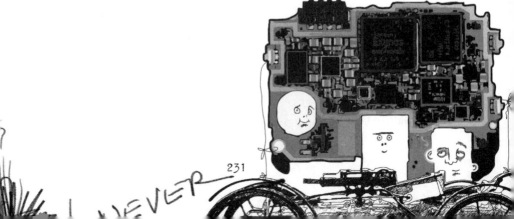

I went into research overdrive.

I gathered any and all information related to the production of drones in China. I read every article I could in any of the languages I know: Mandarin, Cantonese, French, and English. First thing I had to do was narrow down the search criteria to just target places that manufactured cameras for drones. There were dozens of them, many with subsidiaries in China. I scanned through them all, but most were for commercial use. Tunde said this camera was modified, it was advanced. I needed to find a company on the cutting edge of camera research.

Sure enough, I discovered several specialized camera companies that designed camera arrays for military contractors. They were all located in Dongguan.

Linking satellite data with the schematics, I zeroed in on one factory in particular: **Wise Eye Intl. Co. Ltd**. They had a very basic website with little information, but it was enough to begin the real work.

Considering the roughly twelve-hour time difference between Boston and China I was lucky that Rodger Dodger, my microblogger friend, was online.

Painted Wolf: Rog, can you do me a favor?

RoDo: Hey! You all good?

Painted Wolf: I'm all right. A bit crazy right now. I have a request: I need to know what's being made at a factory in Dongguan called Wise Eye Intl. Any thoughts?

RoDo: Okay. You caught me at a good time. I'm visiting All-Star, you know him? He's insane. Brilliant hacker and a supersmart engineer.

Painted Wolf: Of course. Say hi for me.

All-Star: yo, Wolf. Hey. Hang on, let me look.

Painted Wolf: Thanks, All-Star. Thanks, Rog.

RoDo: From what I can find, it looks like they make camera stuff. Mostly lenses and those bubble things on the bottom of drones that take all the pictures.

Painted Wolf: Anything else? Anything new in their internal docs? Few weeks back?

All-Star: yeah, yeah, a new order with a company called Shiva Tech based in the States.

RoDo: I got nothing on them. No websites. Nothing.

Painted Wolf: Anything from Wise Eye about what this mystery company is? What it's doing in China?

All-Star: Hang on . . . Need to get deeper . . .

I realized immediately that Shiva Tech was Kiran's. I assumed it was either a shell company or something he'd spun off of OndScan.

Painted Wolf: Any luck?

All-Star: Getting there . . .

RoDo: So, Wolf, when're we gonna see you again?

Painted Wolf: Soon, next week maybe.

RoDo: Awesome. That last video, man, you killed it.

All-Star: Okay. Okay. It took some serious work but I got it. Shiva Tech is pretty well hidden, but it's part of this conglomerate called OndScan in India. That's weird, 'cause those two aren't exactly . . . Hang on, there's something here. Let me drill down into these plans and I'll hit you in a second.

I waited a few agonizing moments, my mind racing ahead with all sorts of ugly scenarios. What was Shiva Tech really up to and how did it relate to my father? Finally, All-Star reappeared.

All-Star: Those drones are programmed to snoop on people's cell communications. Crazy, never seen anything like it . . .
Painted Wolf: Spy software.
All-Star: They hoover it up. Just, whoosh, get it from the passing towers. Probably e-mail, too.
Painted Wolf: Thank you so much, both of you. See you.
RoDo: Keep knocking 'em dead, Wolf.
All-Star: Rock 'n' roll, baby!

Shiva Tech made spy software that collected cell communications and e-mail. That meant Kiran was in China to get the software loaded onto the drones. It struck me then that Kiran had already told me what Stage One of Rama was. When he was giving me the tour of OndScan, showing me the quantum computer, he said Stage One was called Shiva.

Just like Shiva Tech.

What Kiran had neglected to mention was that he was naming these programs the same way he'd named our teams, after Hindu deities. Rama was the Hindu god of order, reason, and virtue. He made things right. Shiva, on the other hand, was the Hindu god of destruction and transformation.

Shiva Tech, the drones, no doubt that was why Kiran was in China. I recalled what he had said. He'd told me that Stage One was all about bringing down corrupt governments and institutions.

I didn't want to imagine the kind of destructive power someone like Kiran might be able to harness. Making hacking software for drones? Meeting with people like General Iyabo? The puzzle pieces were certainly adding up to an ugly picture.

And somehow, **my father** had gotten himself mixed up in it.

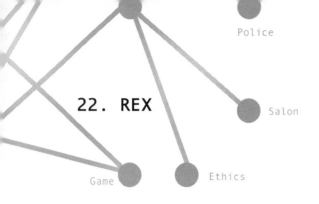

Police

22. REX

Salon

Game

Ethics

01 DAY, 11 HOURS, 28 MINUTES UNTIL ZERO HOUR

"There's this assumption that great coders make great hackers, but it's wrong."

It was after midnight and Kiran sat across from me in his apartment a few blocks from the Boston Collective. Barefoot and cross-legged, he sipped from a glass of sparkling water. The apartment was on the fifteenth floor of an ultramodern building and took minimalism to the extreme. The furniture was low to the floor, the walls were bare, and the color scheme was white, off-white, and gray.

He'd offered me a drink, but my stomach was in knots.

"Thing is, it takes a certain personality to really be successful at hacking. You can't have the sort of moral hang-ups that most people have. I don't want to call it sociopathic, but you need to be able to not care. And, frankly, you care too much. That's not a ding against you. If anything, it's a plus. I knew it was you, Rex. I knew from day one."

"Why'd you let me stay?"

"Because you're talented. You remind me of me, in a way."

"So, am I out? Should I pack up?"

"That's your decision."

I was confused. *What did that mean?*

"Are you going to the cops?" I asked. "I need to know. Now."

Kiran shook his head, gave me this look like he felt sorry for me.

"Of course not, Rex," he said as he stood up. "There are some people I'd like you to meet upstairs. Come on, I'll introduce you and we'll talk more there."

We took an elevator to the penthouse.

Kiran was still barefoot.

During the brief three-floor ride I found myself replaying the day's events. Emotionally, I'd gone from summer to winter in a matter of hours. I wanted to talk to Tunde, to try to explain myself to him. I wondered what Painted Wolf would think. Would she understand? Would anyone?

The doors opened and we stepped out into a crowded lounge.

I didn't recognize most of the people in the room. There were snacks and coffee and energy drinks and the air was electric with conversation. The clatter of fingernails on laptop keyboards was like a storm of cicadas.

If they were contestants, they didn't seem fazed about being out.

As Kiran and I walked through the room I noticed four girls constructing some sort of biological model with straws and toothpicks. A table over from them, two guys ate chips as they worked on a homemade computer housed in an old Connect Four game. Behind the two guys, a boy with a Mohawk was pipetting a steaming liquid over his salad. Next to him, a girl with Coke-bottle glasses was playing three chess games at once.

Who were these people?

"This is the Salon," Kiran said.

We pushed past a large table where a girl had moved aside her plate and tray to clear room for what looked like a tangled pile of multicolored yarn. Freckled, with hair in a ponytail, she was knitting, and she looked up at Kiran and smiled. "What do you think?"

Kiran picked up the yarn. As he did, it fell into shape.

Well, a sort of shape.

It was more like a 3-D squiggle, yarn twisted into loops and whorls, all of it circling back on itself in unpredictable ways. If a hundred cats spent a hundred years in a box of yarn, this is the sort of thing they'd come out with.

Kiran said, "Looks amazing. Almost finished?"

The knitter grinned. "Almost. A few more peptide bonds."

Kiran looked over at me. "Tori's a molecular biologist. This is her protein."

"It's novel," Tori said. "If I can get the microglobulin right, it'll be targeted for connective tissue disorders. Not sure if it'll work, but I call it Henry."

I reached out, took a dangling bit of yellow yarn in my hand, and shook it. "Nice to meet you, Henry. I'm Rex."

Tori chuckled. "You're not the first to think of that," she said. "What do you do, Rex? I'm guessing computers."

"Well, coding, among—"

"Oh, there are a ton of you here," she said condescendingly.

Ouch. Tough crowd.

Kiran stepped in. "Rex is new here."

We moved along, toward an empty table at the back of the Salon.

"So who are all these people?" I asked.

"This is my brain trust. People I've hand-selected to join OndScan for a revolutionary project," Kiran said. "These are my people. These are your people. And these are Teo's people."

22.1

Hearing my brother's name was like being kicked in the stomach.

It left me spinning.

Kiran eased himself into a chair at an empty table at the back of the Salon and motioned for me to sit beside him. I couldn't sit. All the muscles in my body were tensing. How did Kiran know Teo? Why would he bring his name up?

What did he know?

"Tell me where Teo is," I said, my hands shaking.

"I don't know," Kiran said. "But he's not here."

I didn't know how to respond.

Was this a cruel joke?

"He's been gone for two years. He never talked about you or—"

"But he knew me," Kiran said. "Please, Rex, sit."

I sat on the edge of the chair, as tense as Kiran was relaxed.

"Your brother reached out to me, several years back. It was when I had just started transforming OndScan into something much larger. I had epic visions that, over time, only got bigger. Teo and I frequented some of the same sites and forums. We were inspired by the same thing, had the same drive to make the world a better place. Just like everyone here. But, unlike them, Teo wasn't so good at communication. In fact, I haven't heard from Teo in at least ten months."

"Ten months?" I nearly spat it out. "Was he okay?"

"He was fine. Just as passionate as ever. This was all over e-mail, of course. In fact, he'd sent me a self-destructing message through a secure, deep Web URL. One of the first of its kind that I'd seen, very clever."

Kiran was toying with me. I didn't care about a secure URL or a self-deleting e-mail. I wanted to know where Teo was. And just knowing that he was in communication with Kiran, even if it had been ten months ago, was like getting a message from the depths of space. It left me both saddened and newly energized. Regardless of whether I was kicked out of the Game, I needed to make sure that WALKABOUT continued to run. Still . . . Kiran was being coy.

"What aren't you telling me, Kiran?"

"I wanted Teo to join me," he said. "I'm rebooting the world from this very spot. It will be ugly at first. Institutions will fall, borders will be erased, and, sadly, people are going to lose their lives. But out of the ashes, something miraculous will emerge. I wanted Teo to be a part of that. He worried. He thought it was all going too fast. He wanted to slow down the implementation. Honestly, Rex, he was afraid. And fear is crippling. So he ran away and joined Terminal. Despite all the optics, deep down they're just nihilists. They revel in the destruction they cause. For them, there is no endgame."

My blank expression failed to hide the fact that I already knew Teo was involved with Terminal.

"You're not surprised?" Kiran asked. "Well, it's what he wanted. What he believed in. You, on the other hand, you don't have his fear. That's really great. That means you've got your head screwed on right. But . . . you're not driven enough. I don't think you see the bigger picture. That's why I didn't invite you to the Game."

"Not driven?"

I wanted to smack the smirk off Kiran's face.

"You're one of the best coders that I've ever encountered. Hands down. I've done some digging, read through all the LODGE posts, downloaded and messed around with most of your programs. Some of them, with a few tweaks, could be game changers. Real next-level stuff."

"But . . . ?"

Kiran smiled. "But you needed a push. You aren't realizing your potential. You aren't hitting the levels I know you're capable of. I realize now that it was likely because of Teo. That really threw you off track, which is totally understandable. I don't know what I'd have done in your situation. . . ."

He was right of course. But what he didn't know was that I hadn't been idle. I'd sublimated that pain into WALKABOUT, into the program that was running on his quantum computer that very moment.

"I invited Painted Wolf and Tunde and I wondered if it might give you something of a jump start, propel you into action. Force you to jump."

"You mean you *wanted* me to hack my way in?"

Kiran shrugged. "I wasn't sure what you'd do."

"So then why the drama?"

"Well, there are rules. Edith is something of a stickler. Not a bad thing, honestly. But trust me, Rex, if you didn't have the promise I see in you, I most certainly would have sent you packing. But you have even greater potential than I first thought. I'm offering to let you stay if you agree to be part of my team. To embrace what Teo rejected. To be part of this . . ."

He gestured to the busy crowd around us.

"You deserve to be here," Kiran said. "This is the future, Rex. You would have complete freedom. I would encourage all your ideas. Together, we'll tear down the system and put a new one in its place."

"Rama?"

"Yes, Rama."

"And what about the part before that. The tearing-down part?"

"Every revolution begins with action. Sometimes, people don't realize what's best for them until after it's happened. Sometimes, they need a little push to get them to realize. They have to reach a tipping point. A situation that threatens the structure of their lives so profoundly, they have no choice but to embrace change. I want you to be part of that push, Rex. Sure, it will be difficult work. It will—"

"You're talking about chaos. People will die, Kiran. I know you're working with bad men. Killers. This idea of yours, it's crazy. . . ."

"So simpleminded, Rex. So very, very simpleminded. Please, accept my offer. Join me here and I will show you how it will work. If you do that and still decide it's against your nature, you can leave."

"You made this same offer to Painted Wolf?"

"Yes."

"And Tunde?"

X

"Perhaps later, depending on the outcome of the Game."

"Can I think about it?"

Kiran nodded. "Take the rest of the night. Let Edith know in the morning. Why don't you hang out here a little? Don't be shy. You're on the ground floor of the next stage in human history."

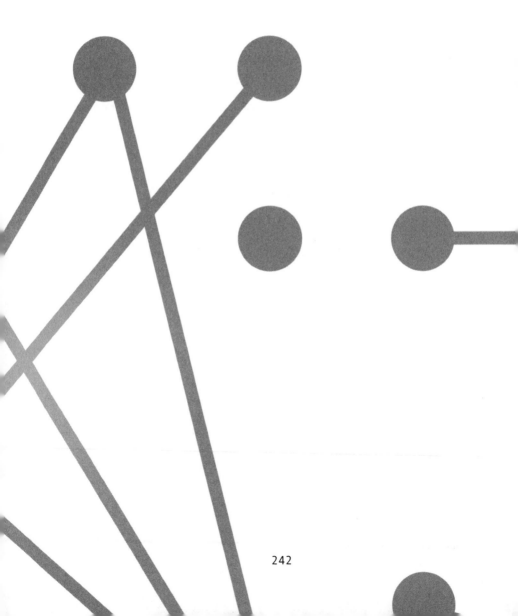

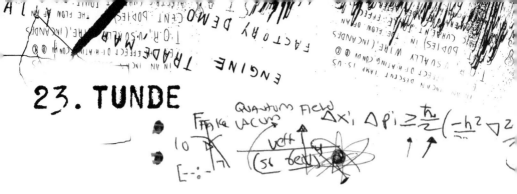

23. TUNDE

01 DAY, 10 HOURS, 17 MINUTES UNTIL ZERO HOUR

Reinvigorated by my conversation with Painted Wolf and still having heard nothing from Rex, I knew I had to return to Team Mitra and our work on Efiko.

She was right. I had to focus.

Luckily, I was blessed with an extraordinary team.

Na we dey run things!

After a short but productive meal of pizza, I marshaled my teammates as I imagined Painted Wolf would have: with an eye to expediency and efficiency. It was crucial that each of us knew exactly what we needed to do and to get it done as effectively as possible.

After a fresh infusion of caffeine and sugary food, Anj, Halil, and I set about creating Efiko. After going over several hand-drawn diagrams I had prepared, Halil and I began transforming the wasted battle robot into a thing of immense beauty. While I was gone, Halil had developed a wiring diagram for a robotic arm the likes of which I had not yet seen.

"This is brilliant," I told him.

"Thank you, *omo*," he replied.

I laughed. The Naija lingo was catching on!

Anj was my go-to for the integration, which was the most

important role on the entire team. It was her job to make sure that we were all on the same page and that each separate piece would fit. This was good for her! She was so very shy that giving her a job that required much communication was a real boon. *Na so!*

As a group we designed the electronics, hydraulics, and servo-controlled driver and vision system for our machine.

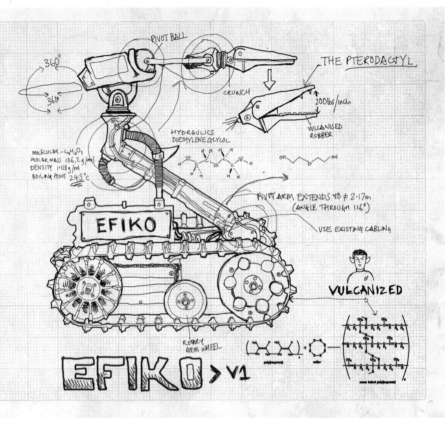

A blueprint for the design of Efiko

Many hours passed in a blur of sparks and motion. Night became day. We were all in our element, working in harmony like a hive of bees. I was so concentrated on the task at hand that I nearly forgot my worry over Rex. Nearly.

That, of course, changed when he walked into the lab near dawn.

I will admit I was stunned to see him.

Part of me had hoped that if he was sent home, he would just leave, without saying good-bye, because I was not sure I could handle it. But a larger part of me prayed that he would come around and talk with me, if only to say good-bye.

"Hi, Tunde," he said, looking at Efiko. "That machine is incredible."

I turned off the torch I was using and pushed my safety goggles up.

My heart was thrumming in my chest and my stomach was a toxic brew. I was happy he had returned, yet at the same time my anger was as fierce as ever.

"I was not sure I would see you," I said.

"Can we talk in private?" he asked.

"I have a few minutes, yes."

23.1

"I'm sorry," Rex said, after we had stepped out of the room and into the hallway.

His voice wavered. He clearly felt terrible about what he had done.

"I don't have any excuse. I was selfish. I needed in to the Game to run WALKABOUT and I should have told you that I wasn't invited. But I was too proud. You have to believe that I never wanted to hurt you or Wolf or put any of this at risk. Don't know what else I can tell you but I'm sorry."

"Are you out of the Game?" I asked.

"Not yet," Rex said. "Kiran made me an offer."

"And will you accept it?"

"Probably. I need to be here for you. But I don't want to make a decision without discussing it with you. This isn't about me anymore, it's about us."

These were nice words, but I was still hesitant to trust him again.

Rex pulled a squashed roll of papers from his back pocket and handed them to me. They were computer printouts and filled with rows and rows of numbers.

"Spent the last couple of hours in the library," Rex said. "Wrote a program for your jammer. Think this might be exactly what you'll need."

I glanced over the printouts but could not make heads or tails of them.

"Thank you," I said. "Please, come into the lab."

Rex followed me inside. Halil and Anj gave him cursory waves, entirely absorbed in their work. Then, sitting at a bench at the back of the lab, I spread out the plans Rex had drawn up. Rex explained as best he could what he had devised, and it sounded good, though my knowledge of this sort of programming was very limited.

"You need this thing to be real. You need the general to be blown away. So instead of just writing a code that would make it a working jammer, I wrote the code for the best damn jammer ever created."

Hearing this, Norbert walked over, leaned in, and read the lines of code over my shoulder. If his quickened breathing was any indication, he found the material very impressive. "Oh man," Norbert groaned. "Unbelievable. I guess I should just toss what I've been working on, because looking at this, I'd say Rex isn't exaggerating. This is a piece of art. I'm totally serious."

That was very reassuring to hear.

"Since you're making this for a monster," Rex said, "I added a back door to the program. There is no way any of the general's people can find it, not unless they're sitting in this lab right now. It's invisible. And it will give us the ability to shut down the jammer from a remote location. Even better, when the jammer's shut down, it can't be reactivated. It will overheat and fry its components, and anyone trying to fix it will think it was user error."

"This is brilliant. Are you telling me that the jammer will break and the general will think he did it?"

"Yes."

I reached over to Rex and we shook hands.

I could not help but *shine my thirty-two.*

"You are indeed an excellent friend. Shall we test it out?"

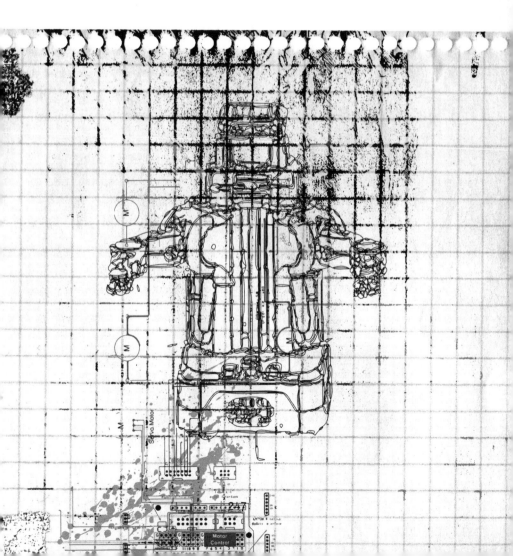

01 DAY, 01 HOUR, 09 MINUTES UNTIL ZERO HOUR

I found Tunde, and Team Mitra, sitting on the lawn outside his dorm.

They had a large suitcase on the ground. Attached to it were numerous wires connected to an array of antennae. At first I wondered if this was what Team Mitra had developed to crack the safe, but as I got closer the device's true significance became clear: My cell phone went into a frenzy in my purse.

I pulled it out to see the screen flickering before it crashed.

"It works!" Tunde shouted as he ran to me. "Did you see that?"

"Yes," I said, smiling because he was so happy. "But what was it?"

"The jammer! It works!"

"I thought it was a **GPS jammer**, not a phone destroyer."

Tunde laughed. "Your phone will be just fine. It was merely too close to the equipment. Have a look over there."

Tunde pointed between some trees, and in the far distance I could see Rex standing on the roof of a building. He waved.

"Rex is holding a GPS device," Tunde explained. "It is completely jammed."

"Must feel good to have it done," I said. "But maybe you should stop testing it here. I'm worried you're going to bring down a plane or something."

"You're right," Tunde said, and quickly shut the jammer off. "I called the general and told him. He was very pleased. He has only one more demand." Tunde's eyes were filled with concern. "I must win the Game."

"You will. I promise you."

As Tunde packed up the jammer, Rex ran over to us.

He and Tunde performed a complicated handshake before he turned to me and smiled. "Walk with me and Tunde for a minute."

We strolled around the grounds of the dorm as the sun played hide-and-seek in the patchy sky. Rex told us about his meeting with Kiran. Both Tunde and I were shocked to learn that Teo had been involved with Kiran. I informed them of what I had found on the disk and how I suspected that the drone spy software was related to Shiva, Stage One of Kiran's Rama program.

"I don't know what he's actually planning," Rex said. "But from what he told me and from what you've discovered, it sounds kind of like the end of the world."

"A little overdramatic," I said. "But not by much. At least your father isn't caught up in it like mine. I don't know what I'm going to do. . . ."

Tunde spoke up. "I do. This means that after we have won the Game, given the general his GPS jammer, and found Teo, we are going to have to stop Kiran."

"Woooooolllllllfffffff!"

I spun around to see Rosa racing toward us, tears streaming down her face.

"What's wrong?" I called, as I ran to her. As sleep deprived and emotionally exhausted as I was, I moved with surprising speed.

"It's Charlie," Rosa said between big gasps.

"What is going on?" Rex appeared at our side.

Rosa looked up at us, lips trembling. "He's dead."

24.1

We found Ambrose in his dorm room.

Charlie lay on his back, legs curved in rigor mortis, in the center of Ambrose's palm. Ambrose looked **surprisingly calm** considering.

"I'm guessing either old age or something viral," he said.

"Stress?" Rex asked.

Ambrose shrugged.

"Can you revive him?" Rosa said between jagged sobs. "I mean, just give him a shock like in the ER. He only has to last another day."

"He's gone," Ambrose said. "RIP, Charlie."

I suggested we should bury Charlie beneath an oak tree right outside the dorm. Though a bit confused by the idea of burying an insect, Ambrose still said some kind words about how Charlie had been a good friend and a hard worker. As soon as the dirt was shoveled over Charlie's tiny grave, Rex said, "How hard will it be to wire up another one?"

Ambrose shrugged. "If we had another one, maybe a day."

"We have a day," I said. "Where do we find another Charlie?"

Rosa said, "It'll have another name, you know."

"I like the name Charlie," Ambrose said. "Woods, maybe. But we're in a city."

"How about a pet store?" Rex asked.

"Yeah," Ambrose said. "But we won't find a Hercules beetle in a pet store."

"What *can* we find?" I asked, trying not to be impatient.

"Probably a cockroach."

Rosa ran off screaming.

We found a pet store on the other side of the river. It was a two-mile walk past a park, but it was cool and not raining. Even though having us all go wasn't the best use of our time, we all felt a fondness for Charlie. Even Rosa. And so we all wanted to be there when his replacement was chosen.

The store was filled with fish tanks. Rosa found some mice, but Ambrose insisted they wouldn't work. "Too intelligent," he said. "And that's gnarly surgery."

In the back of the store, Rex discovered several tanks with crickets for feeding amphibians and reptiles, but none of them were big enough to carry a USB. Ambrose had a heart-to-heart with one of the clerks; turned out they both had **an affinity for** beetles, so he let us see some insects he had in the back room. They weren't usually for sale, but, for us, he was willing to "make a deal."

"You're kidding me, right?"

Rex's reaction was much like my own. The clerk opened the lid of a tank, pulled out some of the leaves at the bottom, and uncovered something that looked like an armored snake. It was ten inches long and had way too many legs.

"It's an African millipede," the clerk said. "Biggest you can buy."

Ambrose beamed. "We'll take it."

We had a late dinner at a Thai place. Rex was very critical of the dishes, but we were all famished. During the meal, Charlie 2 sat in a bag on Ambrose's lap. "I can't let him get too cold," Ambrose explained.

Once we had the millipede back on campus, we split up to get to work. Amazingly, Rosa wasn't as disgusted by Charlie 2 as she had been by the original, so she joined Ambrose for the surgery.

"We're going to attach the harness, then we'll wire up the electrodes. Millipede muscles are different, a lot of legs to work with, but I've got a cool work-around for that," Ambrose explained. We trusted him.

While Ambrose and Rosa prepped, Rex and I worked on the

programming for the USB. Well, really, he worked on it and I tried to help.

Rex coded like a somnambulist. He moved from a computer where his fingers darted across the keyboard to sheets of scrap paper I'd taped to the wall. There, he'd work out the math longhand. After several hours, his fingers were black with ink and his hair was in total disarray.

When Rex was done, we loaded the program onto Teo's USB.

Near dawn, we watched Ambrose and Rosa run Charlie 2 through a pop-up obstacle course in the basement of the library. The millipede was so much **faster** and **stronger** than the first Charlie that we all agreed his passing was something of a blessing. "Though we're not going to ever say that again, right?" Ambrose clarified.

"He's amazing," I said.

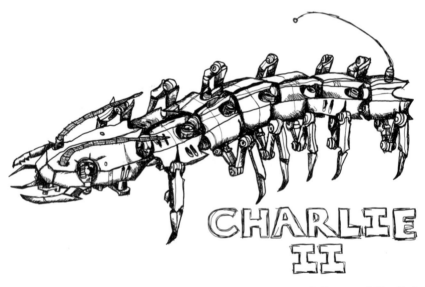

A diagram of Charlie 2

I was so sleep deprived by that point that it may have just been my brain shutting down, but I actually worried that with Charlie 2, we might accidentally win. Rex noticed my exhaustion and dragged me to the café in the student center. We promised to pick up stuff for Ambrose and Rosa; he wanted a bagel, she wanted gummy candies.

"Find sour ones, if you can." She grinned.

"And get a cucumber for Charlie 2!" Ambrose shouted. "He deserves a treat."

25. REX

06 HOURS, 32 MINUTES UNTIL ZERO HOUR

The student center was deserted.

With only hours to go before Zero Hour, everyone else was tucked away with their projects, heads down, putting on the finishing touches.

Painted Wolf was zonked. Her costume was slipping a bit. Her wig, her sunglasses, her earrings. She was tired and even though everything was in place, it looked slept in. Ruffled. Honestly, it was a breath of fresh air. She was always so put together it was nice to see her relaxing a bit.

She grabbed some coffee and an apple. I picked up a big bottle of water, Rosa's sour gummies, and managed to drum up a few cucumber slices. The man working the counter seemed annoyed at having to turn on the register to ring us up. He lit up, however, when I asked him about his sneakers.

"Nice kicks. Chang Pumps, right?"

"Yeah." The guy leaned over the counter to get a look at my shoes. "Dang, Forbes Dunks?"

"Swapped a guy a laptop I built for them."

"Dope."

We exchanged fist bumps, while Painted Wolf put cream and sugar in her coffee and then found a seat near a window. It was threatening to rain outside.

"That thing you do," I said as I joined her, "where you scrunch up your face. I noticed it the other day. It's because you have a feeling, like tingling, right?"

"Yes." She seemed surprised. "How did you know?"

"I get it, too. Sometimes when I come across a particularly amazing line of code, it's just *ziiiiip* across my shoulders. They call it ASMR, autonomous sensory meridian response. It's a weird thing. Totally unaccepted scientifically, but . . . well, it's real. You and I both know it. We have that in common. A shared chemistry."

"I want to thank you," she said.

I wasn't sure what she meant.

What could she possibly thank me for at this point?

"Thank me for what?"

"For not asking me to take off my disguise."

I laughed. "Seriously, I think you look really cool. I'm not just saying that."

"I've gotten used to it."

"I was thinking of maybe getting my own look," I said. "I was thinking something Sherlock Holmes–like, you know? Maybe a houndstooth coat and a pipe? I wouldn't smoke it, just chew on the end and look thoughtful."

"That sounds ridiculous." She laughed. "Besides, I like you as you are."

"I do have nice hair."

I ran my fingers through my unruly mop. That made her laugh even harder.

"It's my parents," Painted Wolf said. "What I do back home is so dangerous. It puts my family at risk. If the authorities or the people behind the people that I expose ever found out who I really was, I would disappear. My parents would disappear as well."

"By disappear, you mean . . . ?"

"There would be no public trial, no jail time. We would be

whisked away in the middle of the night, shoved into the back of a car, and driven off into oblivion. It has happened before, far too many times. I can't take the risk. You understand, right? Any image of me that appears outside of my school pictures or family photos could doom me. There are people like you, people looking to find others, who would use the technology like what you created to track me down. I used to think I was paranoid, but . . ."

"I can't even imagine," I said, leaning in.

"And now with my father . . . It's only getting worse. . . ."

This was the first time Painted Wolf had really opened up about her life, about her life outside of the videos and the subterfuge. I was fascinated and wanted to know more. I prayed she wouldn't clam up.

Instead, she cleared her throat and continued, "It is what it is. I made the choice to live this way, to transform myself. What I do is more important than a social life or anything like that."

"Heavy. But, you have fun, too, right?"

An uncomfortable laugh escaped her lips. "Yes. Of course I do."

"Like what?"

"I . . . I go out with friends. My cousin. We go to movies. Dinner. This . . ."

"So you're having fun here?"

"Yeah," she said. "Despite the insanity. Aren't you?"

"The time of my life."

I wasn't lying. Despite my exhaustion headache and the craziness of the preceding days, I felt better, happier, than I'd felt in years. Part of that was Tunde; it was hard not to be happy around him. But mostly, it was Painted Wolf.

I reached across the table and touched her hand.

It was instinctual. Felt natural. Felt needed.

And as I did, a warm shiver ran up my arm to my scalp.

"I think what you do is amazing and unbelievably important," I said, the words slipping out before I could even think about them. "More important than anything Kiran's stupid prodigy squad will ever do. You're incredible. I think you should know that. And I think you should know that the time we've spent together, here, has meant a lot. You've given me something that I never really expected to find."

"What's that?" she asked.

"Hope."

I couldn't help but lean in toward her, pulled closer and closer by some strange gravity. Even though she was wearing sunglasses, as I got closer, I could see she'd closed her eyes. I could feel the warmth of her skin and hear her breathing.

"What's taking so long?"

It was Rosa. She ran up to the table. "Guys," she said, "we've been waiting so long. I'm starving and we only have like six more hours."

"Six hours is a long time," I groaned. "Besides, we're good."

Ambrose walked up to the table. "Sorry. She's been going a little crazy."

"Hang on, were you two about to kiss?" Rosa asked.

Painted Wolf and I both shook our heads.

"Aw, really?" Rosa groaned. "That would have been so awesome!"

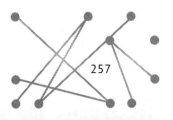

PART FOUR
ZERO HOUR

26. TUNDE

It was here.

The moment was finally upon us. I walked with Team Mitra into the hallway outside the safe room with a feeling of great weight upon my shoulders.

It was as though I held a calf about my neck.

While I was confident of my team and I was confident of Efiko, I also felt *I do skelewu myself.* Troubles had been eating away at my stomach the whole night before. Rex, Kiran, General Iyabo, my family, Akika Village: All of them were depending on me to be successful.

There was simply no other option.

Still, I am not Tunde Oni if I am not optimistic!

And that day, it took only seeing Rex and Painted Wolf at the starting line to rekindle the hope in me. I was not certain that we would succeed, but when Rex waved to me, I did know that our friendship would survive even the most tumultuous trials and tribulations.

Life is a magnificent and incredible journey. One filled with endless challenges. It is a trek across the Arctic! A quest through the Sahara! An interstellar journey! It is true, as Eldon said, that the journey is the destination.

Halil and I rolled Efiko into the hallway, and the appearance of the machine gave the small crowd that had gathered a great surprise. This crowd of a few professors, a few reporters, and a few select members of OndScan was absolutely delighted by the machine.

It was an articulated bot with a single, highly maneuverable arm. I had liberated it: I gave it a brain. Norbert and I programmed Efiko using a refurbished "teach pendant" we acquired from a visit to the engineering lab. Efiko could open a door and pick a safe with merely a few keystrokes!

What a beautiful thing!

We had painted it the brilliant sea-green color of the Nigerian flag.

Efiko was go!

I took a moment to glance over at what Team Pushan had created and was momentarily taken aback. Ambrose held a *new* insect, a millipede like those I have seen at home, and this "Charlie 2" was quite impressive. I looked forward to seeing him in action.

Kenny and Team Indra arrived last.

They came in as loud and rambunctious as I imagine Kenny was at all times at home. Ezra was bellowing, Leleti jumping around, and Fiona spinning about. The machine they had created was a spinning gyro of metal and fury. I have seen honey badgers that appeared less threatening than this monster.

Kenny called his creation DESTROYER and this was painted in capital letters on the side of the machine. Looking it over, I guessed it had started life as a bomb disposal robot. Now it was modified with many spinning blades and many claws. Kenny did not plan to break into the safe but to break into Efiko and the other machines!

Dis boy bad gan!

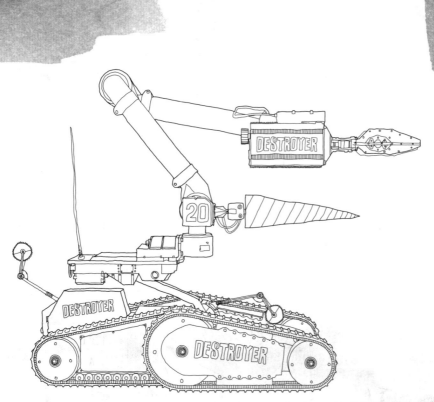

A schematic of DESTROYER

With all the teams assembled in the hallway before the safe room, Kiran arrived in a suit and blocked the door. Edith stood beside him and eyed her tablet computer until Kiran gave her a signal. She motioned to everyone and made a shushing sound. No one was talking at the time, however, so the effort appeared a bit silly. Regardless, Kiran straightened his tie before he began his introduction to the final stage of the Game.

"Welcome, contestants!" Kiran shouted. "There are three teams gathered before me, twelve of the brightest and best minds in the world. We will see in just a few moments how you have put that brilliance to work. As you know, you are not allowed to enter the room itself. Your machine must do that for you. When I sound the buzzer, there are no holds barred. Your machine can do whatever it takes to gain access to the laptop. From there, your software has free rein."

Kiran added, "I wish you all luck and may the best team win!"
With that final proclamation, the buzzer was pressed.

Halil gave a cheer of "woo-hoo!"

Kenny screamed with a wild joy that was frankly frightening.

Then, the door to the room was opened.

26.1

What followed was best described as a death match.

Those machines make like dey wan throw blows at each other!

DESTROYER crashed forward as soon as Kiran stepped aside, and nearly took the door off. Certainly it scraped long slivers of wood from the frame. What a disastrous piece of machinery. Surely Kenny should be designing machines for General Iyabo, not me!

We had Efiko follow DESTROYER into the room and I was delighted to see that Efiko was much faster than the war machine that Kenny had created. Efiko maneuvered right around this fierce opponent and was first to reach the safe!

"We have an intruder," Anj said, pointing to Efiko.

"An intruder? What do you mean?" I asked.

Ah, but imagine my surprise to see that Efiko had a stowaway!

Secreted on one of the stanchions supporting the arm of our beloved Efiko was Charlie 2 from Team Pushan! With Rosa at the controls, the creature must have scrambled up onto our robot while Kiran was speaking. Clever.

As Efiko had reached the safe, it was now time for me to hand the controls over to Anj. She was thrilled to take them and smiled the whole time. She was our expert at picking the lock on the safe.

"It's like cellular metabolism," Anj said as she worked the controls. "A lock can be picked with different tools. Either you

264

have the key or you have an agonist, something that will act like a key."

Anj had Efiko pick up a pin that we had magnetically attached to its side. She then had Efiko use the pin to pick the lock to the Plexiglas safe with an assuredness that was surprising. As Anj worked, fully absorbed in maneuvering the machine, I found my eyes wandering. She had her hair in braids and wore a nicely patterned dress. I must say that I noticed how it moved on her. But the light in her eyes I noticed much more.

As soon as Efiko got the safe open, there was a cheer from the crowd.

I assumed it was because we had breached the obstacle, but it was more for the fact that DESTROYER came charging in behind us and cut a tread from the back of Efiko! Leleti, the South African with long braids, gave a battle cry and high-fived Kenny.

Efiko was damaged and unable to move!

Halil seemed the most affected. He almost crumbled into tears.

With Leleti at the controls, DESTROYER reached the laptop and steadied its USB, ready to plug it in and begin hacking the system. But Team Indra had not anticipated the swiftness with which Charlie 2 could travel and the depth of the hatred Rosa had for Kenny. The insect scrambled down from atop Efiko and crawled in front of the USB port that DESTROYER was attempting to angle into, effectively blocking the advance of Kenny and Team Indra.

This was met with much celebration from those assembled.

Anj handed me the controls and then, very firmly, said, "I know you can do this, Tunde. You can win this. You can win this for all of us!"

As DESTROYER and Charlie 2 fought, I glanced over at Rex, my eyes wild with emotion. He nodded to me very calmly and mouthed these words:

You. Can. Do. It.

I took a deep breath and closed my eyes and focused. The sound of the crowd soon vanished and when I opened my eyes I was as clearly focused as I had ever been in my entire life. It was as though I was atop the Okeke Solar Power Tower, gazing off into the distance, in total peace.

Then, I did the impossible.

I was able to move Efiko! Halil clapped wildly as our beautiful machine pulled itself forward with its arm as though it was a runner who had fallen during a race, reaching for the finish line. Efiko had only to move three inches, but it took such a long time that I worried I would destroy its servos.

Locked in a fierce battle, Charlie 2 was blocking every move that DESTROYER made toward the USB ports on the laptop. Several times Kenny jumped up, ready to break the rules and stomp on Charlie 2 himself, but he was held at bay by stern glances from Kiran. Luckily, Efiko was able to struggle past this scene of machine versus insect chaos. Fiona, the girl with bright green hair, noticed our progress and screamed at Kenny and Leleti to do something.

"Anything!" she shouted.

In the most agonizing minute of my life, I guided Efiko and its arm, with the built-in USB extended, toward the slot on the side of the laptop. In my mind I heard my people cheering me on and saw the faces of my parents. In my heart I felt the strength that had been waiting to explode since the day I had arrived.

With a final flick of keys on the teach pendant, Efiko inserted the USB.

Once the USB was introduced, the screens beside the safe flashed to life and a computer program began to run. This first portion of the program on the USB was designed to function automatically. It took only seconds to spring into action.

Rex and his team were so close!

At the controls, Rosa fought as best she could, but DESTROYER flipped Charlie 2 onto his back (the tech on him was heavy) and was able to insert the USB. Defeated, Rosa handed the controls back to Ambrose.

Regardless, Kenny and Team Indra were inside as well!

We were caught in the eye of a cyclone.

There's a common misperception that the eye of a cyclone is calm, serene even. This is true if you're inside a building or a house and the howling winds appear to have stopped and a glance out the window shows only open sky.

But if you're outside, in the midst of it, you can see a raging wall of chaos, the violence of these subcritical vortices, all around you.

It is like being at the very center of explosive creation.

That is what it felt like in the room that day.

We were, in many more ways than one, at the center of everything.

Team Mitra and Team Indra had just gotten their USBs activated, and while it took Ambrose a few moments to finally flip Charlie 2 back over, we eventually joined the others at the laptop. With a few quick motions, Charlie 2 was able to insert the USB. Honestly, the insect looked exhausted.

Well, as exhausted as an insect can look.

We watched the monitors on either side of the safe to see the progress.

Rex was running the hacking programs from his cell.

"The programs are working on the firewalls," he explained. "They're tough."

"And who's ahead?" I asked, staring at the quickly flashing screens.

"Tunde is," Rex answered. "Norbert's an excellent coder. Kenny's team is getting in with brute force, just smashing away. Norbert, however, is playing smart. His program is all about subtlety. Why bust down the door when you can climb in the window? Hey, there's something I need you to see."

Rex held his cell phone up. A new program had been opened, and in the second window was the WALKABOUT loading bar. It showed the program's progress on the quantum computer just over our heads.

It was at ninety-five percent.

I lit up. "So close," I whispered.

"Look!" Rosa interrupted, suddenly panicked.

Rex and I both turned toward the screen to see Kenny had unexpectedly taken the lead in a matter of seconds. He was far outpacing us and quickly getting even farther ahead of Team Mitra. I looked across the room at Tunde and Norbert. Tunde looked very concerned and Norbert was sweating heavily.

Rosa snatched Ambrose's cell and pushed it into my hands.

"Kenny's winning!" she screamed. "Do something!"

Ambrose shook his head. "Way too risky . . ."

"Painted Wolf can do it," Rosa said. "She can think strategically better than both of us combined." I closed my eyes and let my mind play out all the possible moves. There had to be a way to either boost Tunde or slow Kenny. The solution came to me in a blast of bright light, but it would mean sacrificing our progress.

"I have an idea," I said, opening my eyes. "But it means disengaging."

Rosa grimaced. "Isn't that risky?"

"Just do it," Rex said. "The program's mostly automatic."

"What if there's a problem?" Rosa asked. "A hiccup?"

"Like I said," Rex clarified. "Mostly."

I looked to Ambrose. "It means possibly falling even farther behind."

He nodded, and then I did something **radical**.

With a slide of a finger across the cell phone screen, I released the USB stick from the front of Charlie 2's carapace.

Charlie 2 was now free to maneuver.

I glanced up briefly to see Kenny's eyes widening. He knew what was going to happen. He started shaking his head. "Oh no!" he shouted to Leleti. "Oh no!"

Rosa clapped with joy. "Get him!"

I moved Charlie 2 over to the port where DESTROYER had its USB. Leleti had DESTROYER whir back to life, its metal blades spinning furiously, but they could not reach the small, more mobile insect at its wheels. Ezra appeared ready to run onto the floor and physically stop Charlie 2, but he held himself in check. Barely.

I carefully positioned Charlie 2 so his pincers were set against Team Indra's USB and then I started moving Charlie 2 back and forth. Millipedes, I had learned from Ambrose, are capable of lifting more than eight hundred times their own weight. Getting the USB loose was no problem.

When it fell out and clattered to the floor seconds later, I wanted to kiss that insect. Team Indra's program went down, part of the screen to the left of the safe flickered before going blank.

Kenny screamed as though he'd been stuck with a hot poker and ripped the controls from Leleti.

"I have to do everything myself," he spat.

As I handed the cell back to Ambrose, I noticed Kiran eyeing me. He nodded slowly, very impressed.

With Team Indra out of the way, Rex's program surged ahead.

"We've got a problem," I whispered to Rex.

"I know," he said, eyes on the monitors. "I've got it under control."

Rex surreptitiously slowed his program's progress and Team Mitra soon took the lead. While Tunde was overjoyed, Rosa and Ambrose looked like they might faint. Rosa was shaking with anticipation, the fingers of her left hand digging into her palm. Ambrose was sweating profusely, and he tightened and untightened his jaw in a rhythmic motion. Both had their eyes locked on the screens overhead.

While they were distracted, Rex handed me his cell.

"It'll run automatically," he said. "Just make it look like you're controlling it."

27.1

Team Indra crowded around Kenny as he struggled to get the massive DESTROYER to perform the intricate task of picking up the USB and reinserting it.

At the same time, Rex quietly slipped out of the room.

Everyone's attention was so focused on the Game that no one noticed when Rex reappeared above us and made his way to the quantum computer.

"Is Rex going to be back soon?" Ambrose asked.

"Just had to run to the bathroom," I said. "Don't worry, he'll be back soon."

Ambrose tore his eyes away from the screens.

"Are you kidding me?" he asked.

I shrugged. "Nature calls."

I watched Team Mitra. Tunde stood behind Norbert and cheered him on like a boxing coach. Compared with the chaos erupting in Team Indra's corner, Team Mitra worked in **perfect harmony**.

Minutes quickly became seconds.

"We're winning," Ambrose said nervously. "But not by much."

"Where is Rex?" Rosa was flustered.

"We're okay," I said. "We're still winning."

I clenched my jaw and ground my teeth in frustration as Rex's program moved slightly ahead of Norbert's. This wasn't good. We couldn't win. But the streams of code scrolled across the screens at such a fast pace that I couldn't make out characters; it had become a blur of digital movement, impossible for me to control. Kiran, reading it all, eyes darting, called out the progress.

"This is it," he said, walking closer to the screens. "This is it."

The room grew intensely quiet. The only sounds were the clicking of fingers on controls and the rush of frenzied breathing as Kenny kept DESTROYER kicking the USB around the floor in his desperate attempts to get it back.

Kenny hissed. "No. No. No. No. NO. It's not over yet."

I was so concentrated myself that I didn't notice when Rex reappeared alongside me. "Looks like you're actually too good with this," he said, noticing how we'd pulled ahead. "I'll take it from here." Seconds after he took the cell phone, Team Mitra slipped back into first place. But we still appeared to be neck and neck.

Rex leaned in close to me, so close that I could feel the warmth of his breath on the back of my neck. It sent a tingle of nervous energy down my sides. He held his cell in front of me. The WALKABOUT program screen was open and displayed a single line: an address in New York City.

"It worked?" I asked, a lump in my throat.

"WALKABOUT found Teo."

My mouth dropped open and I spun around and hugged Rex. His eyes danced with excitement, but we didn't speak, because at that very moment, a siren sounded. On one of the screens a plain blue desktop flickered into existence. On it was a single digital file folder. The folder opened and inside was a note with one sentence typed at its center.

Tunde read it out loud. "It says, '**Welcome to the team.**'"

The Game was over, and Kiran raised his hands in triumph.

"The winner of the first-ever OndScan Game is . . . Team Mitra!"

Tunde fell to his knees and we ran over to lift him high. He landed on Norbert's shoulders and Norbert paraded him around the room.

Kiran and Edith clapped wildly.

When Tunde finally hit the floor again, he made his way to Rex and me.

He hugged us both, at the same time.

"See, guys," I said. "Together we can do anything."

"Yes." Tunde beamed. "But our adventure has only just begun!"

28. REX

The Game was over.

Teo was as good as found.

Tunde had won.

Most everyone broke into a frenzy of dancing and jumping and singing and shouting. Well, everyone that is but Team Indra. I didn't hear the commotion, though. I didn't feel shoulders crashing into mine. I was just so, so stunned.

It actually worked.

Painted Wolf grabbed my hands. "Are you okay?"

"Yeah," I said. "I—I think so."

"We did it."

"We really did, didn't we?"

Painted Wolf leaned in and kissed my cheek. "Yes."

Three seconds later, Norbert's confetti bomb went off.

Lightning-fast, the room went from high-end, glass-floored office space to a confetti wonderland. It fell as thick as a blizzard in the Arctic.

Still I didn't move.

Kenny and Leleti were slumped in a corner, despondent. Kenny was actually crying. Ezra angrily packed up his stuff. Fiona just stood there looking confused and watching Norbert leap around the room, yelling with his mouth open wide enough that it quickly filled with confetti. Halil and Anj jumped together and fell to the floor, laughing and making "confetti angels" on the glass floor. Rosa and

Ambrose carefully guarded Charlie 2 as they carried him over to his shoe box.

This was what victory looked like.

I took it all in for a few seconds before a hand landed on my shoulder and squeezed it hard. I turned around to see Kiran standing beside me.

"Congratulations," he said. "You're a force to be reckoned with."

"Was it everything you wanted it to be?" I asked.

"A thousand times better."

There was a commotion in the hallway just outside the room. The party atmosphere seemed to transform instantly from glee to concern as three uniformed police officers walked through the door.

Was someone hurt? What happened?

"Have you heard the news, Rex?" Kiran asked, suddenly.

"The news?"

"Yes," he said, very calmly. "There was just a major security intrusion at the FSB, the Russian Federal Security Service. Someone hacked in and stole billions of top-secret, high-level data points. Countless covert files. It's a global mess. The NSA, Interpol, MI6, they're all scrambling to shut it down, but it's still happening. Just a few minutes in, actually, and it's already the biggest cyber leak in history. The stuff they've stolen, if sent to the wrong people, could start wars. Could change the course of history. Tech security experts think it's the first time a quantum computer has been used to commit a cybercrime."

I was stunned.

"Are you kidding?" I asked. It was the only thing I could think to say.

My eyes were locked on Kiran's, trying to make sense of what he was saying and why he was telling me at that moment.

Weren't we supposed to be celebrating?

Kiran continued, "The word we're getting is that it's the work of

Terminal. Apparently, and this hasn't been verified but I'm guessing it's true, the hackers used the quantum computer in the room just above this one."

"What? I don't—"

My head was spinning.

This wasn't making any sense.

Kiran waved to someone over my shoulder, like he was signaling them to approach, as he said, "Someone broke into the machine, Rex."

The police were walking directly toward me. Eyes locked on mine.

"I—I don't understand . . . ," I stammered.

I backed up, away from the cops, panicked. The lead officer, a big guy with a thick mustache, yelled, "Hands on your head! Hands on your head now!"

I dropped my cell and kicked it across the room just as the cops pulled me to the ground. Kiran scoffed. "Not even putting up a fight, Rex?"

28.1

They led me out of the room with my hands handcuffed behind my back.

Painted Wolf was in shock.

Tunde was pale with disbelief.

The last thing I saw before the door swung closed was Painted Wolf retrieving my cell phone from the floor. At least Teo's address was safe.

Outside, I was pushed into the back of a squad car.

The door was slammed shut.

And off we went.

The following three hours were pretty much a blur. We arrived at the intake center and I was pulled left and right, jostled every which way until my hips and shoulders were sore and my stomach ached. They took fingerprints. They emptied my pockets, even of lint. They took photos. They got my vitals. I sat alone in a holding cell and then an empty room and then another holding cell. The rooms were cold, but I was so numb from everything that I hardly noticed. They finished by reading me my Miranda rights. I had nothing to hide, and being sixteen, I was old enough to waive them.

"You have the right to have an earnest consultation with an interested adult," the intake officer told me.

"An interested adult?"

"Your parents. A family member. Friend. Someone with a relationship to you who is genuinely interested in your welfare and can give you advice. Anyone like that you want us to get ahold of?"

"Do I have to?"

"No," the intake officer said. "But we'll be calling your parents."

"Listen . . . ," I started, but wasn't sure what to say.

I had to protect my parents. This was me, all me, and I would never be able to live with myself if they were deported because I'd screwed up somehow. "I just want to talk to someone here," I said. "I want to explain it all myself. You don't have to get my parents involved in this. They don't know. They don't need to know."

The officer didn't answer. Just said, "Sit tight."

The last room I went to was the interrogation room.

It was the warmest.

I was in there fifteen minutes before a woman in a pink suit and a chubby guy with a red tie walked in. The woman sat across from me. The chubby guy stood. The woman pulled a folder from her briefcase and read through its contents briefly. As she read, she cleared her throat and wiped her nose. It was silly, but I honestly was more worried at that moment about catching a cold than anything else.

Finally, she closed the folder and said, "Rex, I'm Special Agent Lindell. This is Special Agent Rowe. We're with the Federal Bureau of Investigation. Your parents will be in town later tonight, but I understand you've chosen to speak to us without them or another adult. Is that correct?"

"Yes."

"You seem awfully protective of your folks. Why is that?"

She locked eyes with me, her gaze as cold as liquid helium.

"This is about me, right? Not them."

"Are your parents in the country illegally, Rex?"

I didn't answer.

Special Agent Lindell nodded, then took a digital tape recorder from her briefcase, turned it on, and placed it on the table in front of me.

Before she said anything, I leaned forward. "I had nothing to do with it."

Agent Lindell said, "Okay."

"This must be a mistake," I said. "I wouldn't have done anything like this. You can look. I don't have any record. I was just in the competition; I was just a participant. You can ask anyone who was there, I—"

"Says here"—Agent Lindell flipped through some paperwork and coughed—"you were not invited. We have a statement by a Kiran Biswas, who says you cheated your way into the competition."

I choked a bit on that.

"Listen, I invited myself. I assumed it was a mistake, okay? They just forgot to invite me so . . . I invited myself. Kiran and I already discussed this. Did he tell you that? We came to an agreement. It's all been settled."

Agent Lindell made a few notes. Agent Rowe just stared at me.

"You're in very, very serious trouble, Rex," Agent Lindell said. "You've got a stack of felony charges here. You get lucky, say the

278

right things, answer honestly, and plead guilty, you'll probably get off with probation until you're twenty-one. No computers, no phones. That's my guess on the most lenient sentence. But if you're going to fight us—"

"I'm not going to fight you."

"—if, being the crucial word, if you fight us, then you're looking at time in a juvenile detention facility. You ever been in one, Rex?"

"No."

Agent Rowe cleared his throat. "They'd eat you alive."

Agent Lindell said, "How long have you been a part of Terminal?"

I swallowed hard and sat up straight.

"What?"

"How long?"

"I'm not a part of Terminal. I have nothing to do with Terminal."

Agent Rowe dragged a chair over to the table and sat.

"The more you lie to us, the worse this thing gets."

"I swear to you, I am not part of Terminal."

Agent Rowe's eyes bored into mine.

I did not blink. Did not turn away.

"Let's start with this," he said as he pulled an eight-by-ten glossy photo from his stack of paperwork and slid it carefully across the table to me. It was a shot of Tunde's and my dorm room at the Boston Collective. Frozen in the bright, antiseptic light of a camera flash were the notes and calculations I'd written on the walls, the guts of the program for the jammer.

"I don't understand," I replied.

"Had one of our techs take a look at this stuff; he tells us it's for a GPS jammer. Very sophisticated. Large scale, incredibly dangerous, and it looks like it's in your handwriting."

"I was helping a friend."

Agent Rowe glanced over at Agent Lindell. "What sort of friend needs something like this?"

"It's complicated. But he was asked to make it for a corrupt general in Nigeria. You can look him up. He is holding my friend's family captive in—"

"Of course he is."

I was getting nowhere. Frustration was rattling my insides.

"I'm not joking here. I'd be happy to show you—"

"There'll be plenty of time," Agent Lindell said, cutting me off. "Talk to me about the quantum computer. We have surveillance video from OndScan of two individuals breaking into the Boston Collective research lab on the day the computer was illegally accessed. A pretty clean B & E, but these individuals missed a couple of cameras."

I winced internally but kept a straight face.

Could I still talk my way out of this?

"I don't know what—"

"Mr. Biswas has confirmed," Agent Lindell continued as though I hadn't even spoken, "that there was an anomalous program detected on the quantum computer after the Game. The program was linked directly to you. We're still in the preliminary stages of analysis, but our security people tell me that the program installed on that quantum computer was used to commit the hacking attacks against Russian, Chinese, and U.S. government interests."

"That's impossible!"

Agent Rowe delivered the coup de grâce. "'Walkabout' mean anything to you?"

"Yes. But it only finds things, tracks people," I said.

"Not anymore," Agent Rowe replied.

"That's impossible."

"You calling us liars?" Agent Lindell asked.

I rubbed my eyes and tried to drive back the headache that was threatening to explode my brain. "Listen," I said. "I wrote the program. I put it on the quantum computer. But I didn't break into any government anything. That's not what WALKABOUT is for, it's not what it does. I don't do that. I'm not like that. I swear to you, it's the truth."

"Why would you load it on to the computer then?" Agent Rowe asked.

"To find my missing brother," I said. "To do what you guys couldn't."

I realized I was pushing things after I said it. The agents weren't pleased.

Agent Lindell said, "I find it hard to believe that the same person who wrote a program like this one and illegally loaded it on to the highest-end of all computers would have any qualms about infiltrating other countries' government. Call me crazy but . . ."

"I swear to you, I didn't do it."

The conversation went round and round from there.

They said the same thing over and over.

I said the same thing in response every time.

After three hours of this, I went back to the holding cell.

Papa and Ma arrived just after midnight.

The look on Ma's face nearly crushed me.

28.2

We were shown a meeting room at the back of the intake center.

It was small, the furniture was plastic, and the lights hummed.

I sat at the table and ran my hands through my hair in frustration. Papa sat across from me, and Ma pulled up a chair beside me. She held my hand as we spoke.

"Papa—" I started.

He cut me off with a stern glance that was less angry than disappointed.

"Is it true?" he asked.

"No."

"You didn't hack into any government sites or—"

"I said no. I didn't do any of that."

Papa sat back in his chair and sighed. "What about the competition?"

"I cheated to get in."

Ma squeezed my hand and I glanced over to see she was crying again. "Ma," I said, "I'm really sorry. I let everyone down. I was just . . . I needed to be here."

"But you lied to our faces, Rex," Papa said.

"I know. It was the worst thing that I have ever done and it's been eating me up inside. I don't have an excuse, but I do have a reason."

"And what is that?" Papa asked.

"For Teo," I said. "The program they found on the quantum computer, the one they said I used to hack into those government websites, it's called WALKABOUT and I created it to find him."

Papa asked, "Why didn't you just run it at home?"

"I needed a quantum computer. I needed to be here."

Papa nodded as though he understood, but . . . "Why couldn't you just have told us, Rex? We would have figured something out. We would have found a way for you to run the program somewhere. You should have just asked us."

"I know," I said. But that was another lie.

Thing was, even if I *had* told them, there was no way anyone would let a punk kid like me install a DIY program on one of the most advanced pieces of technology in the world. It was a nice thought, though, an idealistic one, and I decided not to argue with my father.

"And you told all of this to the police?" Papa asked.

"Yes," I answered. "They don't buy it."

"Why?"

"Because apparently, somehow, someone messed with my program. It's only supposed to find things, find people. There must have been a second program that ran secretly behind WALKABOUT. I don't know who did it and I don't know how."

"Ma and I have been talking. You need a lawyer. A good one. Uncle Bobby recommended the son of a man he used to work for. He's apparently very good, does a lot of legal stuff with technology."

"And very expensive," I added. "Papa, you—"

"Ma and I have our savings. There's the money from—"

"Papa, no," I interrupted. "I won't let you use that money. That's for your retirement. That's for everything you and Ma have wanted. I won't let you. You guys can't be here. You can't be talking to me or a lawyer or anyone. They're going to find out. They're going to know about . . . our family. And if they do, they're going to send you back."

"Rex, it's too late to worry about that," Papa said.

"It's never too late!" I shouted. "You have to go. Go now."

"We're not going to leave you."

I felt my throat clench and I had to blink to keep the tears from spilling down my face. I couldn't believe this was happening.

Why had I been so stupid?

How was I going to get us out of this?

We were all silent for a moment. The hum of the lights was overwhelming.

Finally, Ma wiped her eyes and took both of my hands in hers.

"What did it say?" she asked me.

"What, Ma?"

"What did your program say? Did it find Teo?"

That's when the emotional dam broke.

"Yes." I let the tears flow.

We cried together, a family, as I repeated, "Yes. I found him."

29. TUNDE

The twenty-four-hour period after the end of the Game left me entirely spent.

It was stunning to me how quickly the mood inside the safe room transformed from one of pure joy and celebration to one of darkest anxiety. Watching my best friend be handcuffed and led outside by police was the worst thing I have witnessed.

Painted Wolf was equally stunned and horrified.

Unlike me, however, she did not let the panic overwhelm her. Her mind is one that ramps into an even higher gear when she is under stress. It was a thing of beauty to see how she handled that situation.

As soon as Rex had been driven away, she pulled me aside and told me to get my things. "When is your return flight to Lagos?" she asked.

"In about forty-eight hours. Why?"

"We don't have much time and I'm going to need you to agree to do some things that you're going to disagree with. Things that are not exactly legal."

"How not exactly legal?"

"Very."

"If it helps Rex, then yes, I will do it."

I found myself agreeing immediately. I was not sure how I felt about agreeing to such a plan but then reflected on the fact that Rex had helped me construct the jammer without a moment of hesitation.

I would not let him down in his time of need.

I called General Iyabo and told him I had won the competition. I told him that I would be home soon to give him the jammer. I feigned humbleness and told him how honored I was to have won for him. He responded as I had imagined he would: "Tunde, I see you soon. Your parents will be quite pleased."

The following hours were a whirlwind of activity.

I was so focused on my small portion of the plan that I did not see the larger picture coming together around me until it was finished. After yet another sleepless night of near-frantic work, our plan was in motion.

Painted Wolf and I agreed to meet on the steps of the student center very early in the morning, just as night was rolling over to daylight. I was not a bit tired. The night had been long, but the adrenaline of winning the Game was surging through my veins.

Though the weather was chilly, I did not have to wait long for Painted Wolf to arrive. I was quite taken aback when a black American sedan with tinted windows pulled up alongside the curb.

Surely this vehicle was meant for someone other than us?

When the front passenger door opened, I expected a dashing and wealthy person to emerge. It was, however, a very old woman with a face as wrinkled as a baked yam and a pile of white, stringy hair stacked upon her head. She wore a business suit, had a Bluetooth headset in her right ear, and carried a leather briefcase. As she walked over to us, I went to her aid, taking her arm, and was surprised to find it muscular, not the weakened limb I had expected.

"Thank you," the old woman said in a raspy voice. "You're very kind, Tunde."

"Do I know you?" I asked, quite surprised.

The voice of the old woman was suddenly different. It was youthful and had a very distinct, very familiar accent. "It's me," she said.

"Painted Wolf?" I was stunned.

Omo, na so I open mouth, ojare!

"Tunde," Painted Wolf asked, "are you ready?"

I snapped out of my daze and nodded.

Halil stepped out from behind the wheel of the car as the rear passenger-side doors opened and Rosa and Norbert emerged.

"Good luck," Norbert said to me. "We're here if you need us."

"Thank you, *omo*. For everything."

Halil hugged me. "My parents' place is available whenever you need a place to crash, and I'd gladly go with you to the junkyard anytime, my friend. See you."

Painted Wolf got behind the wheel and I climbed into the passenger seat. Rosa then leaned in the passenger-side window.

"Painted Wolf's awesome, isn't she?" Rosa said.

"She is extraordinary," I said.

"Did you know she and Rex almost kiss—"

Painted Wolf revved the engine and drowned Rosa out.

I settled into my seat, ready and excited for what was to follow.

"Let us do this," I said.

29.1

Painted Wolf drove carefully despite the pull of the powerful engine.

"Where is this car from?" I asked her.

Painted Wolf replied, "Halil. This is his town, remember?"

"And you have a license to drive?"

She pointed to an envelope on the dashboard. I opened it to find several important documents inside, including a driving license with a photo of Painted Wolf in the old-woman makeup, a badge of some sort, and three round-trip train tickets to New York City leaving that very afternoon.

"What is all this?"

Painted Wolf said, "How we get Rex out. Rosa forged them."

"Incredibly realistic. She is very talented. And the tickets?"

"How we find his brother."

I worried about my return flight to Lagos. I had to bring the jammer. I could not be delayed. Painted Wolf could see my concern as clearly as if I was wearing it as a hat. "Don't worry," she said. "We'll get you back in time for your flight. Everything is going to work out."

"How can you be so sure?"

"I can't," she said. "But we've gotten this far, right?"

I had to agree, she had a point. Still, I was very anxious.

"By the way, we bought this for you." Painted Wolf turned and reached into the space behind her seat. She pulled out a duffel bag and handed it to me. "You'll need to change," she said. "Sorry we couldn't get it to you earlier."

I opened the duffel bag and looked at the clothing folded neatly inside.

"You're my intern."

"And what do I do?"

"What most interns do," Painted Wolf said. "Look useful."

As Painted Wolf navigated the city streets, I climbed into the backseat and changed into the suit. I found that it fit perfectly and, looking at myself in the mirror on the sun visor, I found that I appeared quite debonair. Never having seen myself in a suit before, I will admit I was pleased with the results.

When we arrived at the juvenile intake facility downtown, however, my nerves were frayed beyond all fraying. Outwardly, I remained calm and assumed my role as the assistant to Painted Wolf. Tunde Oni, intern.

Painted Wolf parked the car in front of the building and I followed her inside. She showed her badge to the attendant security personnel and they scanned us both with handheld metal detectors.

Afterward, we were escorted to an elevator bank and directed to go to the third floor, turn left, then right, and ask for Special Agent Lindell at the last door on the left.

We followed these directions in complete silence.

Just before we knocked on the door of the specified room, Painted Wolf turned to me and said, "Do not show any emotion, okay? The only way this will work is if you pretend you do not know the person behind this door. Okay?"

"Yes," I said.

She opened the door, and as soon as she crossed the threshold, she became another individual entirely. She was transmuted!

Rex sat beside his parents at a small table. He appeared defeated, and the expression on his face was so disheartening that it nearly broke me. Though his expression did not change when he looked up and saw me, his eyes did.

They instantly lit up. He knew. He understood.

I kept myself focused, though I wanted to rush forward and carry him out of that place. A severe woman in a blue suit introduced herself as Special Agent Lindell. Painted Wolf shook her hand very briskly.

"I want my client ready to leave in twenty minutes. My bona fides," she said in her old-woman voice as she reached into the briefcase and handed Special Agent Lindell several of the papers Rosa had fabricated.

Then Painted Wolf walked over to Rex and surveyed his condition.

Speaking directly to Rex, she said, "I'm Marsha Osborne-Chang, with Chang, Carlson, Ryder, and Burns, and I've been hired as your lawyer. As of this moment, I advise you not to say anything further without consulting me."

She then turned to Special Agent Lindell.

"Can you please gather my client's belongings? We're leaving."

29.2

We waited in a staff lounge for Rex to be released.

While we sat there, Special Agent Lindell joined us.

Leaning over to Painted Wolf, she said, "We're releasing Rex to his parents' custody. He has a monitoring bracelet on and has been cited back to juvenile court in two days. Make sure he's there. This should go fast because we've got your client on everything."

"That's not what I understand," Painted Wolf said calmly.

"Let me give you a little advice. This is the work of Terminal. If Rex is willing to provide names, gives us locations, IP addresses, access to his network, then maybe we can cut a deal."

"What sort of deal?" Painted Wolf asked.

"A unique one."

"Have your office call mine."

"It's a limited-time offer. Expires at the first hearing," Special Agent Lindell said as she headed for the door. "Tell Rex. He has to play nice. He has to give up everyone and everything."

After Special Agent Lindell left, Painted Wolf turned to me and winked.

"Do you know what you are doing?" I whispered.

"Sort of," she replied. "I've done this in China a couple of times. Procedures here are a little different, but I did some research and it all sounds about right."

Painted Wolf followed this with a shrug and a smile.

If anyone could do this it was her, but *ko easy ra ra!*

Rex arrived fifteen agonizing minutes later. He trudged out the door with his parents, a tracking bracelet on his ankle. In the parking lot, Mr. Huerta turned to Painted Wolf and shook her hand vigorously.

"I don't know who hired you," he said. "But I want to thank you. We don't have much, but I hope that we—"

Painted Wolf waved his words away.

"I would not think of taking a dime," she said. "This is pro bono. Trust me, your son is in very safe hands."

"How can that be?" Mrs. Huerta asked, happy but confused.

"Payment was generously provided by the family of another contestant that Rex befriended over the course of the Game. We all know that these charges are trumped up and I will see to it that all of them are dropped. Now, we do not have much time. Are you staying somewhere in town?"

Mr. Huerta shook his head. "We haven't gotten a place yet."

"No worries," Painted Wolf said. "You can stay with some friends. I'll give you the number for Halil Tawfeek. His parents' place is very close; they'll be expecting you. I need to meet with Rex to do an in-depth interview, which might take the rest of the evening. I can have your son back to you in the morning. Does that sound okay?"

Mr. and Mrs. Huerta took turns embracing Rex before getting into their rental car and driving off. It was not until we reached the car that I managed to take a deep breath.

Two blocks from the police station, Rex let out a huge war whoop!

"You people are insane!"

We all began laughing uproariously. It was entirely nerves on my part.

As the car roared onto the highway, Rex turned around and fist-bumped me. "You did amazing, too, Tunde. I don't even know what to say. I can't believe this. Do you know how much trouble we just got ourselves into? I mean, this is crazy! What are we going to do now?"

"You're due back in court in two days," Painted Wolf said. "But we're going to New York to find Teo before that. I'm sure there are already way too many CCTV cams that have captured images of us in this car. We're going to ditch it at the station and take public transport from here on out. Train leaves in thirty minutes. We'll have Tunde back in the morning for his flight."

"I can't leave the city," Rex said. "I'm being investigated for the largest cybercrime in history, in case you forgot."

Rex held up his right leg, showing us the ankle bracelet.

"You telling me you can't hack that thing?" Painted Wolf asked.

"Well . . . ," Rex said. "There's still a big problem with—"

"Listen," Painted Wolf interrupted. "Did you steal those documents?"

"Of course not!" Rex spat.

"Then that is what you should be worrying about. Someone set you up. The FBI doesn't believe your story. They won't help you. We're going to have to break a few laws to clear your name and settle this thing. None of us want our families involved, none of us want them in trouble. If we're going to make things right, we need to do this ourselves and figure it out as we go. With any luck, we can get to Teo by the time Tunde needs to leave. I know things are really scary right now, Rex, but you have to trust me. You have to believe that we can do this."

I tapped Rex on the shoulder.

"Remember, *omo*, we can do anything together."

A solemn pause passed before Rex turned to Painted Wolf and said, "By the way, you've got amazing eyes."

I changed in the bathroom at the train station.

It must have been funny to see an elderly woman step into a stall and a young, differently dressed woman step out. I tucked all the prosthetics into my carry-on bag and mentally thanked the Boston Collective film department tech crew who had given them to me.

We caught the train in time and had no hassles when we boarded.

As soon as we reached our seats, I settled into mine and tried to relax for what felt like the first time in weeks. But the knot in my stomach wasn't going to go away so easily. I had been recorded on countless video cameras. While my disguises had always been good in the past, this was the FBI. . . . Besides, if the people who had access to WALKABOUT wanted to find us, they could do it in a snap.

That thought chilled me to the bone.

I was thankful when Rex sat down beside me and the train pulled out of the station. I needed to **focus** on the matters at hand, on the coming hours.

"I just want to thank you again," he said.

"Of course. You would have done the same for me."

"You know it. Still, you took a big risk."

Thinking back over the events of the morning, I realized I had acted more on impulse than anything. Whereas before my drive was always to secure a new tape, capture a new confession, when we rescued Rex I was acting almost purely on emotion. I just knew that we had to get Rex out. I couldn't stand the thought of him being locked up; I couldn't stand the thought of not seeing him again. There was simply no other option. I risked everything for him not just because it was the right thing to do but also because I wanted to.

What did that mean?

Thirty miles outside of Boston, my cell phone rang.

It was a BlackBerry I'd picked up that morning both for show (to make Tunde's intern disguise more believable) and so we'd have Internet access not linked to any of us. No one had the phone number. I didn't even know what the phone number was.

"This can't be," I said aloud.

It wasn't a phone call but a video chat.

"No one has this number," I told Rex and Tunde.

"Answer it," Rex said. "But keep the camera covered."

I placed my thumb over the camera lens and answered the call. I was stunned at the face that suddenly appeared: It was Kiran.

"The hell?" Rex whispered.

"Hello, everyone," Kiran said, staring straight ahead as though he could see us. "Nice work this morning, really inventive stuff. Fun to watch. Is Rex available?"

Rex hesitated but then said, "I am."

"I told you at my apartment that you're one of the best coders I've ever met. That was a lie. You're not *one* of the best, you are *the* best. I also told you that the only thing keeping you from greatness is a push. That was true. Two days ago, the world wasn't ready for Shiva. **Now it is**. And I have you to thank for that, actually. Terminal's unprecedented cyber attack was the catalyst I've been looking for, the tipping point."

"I had nothing to do with that. I'm not part of Terminal."

"Of course." Kiran laughed. "That's the point."

Rex glanced over at me, eyes wide, face contorted with emotion.

"What is he saying?" Tunde whispered.

I shook my head, confused.

Rex took the BlackBerry from my hand and held it up so that Kiran could see his face. "Tell me you didn't set me up."

Kiran smirked. "How badly do you want to win, Rex?"

"This isn't a game anymore, Kiran."

"No, that's where you're wrong. I already told you, Rex, you only need a push. So consider this the biggest push you'll ever get, my gift to you. I made sure to alert the authorities that you're on the run. They'll be stopping the train you're on at the very next station. The helicopters, as they say, are already hovering. I look forward to your next move. Oh, and thanks for WALKABOUT. It'll come in handy for sure."

The line went dead. The image vanished.

We sat in stunned silence as the train began to slow.

The conductor came on the overhead. "Ladies and gentlemen, as you may have noticed, we're slowing down to make an unscheduled stop at the next station. I apologize in advance for any inconvenience this may cause and assure you that we'll attempt to make up the time once we're on the move again. We appreciate your patience and will be on our way again shortly."

Rex, Tunde, and I turned toward the nearest window and watched as the train slowed into a station. Police officers lined the station platform.

Rex glanced around the interior of the train, eyes narrowed, clearly looking for something in particular. "Cameras are eyes . . . microphones are ears . . ."

"What do you mean?" I asked him, panicked now.

Rex turned to me. "You ready?"

"Ready for what?"

"Yes," Tunde said, his voice trembling. "What?"

Rex stood up and reached out for my hand.

"**To run**."

FBI field office #2313 — transcript related to investigation #00093837

Transcript of video uploaded to LODGE.COM.

No date given.

Time: 01:40:21

Title: "Homecoming"

00:00:10

Start: Cell phone footage of an unknown person walking down a city street (analysis suggests Brooklyn, New York, though the image is closely cropped) toward a nondescript apartment building. There are no building numbers or street signs visible. The cell camera operator approaches the building and presses the buzzer. The buzzer is pressed twice before the door unlocks and the cell camera operator enters the building. The individual with the cell phone camera takes three flights of stairs before stopping at the first apartment on the left. He (analysis suggests the subject is a male, young, possibly a teenager) knocks on the door. Location analysis identifies this apartment as possibly belonging to a TEO HUERTA (age 18–19, California missing persons case file CA53716B). The door is opened. Just before the video cuts out, the words "I knew we'd find him. . . ." can be heard.

01:40:31

End of transcript.

CC: Special Agent Lindell, NY

0 — False vacuum

5

$$\mathcal{E} = \frac{Mc^2}{\sqrt{1 - \frac{v^2}{c^2}}}$$

ACKNOWLEDGMENTS

Many thanks to Keith Thomas, my creative partner in crime.

To the warrior poets: Holly West & Jean Feiwel . . . *Gracias*.

And Everardo Gout, as always, a lighthouse that pierces the darkness.

To Brent Bushnell and Two Bit Circus for their real-life genius puzzles.

And to JR, Prune, Marc Azoulay, Radical Media, Abhijith Babu, Edo Segal, the wonderful people at Mother New York, The Collective, Bill Robinson, Ken Hertz, James C. Finney, and James Patterson; Thank you for all your support.

THANK YOU FOR READING THIS
FEIWEL AND FRIENDS BOOK

THE FRIENDS WHO MADE

THE GAME

POSSIBLE ARE

JEAN FEIWEL
Publisher

KIM WAYMER
Production Manager

LIZ SZABLA
Editor in Chief

ANNA ROBERTO
Editor

RICH DEAS
Senior Creative Director

CHRISTINE BARCELLONA
Associate Editor

HOLLY WEST
Editor

EMILY SETTLE
Administrative Assistant

DAVE BARRETT
Executive Managing Editor

ANNA POON
Editorial Assistant

FOLLOW US ON FACEBOOK OR
VISIT US ONLINE AT MACKIDS.COM.

OUR BOOKS ARE FRIENDS FOR LIFE.